CALL
ME
ELIZABETH
LARK

CALL ME ELIZABETH LARK

A Novel

MELISSA COLASANTI

CROOKED
LANE

NEW YORK

Published in the United States by Crooked Lane Books, an imprint of The Quick Brown Fox & Company LLC.

Crooked Lane Books and its logo are trademarks of The Quick Brown Fox & Company LLC.

Library of Congress Catalog-in-Publication data available upon request.

ISBN (hardcover): 978-1-64385-682-7
ISBN (ebook): 978-1-64385-683-4

Cover design by Kara Klontz.

Printed in the United States.

www.crookedlanebooks.com

Crooked Lane Books
34 West 27th St., 10th Floor
New York, NY 10001

First Edition: March 2021

10 9 8 7 6 5 4 3 2 1

For my mother and sister

I drowned under pale moonlight, in
shimmering obsidian-colored water and seaweed
clung to my body, worms crawled from my blue
lips and turned into butterflies.
and the newspaper called me jane doe.

CHAPTER ONE

MYRA

Herb says Myra has drowned herself with Charlotte, where the beach is rocky and the tide tinged gray-yellow, its crest effervescent. At the inn, wind batters the wooden shingles like the ocean thrumming the shore at high tide. The squall sends sand whipping through the air. The pier empties of people, except for the lone fishermen who wear rubber boots and heavy yellow raincoats, casting their lines in turbid water. Myra and Herb are ensconced in the inn, wrapped in sweaters and crocheted afghan blankets. Occasional guests trickle in, but not often. People visit the Oregon coast during summer.

Myra doesn't take vacations during the off season, no matter how many empty winters pass. Charlotte knows her mother is waiting. She lived for the scent of the ocean, for the lacquer of salt on her skin. The crabs hidden under mounds of sand and the starfish in the tide pools enchanted Myra's youngest child. Myra supposes this is why Charlotte was so attracted to the mystery of the deep, dark sea. The waves sweep away an entire pool of living things, but with the next tide, they begin again.

And so Myra is not particularly surprised when her dead daughter walks in the door.

* * *

Myra studies the sawdust-covered floor of the musty inn, thinking they should sweep it and install shiny new wood. She spends her free time leafing through the glossy pages of decorating magazines, considering all the possibilities for the place. It should be more modern, like the bigger hotels in Rocky Shores. There are bed and breakfasts with assorted coffees and fresh baked goods; there are vacation rental homes and cabins, some of which come equipped with pools and fitness centers. And the Barkley Inn is an entire mile from the open shore.

When Myra's parents were alive, people shuffled in wearing flip-flops and shorts in the summer, eager for slabs of marbled steak served for cheap on Fridays. Peanut shells and loose sand scattered the floor. Back then, poets read their work on Saturday afternoons. Musicians strummed their guitars and sang with their husky, melodic voices on Saturday nights. Candle-filled Mason jars adorned the tables. Ripples of lavender incense hung sweet and thick in the air.

They have personal touches that have gone back decades—luxurious bath towels, chocolates on the pillows, chilled champagne in the honeymoon suite. But the curtains are a drab shade of olive-green, and antique topaz candelabras cast dim light over the lobby. In the sixties, they were eclectic; now they're just creepy. Perhaps Myra could get one of those latte machines people like nowadays.

On this particular afternoon, Herb hovers behind her as she considers the flooring. She pretends not to notice his wry smile, how he watches her. Age spots dot his thin skin; his eyes are set beneath deep wrinkles, but they glow with a tenderness that has never changed. He will always be her Herb.

"Whatcha up to, honey?"

"Do you think we should get rid of the sawdust? I'm thinking deep mahogany floors."

He says with a playful smile, "Does it really matter what I want?"

Myra rolls her eyes. "I'm just thinking of ideas to spruce the place up—"

A vehicle brakes hard, its screech penetrating the thick storm windows.

Herb cringes. "Good lord. Someone needs a brake job."

Myra peers around the curtains. Headlights dip and rise over bumps in the gravel. Rain has streaked the windows, leaving tracks through the winter grime.

"A guest?" she says, thinking: no one has stopped by in weeks. Who wants to go to the bayside town and get drenched? Perhaps someone is traveling through. Maybe they need directions.

A rusty pickup truck with Washington state plates jerks into a spot.

"Great," mutters Herb. "Here comes trouble."

A stranger with inky hair climbs out of the car. It falls in thick, unkempt chunks around her face. "This one's gonna have a fake ID," she tells Herb. "A really fake one." Myra isn't one to turn away a guest. Everyone has a story—and if they've got information about Charlotte, they might not be exactly on the right side of the law. They don't give *every* guest a room. But they've got a reputation for turning a blind eye to a fake ID, for accepting cash without a credit card as collateral. The dyed hair, the ancient truck. This is a woman running from a man. Myra has seen it before. She could never turn a woman out on the street because she doesn't have a credit card, or she's changed her name. Besides, it's a bed and breakfast—rich folks with good credit tend to stay at five-star resorts. They can't be overly picky.

Herb says, "Shoulda dumped that vehicle a thousand miles ago."

"Maybe she couldn't," Myra says, watching.

The stranger ushers a little boy out of the backseat. She begins to trudge toward them, a duffel bag tossed over her shoulder, clutching the child's hand. The woman stops sharply and turns back to the vehicle. She swipes the underside of the wheel with her palm.

Herb fixes his gaze on Myra. "Don't go soft on me, honey. That girl's running from something, and it's probably trouble."

"Can't be too experienced." She nods to the truck. The girl won't find a tracking device stuck in a wheel well. It's on the damn GPS.

Herb shakes his head, placing his thick knuckled hand on hers. She shoves it away, breath caught in her throat. Hanging his head, he shuffles toward the office. Myra knows what he is thinking. She could climb inside Herb's chest and feel the rhythm of his heart. As much as anyone can know another person, Myra knows Herb.

As the sound of his footsteps recedes, she looks back to the window. The girl is too far away for Myra to make out her features. She slips into her vinyl chair and waits for their nebulous figures to sharpen. Leaning on her elbows, Myra breathes slowly, listening to the rain drum on the roof, run down the metal storm drain, and trickle onto the ground. The damp inn is cozy compared to the biting Pacific Northwest rain.

The bells on the door jingle as the woman pushes it open, water dripping from her clothing. The noxious scent of her fresh dye job wafts inside. She leans over the boy and whispers in his ear. He shoves his thumb in his mouth and looks back at his mother questioningly, and she nudges him toward the front desk. "It's okay," she says. "Let's go up to the nice lady."

The woman's voice is eerily familiar. Myra can't quite place it. Has she come through town before?

Myra glances at the stranger's face as inconspicuously as possible, but she notices how this woman moves, the tilt of her chin, the cadence of her voice as she speaks to the boy—it is so familiar that a guttural pain shoots through her bones, her gut, every last piece of her. The hair may be black, but the eyes are the same. Her breath quickens; the room spins. She leans against the counter, reeling. "My god." The words swirl off her tongue before she can catch them.

"Yes?" says the woman, who is not exactly a stranger, yet somehow strange. She backs toward the door. "I'm sorry. I guess you're full—"

"No," says Myra. "You look like a girl I once knew, that's all."

"We need a room. But if you're full, we can keep driving." She pulls the boy closer.

Myra realizes how bizarre she must sound. She ducks beneath the counter. The woman looks just like Charlotte. Those eyes.

Is she Charlotte?

No. Not again.

Herb is already convinced she's insane. He's probably right in his assessment.

She emerges from beneath the desk and tosses a hand towel to the woman. "You're soaked to the bone. So is your son."

"I'm sorry if I sounded stressed. I'm traveling alone with Theo." The stranger's voice wavers. Rain beads on the boy's apple-shaped cheeks like teardrops. His threadbare pants graze his ankles.

"What's your name?"

The woman hesitates, dropping her driver's license on the counter. "Elizabeth Lark."

"That's a beautiful name," she murmurs. Myra likes it when people choose lovely, poetic false identities for themselves. The lark is such a lyrical bird. Sometimes people come in with names like Moonstone or Pippin. *Too much,* she thinks. Unique is not what you're going for when you are on the run.

Myra studies the driver's license as she boots up the computer. It's well done as far as fake IDs go. The little wheel on the computer whirls to the beat of her heart. "I'm sorry. It's thinking."

Elizabeth pulls her wet jacket around her thin frame, shivering. Her skin is a milky-gray color, and her lips, pale blue.

"You are about the same age as our daughter." Her voice grows husky. She clears her throat and types the information into the computer. "We lost her years ago."

Elizabeth avoids Myra's eyes. The girl already knows. Maybe she has come to see about Charlotte's ghost. Myra's chest is raw and tender. A snake coils in her stomach, lithe and threatening to escape.

"Anyway, it's done thinking."

Elizabeth purses her lips and reaches for her driver's license, knocking over Myra's glass of water. The contents of her purse tumble behind the desk.

"Dammit, I'm sorry." Elizabeth rushes toward the counter, stuffing papers and cards and cash back into the tattered bag.

That's when Myra sees it.

A strand of silver is coiled against the green carpet. It could have been any silver necklace, really. But Myra would recognize the cracked edges of the half heart anywhere. Best Friends Forever. It was a gift from Charlotte to her sister, Gwen, the year before she disappeared. Myra picks up the necklace, locking eyes with the stranger, who holds the boy's hand so hard her bony knuckles turn white. Myra turns it over and traces the initials with her finger.

CB. Charlotte Barkley.

"Where did you get this?" She steadies her voice.

The woman pulls herself to her feet, eyes wide. She takes a deep breath and exhales slowly. "It's mine."

Myra's heart flutters. The snake is ready to pounce.

Elizabeth Lark is not leaving, not until she explains the necklace.

"Yours?"

"From long ago, yes."

The world slows. Myra catches Elizabeth's eyes. They are sapphire-blue, and the closer she looks, she more she is certain. They are Charlotte's. Her little girl face has gone, and it is replaced by sharp cheekbones and an angular jaw. Elizabeth looks similar to Myra's oldest daughter, Gwen. Her limbs go numb. The necklace slips from Myra's fingers, landing in a soft pile on the floor.

"My daughter." The word sticks to her tongue. "Charlotte."

Charlotte does not move. She is stuck in a different time.

At this moment, Herb pads back into the lobby. "What's going on out here? Are you checking in?" He lifts his chin toward Charlotte.

"I don't have any idea what she's talking about." The stranger's face flushes.

Myra closes her eyes. Toddler Charlotte lays on her chest, knees curled up like a prawn, the light sweat from her cheek dewy and warm. Charlotte's squeals as she races her wooden fire truck along the windowsills. Both of her girls would trample in and out, dripping sand and water all over the floor, covered in sticky treats from the ice-cream truck.

"Don't track that water in the house, girls. Stop bringing that sticky stuff inside. Wash your hands!" She hears her own words and wishes she could swallow them. Take them back.

Twenty summers missed. Twenty summers of eclipsed sunshine, of icy heat. These guests wander in with nothing but their fake identities to cover secrets they cannot face, to investigate rumors of a haunted inn. Twenty years of drifters washed up from the frothy shores, looking for a room, dirty and chafed by the combination of sand and rain and heartbreak.

"My god, I have loved you. I have been here, waiting. I never stopped waiting."

Charlotte grips Theo's hand.

Herb takes Myra's shoulders, meets her eyes. He whispers, "This is not Charlotte."

Of course he says this. This has happened before. But this time it's true.

"Look at her, Herb. She looks just like Gwen."

Charlotte stares at them. "I have no idea what to say."

Herb releases her shoulders. He knows when to recede. Myra and Herb dance like this, intricate and poised. They know when to dip forward, when to swing sideways. He knows where he can touch her and what is too tender. And they move gently because their breakable parts have shifted throughout the years, like plates of the earth, scraping against one another deep beneath the surface.

She presses the necklace in Herb's palm. "Look at the initials, honey."

Herb clenches his jaw. His eyes glisten. The jowls on his neck shiver. "Where did you get this?" His voice thickens with emotion.

The wind howls and bristles the door; the tick of the clock over the fireplace throbs in her mind. Warmth spreads through Myra's chest. It relaxes in her stomach, heavy but silent.

"Charlotte's home. This time she really is."

Myra has a million questions. What has happened to her daughter? Who has had her all these years? And how did she find her way home?

Charlotte was only eight. Just a baby, really. And now, she stands before her mother, tears catching in her sunken cheeks.

Sweat beads on Myra's forehead. Tentacles grip her neck. She is drowning, deep in the ocean, where they said Charlotte died. Except Charlotte is here, right in front of them.

Herb steps closer to their daughter, scanning her from head to toe. He turns back to Myra, breathless.

Charlotte is alive. Wondrously, exquisitely alive.

CHAPTER TWO

ELIZABETH

Washington State—One Week Ago

The necklace slips through Elizabeth's fingers and lands in her palm. She inspects the cracked edges of the half heart and turns it over, focusing on the initials carved into the metal. She drops it into her purse.

The cabin reeks of dank mold. Elizabeth peeks out the window, hoping no one will see her, though there is no logical reason for her fear. The cabin is situated in a thicket of deep wood, where lime-green lichen weeps from the trees like gnome hats. Tufts of moss unfurl through the walls where the wood has rotted, while the foundation crumbles precariously beneath their feet. It is as tiny as a dollhouse dropped amid the lush, expansive forest, surrounded by frozen creeks and giant boulders. The moonlight seeps through a lattice of soft fir branches, and the cabin casts a shadow onto the snow. It is swallowed by the forest ahead. On each side of the shadow, crystals of snow glitter like a smattering of diamonds.

No one could find this cabin. No one away from the forest knows they are alive.

"Elizabeth?" Her husband's gravelly voice startles her.

She turns back to her son, who snuggles with his blue blanket and stuffed giraffe on the couch, fast asleep. Elizabeth smiles at Theo and clicks off the television. She slides to the boy's level and perches on the balls of her feet, tucking the blanket under his chin. The cold mountain air seeps into the poorly insulated cabin. His hair tumbles over his eyes, but she won't cut it. A memory of Peter shaving her son's luscious ringlets churns inside her. Elizabeth pushes her fist into her stomach and twirls Theo's stray hair.

"Are you coming, or what?" Peter yells.

She steels herself for the next few moments.

"Coming." She speaks just loud enough for him to hear her.

This is the last time her voice will be low. She squeezes her hands into tight fists.

"Honey, my back is aching. Can you bring me a drink and my pills?"

This is the moment she has waited for. The man doesn't pay the heating bill while he's out of town. And now he wants to be taken care of.

Elizabeth can arrange this.

She swings open the hollow-core door softly, taking care not to let it bang against the wall. He lays in bed, quiet and vulnerable, covered with the only heavy comforter in the house. The curtains are drawn tight. "I'll have your drink and pills in a second. You want food?"

"No. Just the pills. Please, honey."

She hates the word, so thick and sweet off his tongue. She shudders, remembering the tang of his hot breath against her neck.

"I'm sorry about yesterday." He groans in pain. "I can't believe how slippery that ice is. It's like someone dumped water all over the porch."

Her lips curl into a smile. She pours three fingers of Jack Daniels into a tumbler—funny they can afford this, and his Vicodin, when she and Theo haven't been to the doctor, not ever. They haven't left this cabin in years, except to exchange pleasantries with the homesteaders who have cleared trees and built little farms that sprawl down the mountain. They have their own peculiarities, she thinks, because they aren't alarmed that Elizabeth lives in this falling down shack with a five-year-old.

Still, Peter says to be friendly.

"But don't get too close. I'm watching you."

The threat hides beneath his words, like a rat scratching in a dark cabinet.

She drops a pill into the amber liquor, watching it billow into a thick, hazy cloud. And another. It is hypnotic. Venom fills her blood, lurid and dangerous. She swirls it with a teaspoon, and it clinks against the glass like the tick of a clock. She is numb, devoid of emotion, but she depends on this emptiness to survive. Pure instinct drives her down the crumbling hall. Holding her posture straight, she enters the bedroom.

"Here you go, babe." Elizabeth helps him to a seated position. His warm body is sticky with sweat.

"Ahh, thank you. You are a goddess," he says with a light smile.

Don't believe him, don't believe him. He will turn this on you and eventually kill you with his lies.

The whisky sloshes in the glass as she hands it to him. "Drink up." She feigns cheer, but her voice shakes.

"Please don't be afraid of me. I'm your husband. I'm sorry." His eyes are pleading. And pathetic. "Is your arm okay?" Her flesh is mottled with purple finger marks.

She nods with a smile.

"I just don't want to lose you."

11

She and Theo have been trying to escape. And Peter's relentless surveillance prevented them from contacting the nearby homesteaders without his looming presence. However, on one of his work trips, she and Theo walked a mile or so from the log cabin, until they came upon a farm. She got more than fresh eggs and a free-range chicken at the Hart's place.

Mrs. Hart let her use the internet.

Theo played with the Hart woman's children as she typed "domestic violence help" in the search engine. Alice Johnson's name popped up first. She'd apparently been helping abuse victims for decades. Elizabeth sent her an e-mail, wrote down her phone number. But before Alice could respond, Peter rang the doorbell. She heard his voice booming from the front room and slammed the laptop shut. Trembling, she ushered Theo toward the foyer. He put his arm around her, patted Theo's head, and said a sickeningly sweet goodbye to Mrs. Hart. "I was in the area," he said. "I thought you'd appreciate a ride home."

Once they got outside, he transformed back to the Peter she knew. With a sneer, he'd grabbed her by her thin shirt, digging his knuckles into her clavicle. He said, in cool, measured tone, "Mrs. Hart seems nice."

It took month for Elizabeth to get another cell phone and make the call. And for weeks after that, they meticulously plotted their escape.

Peter cuts the water supply when he will be gone for more than forty-eight hours. She and Alice planned to wait for the faucet to shudder and spout, till only copper silt would vomit into the stained sink. But he's become even less predictable. His back injury is an opportunity, perhaps the only one. They can't wait for an out-of-town trip. One might never happen. She cannot predict what electrical line will short circuit within her husband next. There is nothing she can do right when it comes to Peter, because what is right one moment is wrong the next. Every breath she takes is so cold it's hot.

They have one shot.

I'm not the one who should be afraid. Not anymore, darling.

He slings back the drink with another pill. "Damn, that's some strong shit."

"You'll feel better soon. Get some sleep."

Peter leans back on the pillow, his eyes fluttering shut. How lovely it must be to be safe.

Safety is merely an illusion, a trick of the mind. It is never guaranteed.

She rushes back to her son and shoves the last six years of her life into a single duffel bag. Before waking Theo, she creeps back to the bedroom to make sure Peter is knocked out. He's asleep, for sure. But his face is pasty. His olive complexion has turned yellowish, especially around his eyes. His lips are a bluish-gray color. Did she give him too much?

She tiptoes quietly toward him, afraid he'll sit up in bed and pounce on her. He looks really bad. Elizabeth needed to immobilize him for an hour or two, not kill the man. Peter's chest rises, ever so slightly. His neck rolls to the side with a labored breath.

Holy shit. Elizabeth runs to the living room, tears springing to her eyes. She shakes Theo awake.

He looks at her, drowsy and confused.

"We're taking our adventure today, remember? I packed our things. Daddy isn't coming."

"Are you sure?" He chews his fingernail.

She pats his head and smiles. "He's not coming."

Theo glances toward the bedroom door.

"Don't worry." Elizabeth takes his cheeks in her palms. "He's sleeping. We are going on an adventure together, just you and me." She forces herself to smile, heart beating wildly in her chest. "Okay?"

A dubious look crawls across Theo's face.

"He's sleeping. I promise. But we must go now."

"What if he wakes up?" Theo whispers.

"He won't," she replies.

"What if he finds us?"

"He won't. Not this time. Let's go."

"Did you pack my card games, my checkers?"

"Yes. I wouldn't forget those. Come on, now."

"Are you *sure* he won't wake up?"

"Pretty sure." She taps his shoulder. "Enough questions."

Peter might never wake up again. She shoves her hand under the couch cushions, looking for his phone, but he keeps it hidden from her. Maybe she should go back in the bedroom and make sure he's okay. She isn't a murderer. Lord, what has she done?

Maybe Theo won't remember this moment. He is five years old. Maybe he won't remember Peter at all. Peter will wake up, confused as hell, once they are gone, she hopes. He can't possibly be dead. She covers her face with her hands, trying not to cry. Theo has watched Peter hit her, has watched television shows where people aren't typically living in a cabin without heat, and with little food. He's five, and his understanding of the world is expanding, ballooning within their captivity. It's getting harder to hide the truth from him. He asks questions; he's curious about life outside the forest. And she finds herself snapping at him because she can't give him what he needs.

They need to get down this mountain.

Although, deep within the folds of her brain, she realizes that Peter will never let them go. As long as he lives, she is beholden to him. Even once they escape, change their identities, and move far, far away, Peter will be somewhere.

Safety is merely an illusion, a trick of the mind. He will hunt them till his last breath. Maybe it's best he take his last breath now. But still . . . She takes a tentative step toward the bedroom. Oh, shit. Should she check on him again? He could be dying. Should she call someone? They'd help her; they would save Peter.

No, she decides, it is not safe for her child here. There was no other choice but to incapacitate him. Right?

Fuck. They head for the door.

Elizabeth ushers Theo to the truck, dragging the duffel bag behind her. "Hurry," she urges. "But don't slip." The frigid air whips against her skin. Gripping his hand tightly, she instructs Theo to dig the heels of his boots into the ice as he walks. The ground is slick; jagged rocks shine in the moonlight. She clicks the seatbelt over her son's waist, hands trembling, and tosses the bag in the back. Her own seat is awkward.

It has been years since she has driven a vehicle.

She turns the key in the ignition, hits the gas. They slide on the ice, over thick tree roots, into swathes of evergreen trees. The metal truck scrapes against branches, and she hits every gear wrong. But she gathers her bearings. They travel down the mountain, past the Harts', past more pockets of homesteaders with chickens and goats, and away from their captor—her husband, his father. She squirts the windshield with fluid and wipes away a layer of dried mud.

Elizabeth inhales deeply when they hit the main mountain road.

When Peter wakes, they will be long gone. She conjures images of all the possible states Alice might take her to. Someplace sunny, like California. Or a tiny Midwestern town with a big yard for Theo.

What if Peter *doesn't* wake up? She remembers the odd angle of his neck, his shallow breaths. Is she running from Peter—or the police? Could she be charged with murder?

The thought speeds her own heartbeat up. Blood rushes through her capillaries like a broken dam.

Her son looks out the window, enthralled with the road ahead of them. The sunrise spreads over the mountain, clear and wide. Theo points out the window. "Beautiful," he says.

"Beautiful," she agrees.

"Where are we going?"

"We're stopping at a friend's house." She has no cell phone, no GPS to direct her. Only this rusted old truck. She will ditch it when they arrive at Alice's, get on a bus. Elizabeth laughs, deep and throaty. They turn off the main road, crunching through gravel, and up a windy hill to a little blue house.

Her chest bursts with excitement. "C'mon Theo. Let's go meet Alice."

She drags him a little too quickly, and the boy's feet slip on the ice. "Whoops." He giggles as she catches him by the back of his threadbare coat.

Alice is a stout woman, with copper-colored skin and gray-streaked hair. Her smile is empathetic and kind. Several women linger around the breakfast table, holding mugs of steaming hot coffee, the rich scent wafting through the air. A couple of children play in the living room. The space is tight, but it exudes warmth and compassion. A pang of sadness hits her in the chest. She and Theo cannot stay here. It is too dangerous. He could find her among these women. The house is too close to the cabin. Does Peter have friends? He must. What if someone she doesn't recognize tries to find them? He could trail them, set a trap. Theo and Elizabeth must disappear.

And if she's killed him—oh god, she hopes she hasn't killed him—that's murder, right? She didn't technically *need* that dosage to knock him into oblivion. Her brain spins.

"All right girl, come in the back." Alice turns to Theo. "Why don't you play Legos with the other kids?"

He crouches around the box of red and blue and green blocks. A blonde-haired girl helps him stack them into a little building. She takes a deep breath, hope blossoming through her body.

Elizabeth follows Alice down a dark, narrow hallway and into a tiny room with a neatly made twin-sized bed. She rests on the soft blue bedspread as Alice rifles through the closet.

"All right. Here's the plan. You're gonna leave the truck and take one of mine."

Elizabeth opens her mouth to protest. Alice holds a hand up. "Look, girl. You can't take off in the man's truck. They'll find you. And even if you tell the cops what's happened, Peter will kill you and Theo before they can prosecute him. I've seen it before."

Elizabeth decides not to mention that Peter's body might be turning cold as they speak. "But what about you? He'll find the truck—"

Someone will find the truck anyway.

"I'm gonna get in the truck and ditch it twenty miles from here. But don't you worry about that. You take my vehicle." She tosses a key ring onto the bed.

"Alice, I can't take a car from you." She sighs, rubbing her aching forehead.

"You can pay me back someday. Till then, your life is at stake. Don't think about the cheap-ass car I'm about to give you. It's not registered in my name or anything." She rolls her eyes. "Still, you need to ditch it once you cross into Oregon. You'll be conspicuous with out-of-state plates."

"Whose car is it, then?"

"Never mind that. Doesn't matter. All that matters is that the cops can't trace it to you *or* me. Just don't get pulled over."

Elizabeth is bone-tired. "All I care about is getting away from here."

Alice plops on the bed beside Elizabeth. Her eyes are dark brown, and her lipstick reminds Elizabeth of a ripe plum. Alice takes her hands and squeezes them tightly. Teardrops drip down Elizabeth's nose.

"It's going to be okay," she says.

"Promise?" says Elizabeth, feeling very young.

Alice smiles warmly. "I can't promise anything. But you're gonna do your best. I have a good feeling about you."

She clears her throat. Back to business. Alice shuffles through a box of cards, takes a few, and tosses them on the bed. "I made these with the pictures you sent me from the Hart woman's computer. You did what I told you about, wiping your search history, right? And you cleared the photos from the webcam?"

"Yes. But you said a computer can never be fully wiped. That all the information is stored on the hard drive." What if the police discover she contacted Alice on the internet? Her hands begin to shake. If he's looking for her, the first place he'll go is the Hart place.

"Oh sweetheart. All we want is to keep the Hart woman from snooping around. Do you really think Peter is going to report you missing? Let the cops search that dump he's been keeping you in?"

Elizabeth nods. The log cabin is essentially a prison.

It is a prison.

"Where do you think you'll go, Liza? As far as anyone is concerned, you don't exist," Peter had said, with a nonchalant shrug.

Elizabeth's conviction grows. She will leave; she will take her boy far away, where he will never find them.

Unless she's killed him. Then the police will search everywhere, including the Hart's computer. Dammit! Why did she give him all those pills?

"All right. We've got three IDs here. One Oregon State driver's license. One Social Security card, which is essentially worthless for applying for credit or a job. It's just for show if someone doesn't buy the driver's license. Same with the passports," she says, laughing. "That ain't gonna get you out of the country if you plan to return. And I hear Tijuana isn't a fun place to live."

Elizabeth shoves the cards in her purse, beside the necklace.

"You've gotta be careful with fake IDs. Lots of people think giving a person a new first name is safest. To my mind, it's risky. You've been called Elizabeth your entire life. You could not respond to a strange first name. Hell, I've heard of a woman who started to sign the wrong name on a job application. How do you turn back from that? 'Sorry, it seems I've signed the wrong name?' Nah."

"Technically, I've been called Liza. A nickname my mom gave me because she loved Liza Minnelli . . . but I get a new last name?"

"Yup. You are no longer Elizabeth Briggs. Now, you are Elizabeth Lark."

"I love it," she says, smiling.

"Don't get too attached. My work isn't that authentic. We may have to change it again, if he comes after you, or someone else finds out." Alice purses her lips, thinking. "For now, aim for jobs at small companies. Family owned. It's not so much the name, as the Social Security number, which is completely fabricated. Make sure you avoid companies that are gonna do a damn background check." She shakes her head. "That, we do not need."

Elizabeth considers this. "Isn't it strange that this pile of false IDs is no more fake than I am?"

Alice ignores the existential musing. "Next is the hair." Alice reaches into a chest of drawers filled with boxes of hair dye, combs, and scissors. She points to the adjacent bathroom. "Welcome to my spa."

Elizabeth settles into the chair, inspecting her gaunt face in the mirror. Alice works methodically, chopping her long, sand-colored hair to her shoulders. Elizabeth watches it land in chunks on the ceramic tile.

"I'm not trained in this," she says. "But I have a lot of practice. My handiwork will have to do." Alice puts her hands on her hips, squinting a little. "I think we need to go darker."

They turn the chair and Elizabeth leans her head back, letting her hair tumble into the sink. Her neck digs into the cold ceramic. Alice pours a pitcher of warm water over her hair, greasy from lack of a decent shampoo. She massages Elizabeth's temples and scalp with a dollop of Suave.

"You normally wait to wash the hair after applying the dye, but you really needed the wash first." Alice squeezes out the excess water with a towel.

Alice rubs the dye through her hair. The smell of ammonia settles heavily in the stuffy bathroom, stinging Elizabeth's nose. She is woozy from the cocktail of chemicals. Alice peels her rubber gloves off and cracks the window. A shiver runs down her neck. It's funny to think how a whole new life begins with her hair.

"So, how did you end up there?" She tucks cotton around Elizabeth's scalp and behind her ears, then covers her head with a plastic cap.

"Stupidity. Pure stupidity."

Alice perches on the fluffy pink toilet seat. "Tell me about it. Out of all the stories I've heard—"

Elizabeth shakes her head. Alice cannot know. No one can.

Thirty minutes later, her hair is the color of a moonless night. Alice packs her bag with burner phones and rushes them out the door.

"Be careful now." She takes Elizabeth's cheeks into her palms, looking at her with intense, shiny eyes. "You get across the border, into Oregon, and stop for the night. Go someplace that takes cash. Then call me. I'll arrange a bus ticket in my name to your next destination. Keep your head down. Try to be unmemorable."

Elizabeth takes a shaky breath and waves before they pile into the truck. They drive down the forested road in silence, leaving Washington for good.

"Where are we going, Mommy?"

Elizabeth cracks the window and lets some of the noxious smell from her damp hair out of the truck. She takes a deep breath.

"I'm not sure, baby."

But the road takes her toward the seashore, almost against her will, and definitely against her better judgment.

She is going home.

CHAPTER THREE

ELIZABETH

Charlotte Barkley is a legend throughout the country, but for the residents of the small town on the Oregon Coast, she is everyone's daughter. The Barkley Inn is nestled across the highway from a tiny, hidden pier outside of Tillamook County. The marina is weathered gray, with a few boats that seem perpetually docked there. There is a surf shop with an ocean mural painted on its door, an old-fashioned candy store needing a coat of paint, and a fish-and-chips restaurant. Rocky Shores is so sleepy it is swallowed by the lush, endless forest.

Rocky Shores was never a well-known town, not until Charlotte's disappearance. Now, the tourists stop by the bayside for a piece of a secret. Elizabeth wonders what the Barkleys think about this—how they feel about the influx of business their private tragedy has brought. Some of the kids at school whispered that the Barkleys knew what happened to the little girl. Others said that Myra Barkley's obsession bordered on insane, that she would wait at that inn for Charlotte till the end of time.

She kisses Theo on the forehead and tucks a blanket around him. It is the thickest blanket he's ever had. His lips turn up in his sleep, and she wonders what he dreams of.

Myra Barkley doesn't strike Elizabeth as all that odd. She would wait for Theo too.

Elizabeth redirects her thoughts to the plan she must adhere to if they want to escape. She unzips her duffel bag and rifles through it, retrieving the three burner phones Alice purchased from different Walmarts, and the stack of different identification cards.

Don't fuck this up, she thinks.

She holds the phone in her palm. Should she call Alice yet?

No, not until she is sure they are safe. She knows one thing—they can't stay here.

Elizabeth runs her fingers along the silver necklace and squeezes her eyes shut. How will she get out of this one?

Her breath quickens. Elizabeth poisoned the man. She could be guilty of murder. Or maybe it would be considered self-defense. Elizabeth is no lawyer. She's got no experience with cops, and there's no one she can think of to ask without sounding suspicious as hell.

Elizabeth cannot spend one more day incarcerated.

As soon as Myra and Herb retreat to the house, she will gather Theo and sneak out to the truck. Her eyelids are heavy; sleep threatens to overtake her. Even her muscles have gone soft from the hot bath Myra had drawn for her that afternoon. She decides to lie down, just for a few minutes. It is better to wait till deep in the night. She cannot head to the police with Herb and Myra in the morning. Run. That's what she is supposed to do. What she was told to do. Everyone from Rocky Shores is haunted by Charlotte Barkley. The old case will resurface. When the truth comes out, Elizabeth and her son will be filleted by the media. Imposter takes advantage of grieving mother. Her chest aches as she lies beside Theo.

Elizabeth Lark is no one's daughter.

CHAPTER FOUR

MYRA

Everyone is asleep. Myra can't stay at this house, dark and dingy, with thick brown curtains that droop to the floor, and the cracked linoleum that catches beneath their feet. Charlotte doesn't want her. Her daughter, for whom she has waited for so very long, does not want her. If she did, she would let Myra call the police. They should be at the station celebrating with Detective Marlow. They should be drinking champagne, eating cake. Actually, Myra remembers, Charlotte isn't fond of cake. The frosting is too sweet. She prefers ice-cream with a candle. It used to annoy Gwen, that Charlotte didn't want cake.

Who doesn't like cake?

Charlotte should be desperate to see Gwen and Jimi, her sister and brother. Why doesn't she want Myra, who has waited two decades for her to come home, to call everyone with this joyous news?

Myra isn't being fair, she knows. Charlotte has been through hell. Her daughter obviously doesn't want to sit in a crowded police station, where they will ask endless questions. But Myra can't help it. Her vision clouds with angry tears.

She paces the kitchen, waiting for the water to boil, for as long as she can take it. She grips the tea kettle and snatches it off the heat just before it whistles. Gritting her teeth, she smashes it to the ground. Steaming water streams over the floor and splashes on her leg. "Goddamn it!" she yells, unable to keep her voice down. She jumps out of the way and tosses a few dish towels over the mess, shaking.

The last thing she wants is for Herb to see her like this. "Aren't you happy? I expected you'd be thrilled." He'd furrow his brow, a look of disdain on his face. "Come on. She's been through all sorts of trauma. You expect too much." That's what he'd say, and he would be right.

Except she can't help it. She pounds her fist against the kitchen table.

She has no right to be angry with Charlotte. Her vision blurs. Terrible things have happened to her daughter, things she doesn't want to talk about. *How selfish I am!* But her insides twist so painfully. She cannot take this *feeling*. Myra should be ecstatic. Why isn't she happy? This reunion—how it danced in her mind for all these years—was supposed to fix her, glue together the broken shards of her family.

The thick steam fills the air. Fat beads of sweat collect on her forehead and drip into her eyes.

She must be patient, give her baby girl time, she thinks. And yet, she can't do this one thing for Charlotte. What a wretched mother she is. She blinks tears away.

All she has to do is wait till morning. Herb agreed that they should let Charlotte and Theo sleep.

What's one more night?

Myra slams the heel of her hand against the counter and winces in pain. Blisters erupt on her burned leg, her right fist is scraped and red, and a bruise swells on her hand.

This is not how she imagined this moment.

Myra inhales sharply; the hot, moist air cuts her lungs. As she bends down to finish mopping up the water, she feels Herb's presence in the doorway.

"Want Earl Grey?" She wishes he would go away.

"Look at me." Herb's voice is hoarse, almost a whisper. "I doubt one more night will make a difference. It's just twelve hours or so."

She steadies her breath, turning to face her husband. "You think we should call Gwen?"

The burst capillaries in Herb's eyes ripple in thin vines. "I think," he says slowly, "we should get the situation sorted with the police tomorrow."

Myra steels herself for an argument. "You think I'm making this up."

"That is not what I'm saying at all. Please, don't."

"Well, then what are you saying?"

"I don't want you to be devastated all over again." He pulls her close. "I love you."

Myra swallows, choking on the lump in her throat. She pulls back. "She has the necklace."

He stares at the floor. "I hope it's her."

"She has the same face, the same eyes. It's uncanny. She has to be Charlotte," she presses.

"Myra," he warns, "let's wait till tomorrow to get on the phone announcing to everyone that Charlotte's home. She hasn't told us much about what happened. If we go talking tonight, we could ruin a police investigation."

This is logical, she admits.

"Herb. I'm not crazy."

"No, you aren't." He goes to the sink and refills the tea kettle. "Want chamomile? Your favorite, right?" He puts his arms around her. "You have never been crazy, Myra. You were only trying to survive."

"She looks just like her, honey. It has to be—"

Herb rubs years of tension from his forehead. "All right. So, let's say this woman is Charlotte," he says. "What now? It's strange and uncomfortable for us. But we remember the first eight years of her life. What does she know about us?"

"She knew to come back to me," Myra insists.

"How much do you remember from that age? Have you thought about that? You can't go fixing it all so quickly. She claims she doesn't remember where she's been all this time. We can't make a snap decision as to whether she is lying or traumatized. Not yet anyway."

Myra considers this. "I remember my mother working this inn. I remember growing up here."

"Well, I'm not sure about you, but my memories of my parents from that age are kind of fuzzy. And she hasn't grown up with us."

"That's true," she concedes. "I guess we'll have to ask her."

"She didn't want to talk about it earlier, and I'm sure it's hard, but everyone knows about Charlotte's disappearance. Everyone who runs through town is curious about the kidnapped girl's ghost—"

"What are you thinking?" Myra laughs out loud. "That she's faking? I can't imagine what that would accomplish."

"I dunno. Maybe she's nuts. Maybe she's tired and running from something. That much I can tell. And she could have gotten this necklace anywhere. Had it engraved. They're a dime a dozen."

"She's telling the truth." Myra is sure of it. She folds her arms against her chest.

Herb raises his eyebrows. "I just don't want you to get your hopes up. Again."

"Hear me out." Myra speaks harshly. "I didn't even know she was wearing it. It never occurred to me. It's just a trinket she bought for Gwen's birthday at one of those cheap jewelry shops."

"This is getting creepy. If she isn't Charlotte, but she has her necklace, then . . ."

"Come on." She waves her hand dismissively. "I did not report that necklace missing. No one mentioned that she was wearing it. I bet Detective Marlow will confirm what I'm saying."

"Well, it was a long time ago. We were so upset. We can obviously ask her—"

Myra glares at him. "I can guarantee that I never knew she was wearing that necklace."

"That is why I am concerned," he says, slowly. "Maybe she knew about the necklace, had one engraved, and came here for money. What if she saw it in some old media report?"

"Herb! What a terrible suggestion!"

He strokes his chin. "Seriously. Is the safe locked?"

Myra narrows her eyes.

"Okay, okay." He yawns. "But we are stressed and exhausted. We need to get some sleep. That's why we wanted the girl to get some rest. There will be rigorous questioning tomorrow."

The tea kettle whistles, and Herb pours steamy water into a mug. He submerges a bag of chamomile and sets it in front of her. "Here. Drink this." He stands behind her and rubs her shoulders. "It will be okay."

Myra clenches her jaw. Her leg is mottled and hot. Wincing in pain, she wraps an ice pack in a towel and presses it against the burn. "Don't ask," she warns Herb, gazing into the soul of her tea. She takes a sip. "I'll be into bed soon. I'm going to sit and read a bit."

"Come on. Don't be mad."

"I have not been a perfect wife," she says, avoiding his face.

He sighs. "Neither of us has been perfect. That's marriage. But we are good now. So very good."

"Charlotte saved us."

"Why are you bringing this old shit up? It's dead and buried."

She exhales slowly. "You're right. It's just her birth healed us. And the loss of her cracked us again."

Herb takes her hand. "Nothing could break us," he whispers, with bright, shiny eyes. "Nothing."

"I'm sorry," she says.

"Please don't be angry because I'm skeptical."

"I'm not. I've gotten confused before. I understand your worry—but I can't go to sleep just yet." She feigns a smile. "Let me finish my tea and read my novel for a bit."

"All right." He starts for the door. Then he hesitates, hand hovering at the doorknob.

"What?" Myra groans.

He turns on his heels. "Please promise me you will not call Gwen or post on Facebook."

"Hilarious."

"I'm not kidding," he says.

"Just go to bed, Herb. I want to be alone."

He gives no indication that he's going anywhere. Myra ignores his presence, letting the steam from the hot cup bathe her face.

"I'm safe," she finally says. "I promise."

He closes his eyes tightly, as if remembering. "Okay, sweetheart. Come to bed soon, please," he says, voice cracking.

Don't worry, I'm not planning something crazy.

Myra sips her tea, stares at the phone sitting in front of her. She will wait till morning. She promised to wait till morning.

CHAPTER FIVE

ELIZABETH

Elizabeth wakes a little after two AM. She bolts up in bed and searches the room for Peter, heart thumping like she's been running. In the dreams she is always running. And when she opens her eyes, Peter is with her and there is nowhere to run.

She remembers: they have left.

Theo is asleep in the big bed beside her, under the fluffy comforter. The heater rumbles, bathing the room with intoxicating warmth. She yawns and summons all of her strength to keep her eyes open.

They have left.

The icy cabin is far away, up in the mountains, under a shroud of packed snow. Peter could be dead, his rotting flesh and harsh mold mingling into a toxic concoction.

Or maybe he woke up in a hungover daze, enraged. And now he is searching for them. If Peter *is* dead, will she be charged with murder? Will Theo be taken away from her? Christ, she shouldn't have come here. The poisoning wasn't in the plans. She cannot go to jail. She's not a killer.

They are too conspicuous here, in this inn filled with people who are preoccupied with her identity. In a few hours, the police will assault her with questions. If the lie is exposed, the public will execute her for what she's done to Myra. Or Peter will, because the news will lead him straight back to her.

She focuses, absorbing her surroundings. If she could escape that cabin, she can walk out of a public inn. Yes, that's what she'll do. She's made one mistake, and this one can be undone.

Elizabeth can breathe again. They have left.

She had no reason to doubt his threats. Peter's sinewy body was no match for her emaciated frame. She had to disable him for them to escape, to be certain he couldn't trail her. Over and over, she tells herself, she had no choice. Act or die.

He is gone. For now.

She climbs out of bed, sweat tickling her brow, and tosses their tawdry belongings in the duffel bag. The pile of IDs is safely packed in the zippered pouch. She slides one of the burner phones into her pocket. As soon as they get in the truck, she will call Alice and figure out a plan. She is frightened and shaky, but the lump of her son curled safely under a warm blanket soothes her.

It's time for her next move.

Elizabeth shakes Theo gently. "Hey, buddy."

He shifts in his sleep. "Mommy?"

"Time to go for a drive." She wraps the blanket around him and cradles his body. He rests his soft cheek against her chest.

"Is Daddy coming?" His voice is woozy with sleep.

"No, Theo."

She slings the duffel bag over her shoulder and creeps toward the corridor. A single halogen light crackles in the narrow hallway. It is quiet except for light rain pitter-pattering on the roof. Myra and Herb must be sleeping by now, and they'll never hear her. She'll pack Theo in the truck and drive away before they can catch up. Her stomach roils.

Heavy with shame, she pushes the light wood door open and peers around the corner. It looks clear. She may be dead broke and alone, but she will find an honest job. She isn't safe in Rocky Shores. Why did she come here? God, this was stupid.

Theo begins to stir as they round the bend. She shushes him, stepping with care, soft-footed as possible. Holding her breath, she arrives at the end of the hall. The weight of Theo on her shoulder makes her dizzy.

That's when a shock of light shudders in the lobby. Quick footsteps rap over the creaky floorboards. Whispers echo down the hall, growing louder and clearer. She freezes, and considers turning back for the room, but it's too late.

"Char—Elizabeth?"

Elizabeth steps into the lobby. She'll have to be straight with Myra.

"Where are you going?" Myra asks. Her hair is unbraided now, and it cascades over her shoulders in silver waves.

"I needed to get some air." Her voice wavers. "But since you're awake, we should probably talk—"

"Yes, I think that's a good idea," says a woman hovering behind Myra. Her arms are crossed; her jaw is set. She is wearing a pink hoodie and yoga pants.

Elizabeth blinks a few times, swallows hard. Her cheeks burn. She smacks her arm. This cannot be real. Gwen Barkley is standing right in front of her. Unable to contain the shock in her voice, she says, "I really need to take a walk."

"Where were you going with your stuff? And Theo?" Myra points to the duffel bag and little boy asleep in her arms.

"I don't leave my son alone." Elizabeth takes a step back.

"I'm sorry. Of course you don't," she says. Her glasses fog up and tears spill from her eyes. She dries the glasses on her nightgown.

Gwen steps toward her, squinting, as if inspecting a dead bird. "Let's sit down on the couch," she says. "You look pale. This is your boy?"

She nods dumbly. What is there to say? How can she get out of here with this family lurking in every corner? Elizabeth scoots as close to the armrest as possible and arranges Theo on the gold tasseled pillow. He stirs, as if he's about to wake, but she hushes him back to sleep.

"Elizabeth," she says. "I am so sorry for this. I understand my mother can be a bit . . . overbearing. You see, we lost my sister years ago, and somehow she believes Charlotte will still come home—"

"Gwen!" says Myra sharply. "Don't you speak about me like that."

"I'm sorry." She sighs. "Seriously, though. If you're over-whelmed, and you want to leave in the morning, don't stress about it, okay? She does this with strangers frequently." She tucks a piece of loose hair behind her ear.

Elizabeth stares at Gwen. As much as she wants to pack up their stuff, get up and leave, she could slap the oldest Barkley girl for how she talks to Myra. "I'm fine," she replies. "I don't find your mother overbearing at all."

"See, Gwen. I told you. Look at her face. It's her. Your sister is home." Myra's eyes glisten with tears. "Just look."

"Mom."

"Please, tell her about the necklace." She pauses. "The neck-lace. Remember, Charlotte bought it at Claire's. She had the pieces engraved with your initials. I took her to the mall . . ."

"Stop, Mom." She leans forward, studies Elizabeth more closely. "What necklace?"

"It's got the same engraving. CB. You have yours somewhere. We could compare them," Myra says. "Then you'll see." She turns to Elizabeth. "I'm so sorry. You came all the way home, after all these years. Gwen has no right to sit here and demand . . . proof."

Enough of this. They need to get in the truck and leave. "I think it's best Theo and I go."

After an agonizing silent moment, Gwen whispers, "You have her eyes. Are you . . . Is this . . . real?"

Oh no. Sweat beads on her neck. "It's not safe for us here. We'll get out of your hair," she says, nudging Theo awake. "It's just . . . I have a friend. She can keep us safe. This is a mistake. It's all a terrible mistake."

"But you're my daughter. You can't leave. How can coming home be a mistake?" She narrows her eyes at Gwen. "How could you? She's exhausted and overwhelmed—"

"No, I don't mean that. Coming home isn't, I mean it wouldn't be—"

"Okay, okay. I'm just so shocked." Gwen's lower lip begins to quiver. "I didn't mean to make you feel unwelcome. Mom has been waiting here, for you. There have been false alarms." She paces the room. "Holy shit. Where are the police? Why aren't they here?"

"No, no way. I can't deal with the police tonight." Elizabeth peers around Gwen's shoulder, toward the door. She is flustered, can't think straight. She opens her mouth to tell the truth.

Gwen retrieves a pink cell phone from her purse and dials 911. "Really, it's best," she says, waiting for someone to answer. "This isn't something we can handle alone. They'll be here in a few minutes."

She can't let this happen. Gwen is clearly doing her best to sound conciliatory, but the look in her eyes says otherwise. Does she believe Myra is crazy or that Elizabeth is lying? It's impossible to say. The most visceral guilt gnaws at Elizabeth's stomach. But she glimpses her child's thin pajamas, thinks about the hundred bucks she has in her bag. It has to last, has to get her to their next destination. And where will that be? How long will it take for her to find a job?

She is about to do something terrible. This will buy her time before she and Theo have to get on the road. And Alice. Oh shit, what is Alice going to say about the stupid, stupid decision she made to come here?

"It's okay." She hesitates. Taking a shaky breath, she continues, "I remember so little before that day. It's strange."

"I don't find much strange anymore," says Myra.

Elizabeth can agree with this.

The room is dim and quiet except for the storm. She cannot fathom driving that truck through desolate and unfamiliar roads and into the dark, dark night. The susurrus of pine and fir trees crackling in the breeze calm her; the scent of the water is familiar.

The water. The Pacific Northwest Coast has a very specific smell; the breeze is brisk even in summer. When it is warm, this coldness can sweep in and make a person shiver. Each time it is surprising, even to a native—how this cold wetness is icy and crisp despite the sunshine.

Peter is the cutting wind.

Myra probably loved the ocean before Charlotte vanished. Now nightfall must send a chill through her bones. The water was once exhilarating, before her mind conjured images of her baby, cold and alone.

When Elizabeth and her mother lived in Rocky Shores, miles from the inn, up in the mobile home park, the Barkleys were breezy and confident, respected. Gwen Barkley wasn't fond of people like Elizabeth and her real mother—she probably considered them trailer trash.

These people can't seem to let her go. That tea of Myra's sloshes in her stomach.

Sirens wail; she can see red and blue lights whirling through the blackness, and into the parking lot. Why would she stop in her hometown? Alice said not to call attention to herself. And that is precisely what she has done.

That's that. Now the cops are involved. She watches Gwen closely. Does she remember the girl Elizabeth used to be?

CHAPTER SIX

MYRA

Myra rubs the goose bumps on her arms. She's glad she called Gwen, even though she'd promised not to. As difficult as her oldest daughter can be, she's got a way of taking charge that comforts Myra. After the police arrived, they agreed to speak with Elizabeth in the morning. And they said that she and Theo should be examined at the hospital. After all, she's been held captive for two decades. And Theo was probably born at home.

"There is so much we don't know," the officer said.

"Obviously," Gwen added, shooting her mother a scathing look.

She feels like an idiot. Myra should have insisted on getting them medical treatment too, but she was so afraid of arguing with Charlotte, of breaking their fragile connection. And she had a reason to be scared; Charlotte *did* try to leave with Theo in the middle of the night.

None of this is how she imagined it; it's all surreal, the images of eight-year-old Charlotte mixed with this girl—this woman—who has come home to her, damaged, muted. Myra must be hard to recognize too. She was the young, frenetic mother, maybe a little too frazzled, maybe not patient enough, but blessedly naïve. Now she is weathered and gray and wrought with guilt for all the things she did wrong. With a missing child, your life is picked apart. Your parenting. Your secrets. Your marriage. Everything is cut open, left bare and vulnerable and ravaged.

Was her father close to her? Too close? Did you have postpartum depression?

Most of the time it's someone in the family.

"I can't believe she tried to leave," Myra says.

"I can't believe any of this." Herb rubs his forehead. "I just . . . all these years, you knew. I gave up on her."

"You didn't give up. You tried to move on." Myra runs her fingers down Herb's flannel shirt. She reminds herself that this is real. Tears flood her vision. The sound of gurneys rolling along the wax floors is grating.

"When are they coming back?" Herb rubs his hands together.

"I guess the cops are finishing up with her." Myra can hardly breathe. Waiting, waiting, waiting. Dammit, hasn't she waited long enough?

She envisions Charlotte screaming and terrified as she was snatched from the beach. Myra clenches her jaw, willing the thought to dissipate.

"Don't think about it," says Herb. "It's best not to think." He rests his head on her shoulder, running his thick fingers through her hair.

She relaxes in his arms.

"We have her back now. That's all that matters. Elizabeth is a perfectly fine name." He nudges her side, a half smile on his lips.

"I just hope the police don't say—"

Someone raps on the office door. Myra is weary of repeating the story. She can only imagine what her daughter is going through. Elizabeth. She rolls the name on her tongue.

"Detective Marlow," says Herb, "Can you believe it?"

Sarah Marlow howls with delight. "I've been waiting for this day." She smiles. "Well, you know, Myra. Charlotte got me in the heart."

Myra embraces the detective. Her windbreaker is damp with droplets of rain, but Myra doesn't care. She presses her cheek onto Sarah's slick coat. Over the years they've developed a friendship, though the rest of the police department was sure Charlotte had drowned that night. Kidnapping is rare. Death by exposure or injury is more common.

"She looks more like Gwen than the age progression photos, even." Sarah shakes her head. "All these years later, she knew to come home."

Herb clears his throat. "So, what has she said?"

"Well, if you're asking if this woman is your daughter," Sarah says cautiously, "we think so."

"Oh my god, Herb." Myra throws her arms around him. "I knew it. I just did."

"Let's hold on, before we get too excited," says Sarah. "We'll need a blood test to be sure. We can get DNA pretty quickly. A couple of days. But her story matches that evening. She knows all about your family, as much as she could, disappearing so young—"

"I know all of that. And I don't need a test," Myra says, feeling a sudden need to explain. "She came in with the necklace. Her necklace. She looks just like her older sister. Like Charlotte's baby pictures. There is no doubt in my mind that she is my child."

"It's just you've had a few . . . false alarms in the past." Sarah shifts uncomfortably, cheeks flushed. She rearranges her red ponytail. "I recommend the DNA test, Myra. She signed for it."

"All right," says Herb. "Let's not get into it. Not now."

Myra doesn't want to talk about it either. Her mind is on the homecoming. That's all that matters. "What's next? My biggest concern is finding this man."

"Elizabeth's afraid, of course. The boy is too. Neither of them will speak. All we know is that she was kidnapped, taken by a man on the beach to some cabin in the woods. Which is so vague, it doesn't help us much."

"Elizabeth." Myra furrows her brow. She had hoped Charlotte would take her real name back. An image of a dilapidated cabin forms in her mind. She holds her stomach, rocks on her heels.

"She wants to be called Elizabeth." Sarah pauses. "It's what she's been called most of her life."

Myra swallows a deep and heavy pain. It radiates through her body, as it has since they lost her. Except she is no longer entitled to it. Other mothers never see their children again, never experience this moment. Charlotte is back, she reminds herself. Even if she wants to be called a different name.

"That . . . man," Herb spits the word out.

"He's my grandson's father." Myra's voice is hoarse. "So that means—"

Sarah takes a deep breath. "It would appear that way, yes."

Herb puts his arm around Myra's shoulder. "At least she got free."

"We need to convince her to talk. Right now, all she knows is his name is Peter Briggs. Which he certainly lied about."

"Could there could be more victims?"

Sarah adjusts her collar. "I can't say so. Not yet. I'd like to pick her brain, when she's stable. To get some kind of idea about the location."

Herb stands and leans on the table. Myra avoids the wild look in his eyes. "If he's even still there. He could have bailed town."

Sarah's voice tightens. "That's the issue. We don't know. That's why we need to find him. Immediately."

"He could be searching for her, Sarah. Hunting her," Myra says. "You don't keep a girl hostage and then just accept it when she escapes." This is what Myra assumes, anyway. Based on what she's heard about abusive marriages. "Right?"

"This isn't a case we usually see," Sarah says softly. "Not one I've ever seen."

Usually, the victim is never found. Because she's dead. She puts her hand in Herb's and he squeezes it.

"It depends," Sarah continues, "on whether he's more motivated to get Charlotte back or to get away from the cops."

Myra doesn't want to think about Peter Briggs. About the night on the beach. She focuses on Sarah's face, tries to stay grounded. This is the moment she has waited for. It isn't time to relive the past. "Where is she? I just want to bring her home."

"I know the impulse is to rush her home and reunite her with family. But we need to proceed carefully. The hospital is releasing her. Physically, they are both okay, aside from malnutrition and dehydration."

"It's so strange," says Herb, "seeing her now, all grown up."

She knows what he's thinking. Eight-year-old Charlotte is gone.

Myra takes a breath. "When are you going up there?"

"The police are questioning her now. Looking at maps of the area. As soon as we have an idea where this cabin is, we'll drive up with her."

"Are you sure that's a good idea?"

Sarah sighs. "We're taking it as slow as we can, considering how urgent it is that we find this man. She is stable."

"Physically, perhaps." Myra smooths her shirt. "Emotionally—"

"She needs therapy, and so does Theo. They're giving her some anxiety meds." Sarah pauses. "We tried to trace the vehicle."

"And?"

"No luck. The last person it was registered to died fifteen years ago. She says the man drove it, but he didn't tell her anything useful about his work. Trucking, he said. Probably a lie."

"What else did she say about him? About that night?" Myra presses.

"She remembers only bits of the night she was abducted. Don't push her." Sarah taps Myra's shoulder. "You've got to keep it together. Gwen and Jimi are waiting in the cafeteria. You should talk to them while the doctors finish up with Charlotte and Theo."

Myra exchanges a glance with Herb. "Well, then. I wonder what Gwen has said to Jimi."

Herb sighs. "Let me do the talking this time. Please."

Jimi and Gwen are at the cafeteria, ashamed of her, once again. Except she is right this time. This has always been her battle, and now it is over. She can face the children, who think she's insane. Their family will heal.

Charlotte is home. This time, it is certain.

CHAPTER SEVEN

MYRA

Half the fluorescent lights flicker in the dim cafeteria, buzzing like a dying bee. Myra sees Gwen first, who is scrolling through her iPhone. She taps her foot as if annoyed that her evening has been interrupted. Myra squints, trying to compare Gwen and Elizabeth's features. The eyes are identical. Elizabeth is just so thin, and with her hair dyed such an unnatural shade of black, there are differences too. Well, she assures herself, the resemblance is clear. They aren't twins, after all. But Charlotte and Elizabeth—those pictures are so alike. Except in her baby pictures, she was healthy. Now, she's gaunt, pale. But the eyes are the same.

But Charlotte and Gwen have always had opposite personalities. Gwen is a skeptic, of everyone and everything. Like right now, Gwen is either posting this news on Twitter or bored because she's decided this is one of Myra's crazy false alarms. Probably the latter. And she's going to be very surprised to find out she was wrong. Myra can't help but smile, imagining Gwen's face.

Jimi digs his fork into an ice-cream scoop–shaped ball of mashed potatoes and shoves a big bite in his mouth. He wears his typical black garb, his hair in a long ponytail. When he notices them approaching, he stabs the plastic fork into the potatoes, where it stands upright.

"What's going on?" he asks. "Did you scare some poor girl this time?"

"I hardly think that's called for," says Myra.

Gwen slips her phone back in her purse and says in an even tone, "Mom, I really think you should speak to a therapist about this. You understand how weird this is, right? Calling me at two A.M., insisting you've found Charlotte, and she is sleeping in one of the hotel rooms? I get that you're on your meds and all. I promise this isn't an accusation—"

Jimi scoots out of his chair. "It's time for a damn intervention," he says. "You have to accept that Charlotte isn't gonna come plodding in the door, Mother."

Herb clears his throat. "Well, that's exactly what happened this evening. It's impossible to fathom for us too," he says, eyes shiny with tears, "but Charlotte is home." He slumps in his seat. "She really is."

"What the—Dad? Are you seriously falling for this too?" Gwen's mouth falls agape, which is not unusual for her. Myra wonders how a person can go through life perpetually gobsmacked over one thing or another, but she supposes this is what happens when you spend far too much time on social media.

"Please don't tell anyone yet." Myra speaks evenly. She must be rational; she must make them see that she is a reliable narrator of the event. Straightening her posture, she continues, "Would anyone else like something to eat?"

"Holy crap." Jimi rubs his temples.

"Dad? Are you serious?" Gwen's voice raises an octave.

Herb nods.

"Holy shit," Gwen continues. "What happened? Where has she been?"

"Wait. Just hold up." Jimi raises his palm. "Some girl is claiming to be Charlotte Barkley. I'll bet that's what it is this time. And you're falling for it. You better get a DNA test. I saw a film on this recently. It's happened before. The family fell for it out of desperation. Hook, line, and sinker. This is common knowledge. She probably wants money."

Myra and Herb exchange a glance.

"Please don't tell me you're falling for this shit too, Dad," Jimi says.

"Stop." Myra speaks firmly now. "Jimi, sit down and stop talking. I haven't eaten since yesterday. I am going to get some food while your father fills you in on the details. I'm not going to be disrespected by you two anymore."

Myra marches off and grabs a tray. She rolls it down the slanted metal tubes. The café is empty except for the young man working the register. She reluctantly accepts a round plop of mashed potatoes and some type of meat—Salisbury steak? Whatever. Her eyes are gritty and swollen from crying. The man smiles tentatively.

"No, it's good news," she says.

She collects herself and takes her tray to the table. Herb squeezes her shoulder in solidarity. *"Thank you,"* she mouths.

Gwen dabs her eye with a tissue. "I suppose I should text Kevin. It will be awhile," she whispers.

Her hair is smooth, makeup expertly applied. For a middle-of-the-night trip to the hospital. Her oldest daughter has always been abrasive. Deep and twisted roots tangled between them long ago. Gwen has had this haughty attitude, firmly convinced that her mother stopped loving her because she lost her little sister at the beach.

That was hard to forgive, Myra admits.

* * *

It was a warm evening in July, and Myra was heavily pregnant with Jimi. She and Herb sat across from each other, al fresco. This was one of the last dates they'd have before the baby was born. The candle between them wavered slightly in the breeze, the smell of hot wax meeting the salty air. Dishes clanged and waiters swished about, taking orders and making polite conversation with the patrons. All around, a pleasant vibe radiated through the restaurant. Her son wriggled in her belly. Myra and Herb had been good together lately. The rough edges of the early days of their marriage had been sloughed off. Now they shone, a reward for putting in the hard work. Herb slathered a roll with butter.

"I feel a little bad about making Gwen babysit." Myra took a bite of decadent food.

"Don't. She can watch her sister now and then. The kid is paranoid we're gonna pawn the baby off on her all the time too."

Gwen babysat about three times a year. Every time, she had a dramatic meltdown, as if she were Cinderella, stuck home while the other kids danced at the ball.

"I suppose you're right," she said. "She laid a guilt trip on me about some party on the beach tonight. We're not remotely strict, I told her. I even gave her twenty bucks for babysitting." Myra frowned.

"Aw come on, honey. She's a teenager. Let's have fun, okay?"

Myra picked at her eggplant parmesan. The sauce was supposed to trigger labor. The oregano. Something was about to happen. Maybe it was anxiety about the new baby. It had been eight years since they'd had a newborn, after all. Inhaling sharply, she focused on the clear, starry night. The full moon cast patches of pale light onto the ocean, like milk poured over the darkness. Somehow, the crash of the waves made her teeth shudder; she could feel her bones crack against driftwood poking up on the shore.

It was the impending labor she was afraid of, she thought. Her mind traveled to their preparations. The midwife was on call. She had a bag packed. Was there something she could be forgetting?

"What's wrong now?" Herb sighed. He was frustrated with her—again.

"Nothing," she replied, picking at the flesh of her eggplant. "Food just tastes a little bitter. Pregnancy hormones can do that, I guess."

"Mine's just perfect," he said, twirling pasta onto his fork, in the shape of a tornado.

The next hurl of the tide pierced her ears. She set the fork down.

"What is it?"

"I'm not sure," she murmured.

"Should we call Dr. Mills?"

"I don't need the psychiatrist," she said, irritated.

He opened his mouth to speak.

"It's not the baby either. I think we should go home." Her mind spun with a strange electricity. Something wasn't right.

Herb furrowed his eyebrows. "All right. I'll get the check."

The waiter maneuvered swiftly through a crowd of people. "Myra Barkley?"

That's when she knew.

"Yes?"

"Phone call from your daughter. She sounds hysterical. You better take it." The waiter handed her a cordless phone and hovered beside them.

A choked sob echoed through the phone. "It's Charlotte. I can't find her. We lost her on the beach."

Myra stood and looked out at the bay. Before her own panic could catch up, she said, "Gwen, what were you doing with Charlotte on the beach?"

Now, the truth cuts through Myra's mind with startling clarity.

They'd left her.

And she was presumed dead.

*   *   *

Gwen confounds Myra. Gwen is a very good mother, much better than she was. Myra would go insane with all Gwen manages. Little Savannah and Cora are in three sports for their self-esteem—gymnastics, ballet, soccer—Myra can't keep track of it all. Gwen and Kevin live uptown with the rich people. All of this suits Gwen, which is perfectly fine, but she and Myra live on opposite poles of the earth. How can you identify with a child you don't understand?

Myra and Herb are former hippies who run a bed and breakfast on the rocky bay. She has spent many years trying to puzzle out why there is such a disconnect with her oldest daughter. Now, she watches Gwen tap her fingernails, painted pink, with delicate flowers dotted over the tips, and it finally occurs to her.

Gwen is a cat person. She is a cat person in a family of dog lovers.

"They say not to overstimulate her or the boy," Herb says. "Post-traumatic stress."

"Fine." Jimi sighs. "I still worry about Mom getting attached to this woman and her son without DNA to confirm she's who she says she is."

"Oh, Jimi. Just look at the picture!" Gwen points to the Polaroid taken by the police. "She looks like me. You're just suspicious because you didn't know her—"

Jimi scoffs. "Yeah, well. I was born three weeks after she disappeared. I have heard nothing but Charlotte this and Charlotte that my whole life. So, I think I know her pretty damn well."

"Why are you doing this?" Myra asks in a soft voice. "Why do you want to take this moment away from me? I've been waiting twenty years. Twenty years!"

"All right. Let's all calm down. It's been a very overwhelming day." Herb squeezes Jimi's shoulder. "The police are fairly confident." He meets his son's eyes. "We need to support each other here."

Jimi glowers. "Are you suggesting I wouldn't be happy if this woman was really my sister? I'm only trying to protect you. Trying to be reasonable."

Myra bites her lip. She isn't going to take the bait. Heat prickles her skin. Blotchy red patches mottle her neck when she is stressed. She rearranges her scarf discreetly.

"We appreciate that. But you need to let your mother and me handle this, Jim." Herb comforts him, like always. Her stomach hurts. The mashed potatoes are like glue stuck to her insides.

"Yes sir." Jimi picks up the plastic tray. He dumps the food in the trash with a clatter. "Whatever you think is best. I hope to god that DNA test proves she's who she says she is. I just don't want this family destroyed all over again."

Myra doesn't intend to force a DNA test on Charlotte. She is their daughter. Myra knows it to her core. Except there's no benefit to explaining it to Jimi and Gwen. They will only dissuade her. Steal her happiness.

Tears dribble down her cheeks and onto the table.

CHAPTER EIGHT

ELIZABETH

Theo falls asleep on the way back to the Barkley place. Elizabeth taps her foot to the rhythm of the rain pattering against the windshield. Not a sliver of moon cuts through the clouds. She leans her head against the window, relaxing into the hypnotic buzz of the glass against her cheek. Other than the rustling of wind and rain and the tires humming along the road, the car is eerily quiet. Rocky Shores is the same as it was when she left with Peter, though the inn is a little shoddier than she remembers. The family put so much pride into it back then. The paint was fresh and bright in contrast to the peeling, ocean-weathered sorrow it bleeds now. Even outdoors, the place smells musty and antiquated, a museum dedicated to Charlotte Barkley.

She wishes she could sink into a puddle of mud and disappear. At any moment, Myra and Herb will recognize her. *Isn't that the little girl from the trailer park?* She can hear Gwen's snarky teenage voice, sense her presence.

Except, when the door creaks open, she understands why everyone thinks the place is haunted. Charlotte Barkley's legend or not, the 1960s decor and wood-paneled walls are creepy. A million ghosts could live in the folds of the thick curtains.

"Any guests tonight?" She can only hope. The thought of staying here alone with Herb and Myra, as they whisper about her while she sleeps, makes her bones rattle.

"Nope, not many in the winter," replies Herb. "We figured you'd stay at the house."

The house? She searches her mind for an excuse. There is no way she is sleeping in the Barkley house. In Charlotte's bed. Goose bumps prickle her skin. "We're already set up in the room downstairs in the hotel. I think Theo would prefer to go back." She tries to hide the tremor in her voice. She has no reason not to trust that the Barkleys are who they claim to be. But maybe she isn't the only one hiding something.

Herb opens his mouth to protest, but rain plunks harder. The wind nibbles at their thin clothing, and the dense fog blows like a cold dragon's breath. "It would be a pain to move your things to the house in this weather." He wipes droplets of rain from his cheeks with his flannel shirt. They hurry inside.

A brass chandelier flickers in the lobby. Half of the candlestick lightbulbs are burnt out, creating a shadowy semicircle of soft light. The furniture is a mismatch of dusty antique tables and newer couches. Elizabeth creeps back a step, cradling Theo tightly in her arms. It is so much darker than when she arrived. The emptiness is palpable. What could be hidden in the crevices of each room, going up three floors?

"We're working on renovating the place," says Myra, as if reading her thoughts.

The warmth contrasts with the wind chill outside. Her hands are freezing, yet heat floods her cheeks.

"How about a cup of tea before you go to bed?" Myra asks.

Is this family as strange as they seem? Or are they just completely dysfunctional? If so, Elizabeth is making everything worse. She imagines Myra Barkley's face when she finds out the truth. The woman will crumple into nothing.

If Charlotte didn't drown that night on the beach, what happened to her?

Herb wraps his arm around his wife. Elizabeth's guilt intensifies, builds in her stomach till she might cry. "Both of you need rest," Herb says. "You should get Theo to bed. It's just been so long. Your mother has waited for so very long." His voice cracks. Deep lines web his skin. His eyes are bloodshot and red-rimmed.

Mother? Elizabeth flinches at the word.

"I suppose one cup won't hurt." Elizabeth can't sleep tonight anyway. She needs to figure out how to get the cops to Peter. After that, she'll find Alice. Unfortunately, her truck has been impounded.

Elizabeth wonders if her trailer is still vacant. She yearns to go to her childhood home. That was the plan. Why did she deviate from it? Maybe she's no different from the neck-craning tourists who pry into Myra Barkley's life, reveling in her obsession.

Herb parks himself in the loveseat across from Elizabeth. "Quite the night."

She arranges Theo on a gold-tasseled throw pillow. An awkward energy passes between them. She isn't sure what to say, what Herb expects of her.

"This is all new for you," he says. "You don't need to rush over to your old bedroom right this moment."

Elizabeth raises her eyebrows.

"Or ever. If you don't want. I'm not sure how I'm supposed to act. I never expected this, Charlotte—"

"Elizabeth, please. Call me Elizabeth. It's what I'm used to, okay?"

She squeezes her eyes shut and wills herself out of this crumbly old hotel.

"I'm sorry." He frowns. "She's never thought about what would happen if you really came home. You're twenty-eight years old now, for god's sake."

Before she can speak, Myra enters from the breakfast nook, balancing a wood tray with three teacups. Spoons clink with her movement. She maneuvers toward them and eases the tray onto the beveled glass table. Her silver braid hangs over her shoulder, and a long, flowered skirt grazes her ankles. A coral and turquoise beaded necklace encircles her neck. Even at her age, she's still the salt-of-the-earth woman she was when Elizabeth was young.

"I have so many questions," says Myra, taking a seat beside Herb. "And yet I don't want to overwhelm you."

"Maybe we should do this later," Elizabeth says in a low voice. "Okay?"

"What was he like?" Myra quickly covers her mouth with her palm, clearly embarrassed.

"Myra," Herb warns, "that's too much for now. She just arrived and we aren't going to pressure her. *Elizabeth*." He emphasizes her name.

"Elizabeth," Myra says, tasting the word, obviously foreign to her tongue. "I'm sorry."

"I've spoken enough about Peter tonight." Her lower lip trembles. She wants to leave, to hide away. Why must Myra bombard her with questions?

Elizabeth tries to breathe but can't seem to fill her lungs. They have left the woods, and yet she is engulfed by the immense, dark forest where monsters hide in the night.

Peter slipped into her life and stole her youth with his charm. She remembers a sweet summer evening, resplendent with wildflowers and dreams. She had asked, smiling, with a hand on her swollen belly, "When will we start the farm?"

He shook his head. "We'll build when I have the money, Elizabeth. Stop pressuring me."

"I didn't mean to—"

She remembers his furrowed brow. His expression was dark, unrecognizable. Theo swam in her belly as if he knew their future.

"I need you to respect me, Elizabeth." His voice dropped to a cold whisper.

And as sudden and shocking as the beginning of a nightmare, he kicked her, swept her from her feet. Protecting her belly from impact, her palm smashed into the dirt.

Elizabeth shouldn't have pushed. He convinced her that he was stressed. She understood the strain of financial problems. It wasn't his fault. She'd touched his insecurity and he'd reacted.

His blank stare skitters through her mind.

Peter is a stinging nettle. He grows in thick clusters; they hide in the shadows with heart-shaped leaves. But inside, there are stinging, insidious hairs. Teeth skulk beneath his flowers, waiting to sink into unguarded flesh. The nettle flourishes in lushness, blends in with beauty. She could not have known.

Her palm goes to her leg, ensuring she's cut him off at the roots.

She catches Myra's desperate gaze, and it hits her: she has nowhere to go. It is cold and early in the morning. Her head aches. "Theo is exhausted." She motions to the boy, whose chest rises and falls, followed by little snores.

"You don't have to talk about him ever if you don't want. Just help the police. We're so happy you're home." Herb's face twists into a pained expression.

Weird as they may be, Elizabeth can't crack their world tonight.

"So very happy. It's like I'm in a dream." Myra moves beside her, and before Elizabeth can protest, buries her head into her chest. "Oh, my darling daughter. You're home. After all these years."

Elizabeth pats her back. What the hell has she done?

CHAPTER NINE

GWEN

Gwen sits cross-legged on the bed, tossing old treasures out of a large box into two piles. Left to throw out, right to keep. Everything she owns is organized, with the exception of this battered moving box. Her earrings are arranged in neat rows across a velvet jewelry box. The tennis bracelet Kevin gave her for Christmas encircles a bracelet stand. Even her yoga pants are folded in soft piles.

Something terrible is about to happen. That man will get her children. Gwen takes a Xanax with a gulp of water.

This box is a tattered mess of broken memories. She finds yearbooks, a cheap necklace from her first boyfriend (Gwen has always loved jewelry), even the terrible poetry he wrote her (he thought he'd be published someday, but she didn't have the heart to dissuade him). The one thing she cannot locate is the half-heart necklace Charlotte bought her from Claire's at the mall twenty years ago. Her forehead breaks out in sweat.

Gwen flops forward on the bed, stretching her arms out in child's pose. She reaches her fingertips as far as they will go, screaming into the darkness. What will she tell her sister when she can't find the necklace? Her sister has been imprisoned for twenty years, holding onto that necklace, now rusty and tarnished, and Gwen can't even locate her half.

Her stupidity was mind-boggling. Jared was the one who wrote poetry and love letters, who made her swoon with his surreal level of attractiveness. He was older than her, and she thought she was in love. That evening, Charlotte's eyes were droopy, and all she wanted to do was watch cartoons. Her parents glowed at the thought of one simple evening alone, not tending to the inn. But Gwen couldn't skip one party.

Her mistake ruined everyone's life. There is no skirting the truth.

And now, Gwen has Kevin. They have date nights. Their children stay with a responsible friend or her mother. Her chest burns deep inside. She deserves none of it. Gwen dragged her little sister to the beach, and in a passionate argument with a boy, she failed her.

She had applied a generous coat of mascara in the bathroom, complaining to her friends about being stuck with her baby sister. Gwen knew Charlotte could hear her prattle on. Childish exasperation surged through her blood. She *wanted* to make her sister feel like a burden.

Shut up, she'd said. Don't be such a baby.

Worst of all, she imagines Charlotte, sitting alone by the jagged rocks. Perhaps she was fingering the necklace, shivering and crying to go home. Gwen will never know what Charlotte, with the messy hair and the flamingo-colored flip-flops, was thinking when the strange man grabbed her from the beach and drove her up that mountain. Was his hand smashed against her face to keep her quiet? Or did she scream all the way to that truck, but no one noticed? No one noticed because they were too busy drinking beer and toking weed out of a bent soda can, basking in the glow of the fire.

First, she lost Charlotte, and then she lost the necklace.

She didn't even report the necklace along with what Charlotte wore to the beach that evening. Pajamas. She couldn't remember what color they were. Pink? Purple? Gwen's cheeks burn with shame. She thinks of her own six-year-old daughter, Cora, and tears prick her eyelashes.

Gwen plans her children's outfits every morning. And then she notes them in her phone. She will never forget again.

Gwen jumps off the bed and gets into downward dog, stretching her leg up and to the right. But yoga is not enough today. After a few more stretches, Gwen eventually slips into the walk-in closet, shuts the door, and screams and screams until her throat is raw. Primal screaming heals the soul. There was a whole article about it on Pinterest. It cures numerous stress-induced ailments, supposedly, and seemed harmless enough to try. So far, the only side effect is a sore throat.

Gwen is very good at fixing problems. She has two children, after all.

She takes a slow, measured breath and exhales, pulling in her belly. She puts on her skinny jeans and an off-the-shoulder sweater that covers a few unfortunate stretch marks. They have surgery for this, of course, but her Instagram followers assure her that it's best to be grateful. At least you don't have a muffin top, they say. And those are not stretch marks—they're tiger stripes—to remind her of the children that grew inside her belly.

Gwen is not particularly grateful. But the other mothers will judge her if she surgically removes the evidence of her pregnancies. Some women are infertile. Her soul ought to be filled with Zen. She knows, better than anyone, the importance of keeping a decent reputation. It's bad enough that everyone thinks the Barkley Inn is haunted. And that her mother is batshit crazy.

Jimi calls himself the invisible son. "I'm here, Mom. I'm still here." He said this with his eyes, with the way he trailed after her as a toddler. Gwen took over for the first time in her life. She mothered Jimi when her mother would not—could not.

It is important to break the cycle.

Gwen crosses her legs again and sits with her spine straight, hip flexors flat. She says the serenity prayer to herself. With Charlotte's homecoming, she cannot afford to play the blame game. Tragedies happen. Bad things happen to good people.

She flops backward onto the mattress.

Fuck it. Her mantras don't work. Years ago, she didn't believe in affirmations. When she broke up with Jared and Charlotte was presumed dead, she would have told you this affirmatively.

She rushes into the bathroom and brushes all her pink and yellow Post-it Notes off the mirror. They flutter to the ground like leaves falling from the cottonwood trees. Her branches are skeletal; her roots are shallow.

That's all I am, she thinks. An empty soul full of flimsy bullshit.

She slides open the bathroom drawer, where her collection of Sephora makeup is artfully arranged, and selects a palette of colors. Fake. Fake. Fake. Perhaps she'll get the tummy tuck and boob job to go with it. What do the ungrateful mothers call it? A mommy makeover. Yes, this is exactly what she needs. She drags a mascara brush through her eyelashes and plucks a few stray hairs from her brows.

Just as she puts the finishing touches on her makeup, she hears the key turning in the lock of the front door.

"Who's there?"

No answer. What if Peter Briggs finds her family? She's happy her sister is home—of course she is. Gwen got her sister kidnapped; now she's escaped, and the son of a bitch will come for her kids next. That's the way things go for Gwen.

"It's just me, Gwen." Her husband shuffles around downstairs. The mudroom door screeches open, and she hears him talking to the girls. "Put your backpacks away. We line our shoes up in the cubbies like Mommy says, right?"

Cora and Savannah grumble about wanting a snack.

"Your mother went to a lot of trouble to organize this, girls," he says, sounding weary.

Kevin tries so hard. She shoves the mess from the bed into the box and hides it in the closet. She exhales.

"Coming," she yells.

Gwen dashes downstairs, trying to look composed. Kevin's eyes are puffy and dark. He offers a weak smile.

"Have you thought about getting someone to Feng Shui your office, babe? Accounting is a stressful job."

Kevin sighs. "Not that shit again." He inspects her face. "Why are your eyebrows so inflamed?"

"It's called grooming," she snaps. "You could learn something."

"I find arranging people's finances calming, I suppose. Girl Scouts is stressful."

Gwen laughs at this. "It really is. How was it?" Her mind is ragged, stomach churning. She almost wishes she hadn't sent Kevin with the girls to the weekly scout meeting, considering she *never* misses the girls' activities, particularly scouting, as she is the troop leader. She feigned illness, but everyone must know. They're talking about Charlotte's homecoming, whispering about how it was Gwen's fault. Maybe they think she's a negligent parent. They probably won't let their children come to her spacious house, which she had designed especially for nurturing young minds and childproofed with every possible accident considered: they have no trampoline, pool, guns, or Tide Pods.

Kevin catches her eyes, and tired as he is, he'd do anything for her, for their family. "I don't think anyone judges you for Charlotte's disappearance. They are just happy she's home."

Gwen looks at the ceiling. "I couldn't find the necklace, hon."

"You were a teenager. Do you keep every little craft the kids make in school?"

Gwen does keep all of their crafts. They are organized alphabetically and color-coded by holiday and grade level.

He throws his hands up. "Never mind. The point is, stuff like that gets lost. You didn't expect she would be abducted—"

"Stop," she whispers. "Just stop."

"I love you, Gwendolyn Barkley," he says, wrapping his arms around her. "I know who you are deep inside. And I only wish you could know too."

She smiles sadly, wondering why Kevin loves her, after all this time. Her beauty has faded; she has stretch marks and saggy breasts no exercise can fix, and she's not even particularly nice much of the time. Kevin is naturally sweet and funny, maybe because he was nurtured as a child.

And Gwen, well, a vague sense of irritation buzzes off her most days. She is frayed and jaded straight to her core.

"Why don't you take a nap?" he says.

A familiar shame rises inside her. Kevin loves her. But he doesn't *know* her.

"I suppose a nap would be good."

He kisses her nose. "I'll take the girls and pick up pizza. Give you a break"

She had planned to make salmon, brown rice, and kale for dinner.

"Gwen," Kevin warns, reading her mind again. "You can have a salad with it, if you want. Throw a superfood on your greens. But damn it, let me help you."

"Okay." She blinks tears away.

The kids bound into the kitchen, bright smiles on their faces. "Are we going to see Theo?" asks Cora. "One of the moms at the meeting today said he needs friends."

Gwen raises her eyebrows, leaning against the granite island. "They are talking about us."

"Girls, go get ready." Kevin says quietly.

Savannah and Cora exchange a glance and shuffle back to the mudroom, whispering.

"Well, are they? What are they saying?"

He looks weary. "No one judges you," he reiterates.

"Oh Kevin, you just can't appreciate how they are." Gwen shakes her head. "These women want gossip. That's what this is about. Don't you see?"

But Kevin doesn't see. There is such pressure to be a good enough mother, a good enough woman. To feed your children a perfect diet. The photos of her Facebook friends' artfully arranged meals kill her appetite. Because her children hate quinoa. They won't even eat onions hidden in a casserole.

Gwen will never be enough.

CHAPTER TEN

ELIZABETH

Elizabeth's mind races. She is out of money. The place is surrounded by cops, and her picture is plastered all over the internet. She dials Alice's number. Please, let Alice be okay. If Peter gets to her—Elizabeth refuses to think of it.

Wait. She shouldn't call Alice from the hotel. She hits "End" and shoves the phone in her bag. It's better to make the phone call once she gets on the road. Her blood pools with rage. Peter's venomous face lingers in every corner of this weepy hotel. Detectives and the FBI are packed in the kitchen. They think they are protecting her. They think they are in charge.

They are mistaken.

She finishes packing, moves briskly. Breathless, she tells Theo to get his shoes on. He gives her a sideways glance, twists his lips as if he is about to speak, but he complies. They have learned to sense danger from one another. He knows when he can argue and when he must listen very closely. She ties the red sneakers Myra bought him, sweat trickling down her neck. Her pulse quickens. They must leave now.

She presses her ear against the thin door.

Detective Marlow speaks, "Peter won't take the chance and come after her. Especially with the Feds surrounding the place. That would be a stupid choice."

"How did these pictures get out?" Myra asks, incredulous.

"Easy enough. Nothing stays secret for long in this town," Herb says. "Besides, everyone and their brother has a camera phone."

"Come on now," another voice interjects. "We all knew it would be only a matter of time. This is big news everywhere. There was no stopping it. Only slowing it down. Like Detective Marlow says, we have the situation under control. There's no way around a press release, but we'll keep the information minimal . . ."

Press release? Elizabeth might throw up.

"No one leaves the hotel until we verify their identity . . ."

Elizabeth assumes this includes her. If it comes down to it, she will admit the truth just before she skips town. She reaches behind the bed. The space is tight, and her hand scrapes the wall. Spreading her fingers out, she touches the phone she hid there. The last pay-as-you-go phone. She grasps it and slides it up on the bed.

The window is cracked open an inch or so. Wind splinters the old structure; it is a warning. Elizabeth shivers. The pier across the street is vacant; the screech of plover birds over the water is eerily piercing.

"C'mon, Theo. Now," she says.

She pulls him onto her, and he throws his arms around her neck. His tears wet her hoodie.

"Oh baby. I'm so sorry. We are going somewhere safe. I promise." Her own eyes water, but she refuses to cry.

Do not lose your shit, she tells herself. *Not now.*

"Let's go," she insists.

Elizabeth grips Theo's hand and marches into the kitchen. She ignores the police and FBI team. "We're going for a walk," she tells Myra.

Myra looks momentarily startled and exchanges a glance with Sarah Marlow, who shrugs.

"Do you want a ride?" Myra says. "It would be safer. Plus, it's raining."

"No, I really need some air."

"That's perfectly fine," Herb says. "Call if you want a ride back, okay?"

Elizabeth nods; relief floods her veins. She expected some sort of resistance from the Barkleys. Directing Theo toward the lobby, she says, "I just can't stay inside all the time. It makes me claustrophobic."

Elizabeth's doesn't wait for a response. They step out into the fresh air and start toward the bus stop. She pauses for a moment and changes course. Elizabeth's head swims. Which way? She gathers her bearings, grips Theo's hand. He is breathless but scampers up beside her. Their feet clack against the aged slats of wood. Sand lashes at their skin like shards of glass. Blinking, she shields Theo's face. Her hands freeze; her heart palpitates under her ribs. The wide-open space is at once freeing and terrifying. Ragged seaweed clings to the poles. The water is rough and moody. Green patches of phytoplankton float on the surface, but they are swallowed by choppy waves with each new tide. Sulfur permeates her nose. No one fishes today. Signs are posted where people usually gather—even in winter, they wrench their fishing poles against the squall. The signs say "Do Not Fish or Swim. Bacteria in the Water."

They slow their pace. She breathes in her surroundings—the wildness of the frothy green water, the thick clouds layered over them, the bitter gale that licks at their faces. Theo is silent, as if he knows there is something special about this moment, about this pier. Her blood surges through his; he melts into her. The chocolate store is closed for the winter. She remembers lingering outside, watching the other children line up for saltwater taffy or chunks of fudge. Sometimes, after payday, her mother would give her a couple of bucks for candy, but Elizabeth rarely spent it. She stuffed it under her mattress in case they needed it for a dire emergency, one that sent her panicked mother to the pawn shop with her collection of old vinyl records. Elizabeth offered her the money, proud of her resourcefulness, but it was never enough.

Nothing was ever enough.

Elizabeth quiets her mind, listening to the waves roll. She takes in the moisture that sticks to her cheeks from the billowing clouds. The gray comforts her. She relaxes her grip on Theo's hand, realizing how tightly she'd been holding onto him.

They can't get on the bus, she decides. Too risky. There are too many people with cell phones. All they'd need to do is snap a picture and post it to Twitter or Facebook before she reaches her stop. She cannot predict Peter's next move, doesn't know his friends or how he makes money. Danger could be in plain sight.

The blustery walk clears her mind. Leaves rustle around them, and the presence of water smooths her frayed nerves. Theo doesn't complain, though their destination is three miles away. She must stop this nightmare before she believes her own stories. What she has done is unforgivable. She wasn't raised to keep secrets, to tell lies. Then again, she wasn't supposed to fall for a psychopath. Alice assures her this can happen to anyone, yet Elizabeth is buried in shame. There is shame in dependence. In poverty. And Elizabeth has spent her life in both.

So, she takes her son home.

Her lip trembles at the sight of her trailer. The windows are broken. Moss sprouts up the walls. The shingles dangle from the structure, battered and lifeless. The buttercup-colored paint has been sloughed away. A "For Rent" sign rattles in the wind.

She may as well try her key.

Her hands shiver. She considers turning to leave. This is breaking and entering. She spins around, checking out the neighborhood. Leaves are piled on the lawn like a burial mound. Skeletal tree branches have crashed onto the saggy roof.

The ramshackle trailer emanates her mother's life and death. It's better than Mom's hollow frame, better than those days with the hospice nurses. She can smell the putrid scent of cancer mixed with orange air freshener, pungent in her mind. It's not here anymore, she knows. And neither is her mother.

She takes a sharp breath and inserts the key. It's a little rusty, but she jiggles it till the lock turns with a teeth-chattering screech.

The place has clearly been abandoned for some time. It smells musty and dank. Black mold sprouts from the walls, and the carpet near the broken window is soaked. A mossy green substance grows beneath the window, and the ceiling is dirty. It looks nothing like it did when she left with that man. Tears stream down her face. She coughs in her arm. Acrid bile burns her throat.

"Mommy, where are we?"

"My home," she says, though one cannot call this place a house. Not anymore. Elizabeth takes Theo in her arms and carries him into her old room. She flops on the blackened carpet and curls around her son. Her chest is tight with anxiety. She swallows hard, tries not to cry.

She's taken Myra on a new and terrible journey predicated on yet another lie. They should leave, get it done with. If they go to Alice's *right now*, Myra will eventually recover. She flashes her son a half-hearted smile. Theo doesn't buy into fables or fairy tales.

"This place smells too," says Theo.

"That's not nice to say," she retorts. "This was a friend's house. We can't say mean things about it."

"When are we going back to the hotel, Mommy? That family is nice, and it's warm there."

She studies the moldy walls, then the broken window. To Theo, this is the simplest choice in the world. There is no way to explain that she has lied. That they don't belong with the Barkleys.

"Why are we *here*?" His voice is filled with disappointment.

She sighs. Her mother's house is so cold and dank it almost resembles the cabin they just escaped. "Theo, I love you very much."

He looks up at her and says, "Then let's go back."

Myra and Herb will be utterly frantic. What has she gotten them into? What has she gotten herself and Theo into? She rubs her temples. Driving Theo wherever Alice sends them will be a nightmare. At the inn, he is warm and dry and cared for. She circles the room, thinking. They should not go back; it will only worsen the situation. But what else can they do now? It would be so much easier if she had time. She had hoped there would be time, but they can't stay here. It's freezing, and the mold is probably toxic. Mice are probably scurrying in the walls.

What if the cops alert the media that she has disappeared for the second time? If everyone thinks she's been kidnapped again, that could lead Peter right to her. It would be far better if he thought she was with the Barkleys, at least till they get out of town. That inn is crawling with police. Peter is not a fan of law enforcement.

She reconsiders her plan. "Okay." She hopes she isn't about to make another huge mistake. "We're going back to the inn now."

He looks at her intently. "Got it, Mommy."

She imagines Myra Barkley's pleading eyes. God, the woman *wants* to believe Charlotte has returned to her. Who is Elizabeth to take that away from her?

CHAPTER ELEVEN

MYRA

Myra taps her foot, paces, tries to take steady breaths, but she cannot get Elizabeth and Theo out of her mind. The inn is devoid of guests; her daughter and grandson spend all their time in the hotel room. She bakes three dozen cookies throughout the afternoon, hoping they will come out.

Eventually, she pads down the hall and knocks on the door.

Elizabeth pokes her head outside. "Hi, Myra. We were just about to take a nap—"

She's dejected, but not surprised. "That's okay. I made cookies. Just came down to see if you wanted to try one." Myra waves her hand and turns away. "Have a nice nap."

"Um . . . Myra?" Elizabeth widens the door.

"Yes?"

"I suppose we could come out and have a cookie."

"Really?" she says. "I mean, sure. If you'd like." Her heart is soaring, but she tries to keep her voice steady.

They sit down on the couch, and Theo chews his cookie voraciously. "These are great," he says.

Elizabeth nods. "They really are. Thank you."

Myra does bake very good cookies. Her mother was not remotely domestic. In fact, her parents were too hippie for Myra's liking. They preferred bourbon to baked goods. But her mother taught Myra all she knew about art and poetry and music. Myra was a little embarrassed about her life at the raucous bar in contrast to her friends' lives. Their mothers were housewives and catered to their husbands rather than a roomful of patrons. Still, Myra learned to paint. The other girls were enthralled by her mother's art, by the various brushes and tubes of oil colors, by the canvases stacked against the walls.

Myra turns her attention to Theo. Her grandson. "What's the giraffe's name?" She remembers Charlotte's pink kitty. It turned light gray because the little girl dragged the thing everywhere. No stain remover could return Pinkie to her original plushness or bubble gum color.

"His name is Freddy."

Theo is adjusting more easily than Elizabeth, it seems to Myra.

Theo shoves the last bite of cookie in his mouth.

She twirls the end of her silver braid in circles. Sitting in this house is driving her mad. They're all waiting for Peter Briggs to hear about Charlotte's return and show up at the inn. The familiar panic claws at her chest. And she can feel Elizabeth's anxiety buzzing in the air. She needs a distraction. They all do.

Theo glances at his mother sideways. "Why are you being so quiet?"

"I'm not. Just tired, is all." She chews at her cuticle. They're about to rush off to the hotel room again. Myra's stomach swims.

She thinks for a moment. "Why don't we paint a picture?"

"With a real brush?" Theo says. "I've only seen those on TV. Daddy brought home coloring books sometimes, but those are kinda boring."

"Yup. I have lots and lots of colors too. Get your jacket."

They gather their coats and head to her shed, shielding their faces from the rain. Her stomach flutters with anticipation. As they approach, Myra says, "Well, here it is."

Myra has had the little studio behind the house since before she and Herb married. It is a simple prefab shed, like a mini-barn with wooden plank walls and enough room for her equipment and the paintings that line the walls. It is cold and damp in the winter, but oil paints fare well in the shed, though the lighting isn't optimal. This doesn't bother Myra. Her dream of becoming an artist faded years ago, like the charcoal sketches smeared and buried in a box somewhere. Painting keeps her hands moving, quiets her mind. This is all she expects from her brushes and paints. All that accompanies her is the scent of fresh rain, the swish of her brushes, the scrape of her palette knife.

She guides them toward the shed, helping him avoid pockets of mud. They are almost there when Theo stops.

"Wait." He stiffens, squeezing her fingers so tightly they go numb. "What's that?"

The wood door swings open on its hinges, croaking like a raven.

"Go back to the house. Get my phone." She nudges Elizabeth. "Take him."

Elizabeth scoops Theo up into her arms and flees, soft-footed.

Myra's pulse hiccups in her throat. She rushes for the shed. "Anyone there?"

No response. She flings it open.

Her paints are aligned in rows, just as she left them. The paintings are in order.

She exhales, shaking her head. How silly. She must have forgotten to shut the door. Still, she picks out the colors as quickly as she can. The shed is icy cold. Red, yellow, blue. They can make more colors out of these . . .

Her eyes are drawn to the wooden stool where she sits to paint. Its back is swiveled away from her equipment. Something is off. Is she losing her mind? Her thoughts dart in circles. The soft halogen bulb flickers, taunting her. This is all her imagination. Maybe Herb came out to look for her and forgot to latch the door. The wind could've blown it open.

A painting of a newborn baby lies haphazardly on the floor.

It is usually hidden behind stacks and stacks of old canvases. A layer of dust has been swept away from the center and collects along the edges. Her hands slack numbly at her sides like a rag doll with ripped seams.

The baby's face is missing.

She turns and runs for the house, screaming, "Theo! Elizabeth!"

Silence.

She rushes through the icy rain and into the house. Theo and Elizabeth hide behind the couch, holding her phone.

Patting his back, Elizabeth says, "Shush. Shush." They huddle together. He throws his arms around his mother's neck. Myra fumbles with her phone and dials 911.

Peter Briggs has found them. He was here, at her house, slashing her painting.

* * *

The cops huddle around Myra's painting, lying on the dining room table. She and Elizabeth stand off to the side. There is a sharp division between the two women and the police, who argue about what might have happened, about what must be done. Above the hum of the detectives' conversation is Herb's electric screwdriver, howling and catching, ratcheting and stopping, as he installs new deadbolts on every door.

"Are there security cameras around the building? Anywhere?"

"Yes," Herb says, his voice distant.

"Check the camera feed," Sarah tells one of the uniformed officers. "Maybe we can get him on tape . . ."

Myra's belly is raw and empty. She and Elizabeth are silent because no one would hear them anyway. Myra twirls the end of her braid and squints at Charlotte's missing face. Her fingers are numb and cold, and she's mesmerized by the decapitated baby, the canvas's frayed edges,

Sarah taps her shoulder. "We're on top of it, Myra. Could've been him, could've been a copycat. You know how that goes."

"He knew it was Charlotte. It's like he's telling us something. That he intends to tear us apart again. To return for her." she says.

"He carved it with some sort of knife. It's not one from the house, is it?"

"We haven't found the knife. Looks like something sharp, precise. A pocketknife or an X-Acto knife. Did you have anything specifically for crafting?" Detective Schumer is Sarah's partner, a tall Black man with a light stubble and a trim build. He wears a serious expression as he paces the length of the room. The moment is surreal. Myra conjures a memory of the two detectives in her house after Charlotte's disappearance, similarly pacing, positing questions, searching for reasons, and coming up without answers. They were so much younger, so much greener.

She runs her finger along the severed canvas and considers this. "No, not that I know of."

"It's the only newborn painting. He could have assumed it was her without knowing it, Myra. He doesn't know what you painted, years before he took her. That's a huge stretch," Sarah murmurs. She turns to Schumer. "Let's keep searching for that knife."

Elizabeth shakes her head. "He's been here. He's not stupid enough to be traced or leave a knife behind. This isn't safe for any of us." She steps back toward the hotel room. "I'll call Alice. We need to go."

Myra follows, a great pain spreading through her body. "You've only just returned."

Elizabeth lifts her chin. "Don't you see? This is dangerous for you too. I can't drag you down with us. And now that he knows where we are—"

"The police are here. They'll find him and arrest him." Myra's voice trails off, realizing how impotent she sounds. Who are they kidding? How can the cops protect them? Obviously, it didn't take long for Peter to locate Elizabeth.

Sarah appears in the doorway, arms crossed against her chest. "Let's all take a deep breath. We'll keep a patrol car here. Herb is changing the locks."

Elizabeth shivers. "I know him."

Myra meets Elizabeth's eyes. "You are safe."

"Okay," Elizabeth says weakly. She sinks into a chair and puts her face in her hands.

CHAPTER TWELVE

ELIZABETH

She paces the musty hotel room. Maybe someone else destroyed the painting, she tells herself. The police said this had happened when Charlotte disappeared. Some copycat. They aren't exactly dangerous, Detective Marlow said. Just some bastard trying to scare them.

Elizabeth wants to believe this, but fire flickers at the nape of her neck. It is that same flash of heat she felt when she and Peter met, the one she ignored. An instinct. Someone is toying with them, and she understands Myra's fear. Even if Peter hasn't found them yet, someone has. And this person doesn't have benign intentions. She knows it, knows it deep to the pit of her soul.

Her fingers tremble as she dials Alice on the pay-as-you-go phone. "Please pick up. Pick up."

Alice answers on the first ring. "Girl, thank god it's you."

The cadence of different voices in the background dissipate. Alice must be heading to another room.

"Is everything okay there?" Elizabeth asks.

"We're okay. Do you need me?" Alice speaks in an even tone.

"Some shit's gonna come out soon. About Peter, and the cabin." She pauses. "He is looking for me. The FBI is involved."

"What the hell? Where are you?"

Elizabeth hears Myra approaching. "Look, I gotta go. I'll call you tonight. After this family dinner thing—"

"What the—what the hell, girl? I'll get you a bus ticket. Ditch that truck."

"I'm sorry," Elizabeth whispers. "I have to go." She presses "End," takes out the batteries and places the phone under a pillow. She crunches it with her boot. Myra had said she could take the car anytime. Elizabeth hates taking from these people. But her only option is to drive out of town and get on a bus. He could have taken her and Theo by now. But he wants to make her pay. He isn't finished yet. She cannot let her guard down; he will pounce. He will take Theo far away and murder her without a sliver of remorse. She grasps Theo's hand and says absentmindedly, "I guess it's time for dinner . . ."

"Are Savannah and Cora going to be there?" Theo says.

"I think so." She leads him out of the inn and to the Barkley house.

"Cool," he says. "This will be fun."

Elizabeth's nerves are frayed; she can't stop trembling. The last thing she wants to do is sit around the table and eat a meal with the Barkleys. Her mind is spinning. Myra invites them inside.

The scent of food makes her stomach swim. Olive oil sizzles in a cast iron skillet, the scent of crispy chicken wafting through the small kitchen. The edges of the thighs curl up in the rendered fat. The room is hazy with light smoke. Myra cracks the window.

"Can you chop this onion?" Myra says, knocking Elizabeth out of her reverie.

"Oh, sure." Elizabeth takes the onion and slices it in half. Its skin crinkles and stings her fingers. The rhythm of chopping soothes her.

Myra sets a bunch of carrots on the cutting board. "Would you mind cutting these up too? I'll put the chicken in the oven."

"Sure." Elizabeth smiles lightly, eyes watering from the onion. She holds a carrot in her palm and shreds the tough outer skin into the sink. The orange root is bright and smooth in her hand. "I'm sorry about your painting."

"Not your fault." Myra chops the red potato with a methodical flick of the wrist. The potato piles up into precise little cubes. "That man." She smacks the cutting board harder. The veins in her hands pop out.

Elizabeth steals a glance at Myra. She ducks away from Myra as she cooks, maneuvers her body so they won't bump into each other in the tight space.

Don't they remember her? How can Myra not remember Elizabeth and her mother? The woman is convinced she's her missing daughter, she understands. And she hasn't seen Myra up close since she was very young. Still, this disturbs her.

"I am so glad you're home." Myra takes a shaky breath. "I never stopped waiting. Never stopped loving you. You've always had a place in this family."

I am no one to you. No one but the maid's daughter. How forgettable we were.

Elizabeth can't seem to get through to this woman. "He's going to do something violent. I know you don't believe it—"

Myra wipes her hands on her apron. "The police will catch him. He won't risk being so close again." She angles her chin toward the floor.

"He'll be back," Elizabeth says.

Myra turns to the cutting board and dumps the vegetables into the pan. Hot oil splatters on the stovetop. "He won't if he knows what's good for him."

Elizabeth does not respond.

*   *   *

Myra won't stop staring at her with those watery eyes. Oh, it kills Elizabeth how Myra trails her every movement, follows her around. The family sits around a large dining table, passing bread and eating roasted chicken and potatoes. Spots have been cleared for Elizabeth and Theo. And they are not guest seats, with chairs wedged in wherever they will fit. No, these are solid, permanent-like places. The middle leaf has been taken out of the garage and put back in the table, where the Barkleys assume it will stay.

This is not your family, Elizabeth reminds herself. She picks at her cuticle till blood drips down her thumb; she is trying to act normal. She'll get on the phone with Alice, explain how this mix-up occurred. Surely someone has screwed up their escape before. She glances at this family, gathered around and happy.

No one could possibly fuck up like this.

"You need to eat more," Myra says, assessing Elizabeth's half-filled plate.

God, stop telling me what to do!

"Never mind." Myra's face flushes. "Do the best you can." She sits between Elizabeth and Theo, taking up a formidable amount of space.

"I just don't have much of an appetite." Elizabeth sets her fork down.

Gwen Barkley and Elizabeth do look similar enough to be sisters. Gwen's cheeks are full, and her hair streaked with soft blonde highlights.

Though Elizabeth can't wrap her head around Myra's logic. Plenty of siblings share little resemblance. More importantly,

Elizabeth and Charlotte have the same color eyes. That's the one thing that doesn't change much throughout a person's life, the one thing, she reasons, that would completely blow her cover. Charlotte had dimples; Elizabeth doesn't. But these differences can be attributed to age and malnutrition.

And desperation. Myra wants Charlotte to be home. She isn't exactly thinking critically.

Elizabeth didn't intend on taking advantage of this grieving mother. She cringes, ashamed of herself.

Gwen is obviously a good mother. She brought a stack of brand-new books and clothes for Theo, and a bag full of toys and puzzles from a specialty shop up the road. Her daughters read him *The Velveteen Rabbit*. She's offered to take Elizabeth shopping, or even take her measurements and order her clothing online—"In case going to a shopping mall is too overwhelming."

She catches Elizabeth watching her and smiles. Elizabeth quickly looks away, embarrassed. Either the smile is genuine, or Gwen's a damn good actor. She decides to reserve judgment.

Gwen looks at Theo and smiles. "You have such wonderful language skills." She addresses Elizabeth. "His speech is so advanced, considering. Now, the science says there is no rush, and there isn't. But . . . can you read to him?" Her cheeks turn pink.

Gwen must assume Theo is a feral child, raised in the woods. She's probably surprised he can use a knife and fork, that he can speak at all. Elizabeth is offended . . . yet given that Charlotte would've been in that cabin since she was eight, Charlotte wouldn't have continued her education. Theo *was* born to a mother who'd lived most of her life in society. Still, it burns, this superiority. She will have to make Gwen believe Peter did give her the opportunity to learn. She sips her water, and says, "We were allowed books, Gwen. And Theo learned games like checkers . . . cards . . . because Peter wasn't always terrible. I have read to him." Her voice drops to a whisper. "I'm not stupid."

"No, no. I didn't mean that." Gwen trips over the sentence. "You were a brilliant little girl. And now you're a wonderful mother. Of course, you blossomed and learned despite that man."

Kevin looks ill. He'd rather be anywhere than here.

Theo sets his fork down. "I don't know all the letters." He draws his lips into a frown. "Am I supposed to?"

"Oh gosh. Nothing like that," Gwen says, clearly trying to rescue herself. "What an idiotic thing to say."

"He is a smart boy." She twirls one of his chestnut curls, glares at Gwen. "You are, Theo."

"I'm sorry. Of course he is. Why do I constantly say the wrong thing—"

"It's fine," she says, though this is not fine. She squirms in her seat. "Let's change the subject." Elizabeth wants to hide under the table. It's impossible to know how to respond. And dammit, she feels insulted.

"Yes, let's," Myra says. "This is inappropriate, Gwen. Seriously."

Looking at her mother, Gwen says, "I'm sorry. I'm just worried about this man. What if he returns? And he could find me and the girls. Mom, we need cops surveying the place. Someone needs to protect us. This is scary. What did the security cameras show?"

"Nothing," Myra says softly. "They were disabled."

"Oh my god, Mom. This is horrifying." Gwen covers her mouth with her palm. She turns to her husband, Kevin, lips pressed into a straight line. "Don't you think?"

Elizabeth is endangering them, and Gwen knows it. Heat blossoms through her cheeks.

He says quietly, "I'm sure it's being handled." He swallows hard and smiles at Elizabeth. "Really."

"I'd think you'd take this seriously." She picks at her chicken. Her hard expression makes her youthful skin wrinkle like parchment paper.

They know I'm lying, Elizabeth thinks.

"Okay," Herb says, "we need to stay calm and let your sister settle in. This is making her feel bad, I'm sure. This entire conversation. It's not her fault—"

"Dad, I'm only saying we need to figure out a plan. It's not some kind of accusation." Gwen's voice rises.

This is the Gwen Elizabeth remembers.

"You're talking about her like she isn't here," Jimi says. This is more of an observation than an admonishment. Myra glares at him as he gulps his wine.

Elizabeth concentrates on the ticking of the clock; it calms her breathing. The swish of the tide outside swims in her ears. Out, out, *out*. Fifteen minutes and she'll call Alice.

"I didn't mean it like that," Gwen says, and slides her chair out from the table. She steps toward Elizabeth and Theo, looming over them. Her muscles clench, an automatic response to danger. She pastes a tight smile on her face, grits her teeth. Pretty soon they'll go ahead with the DNA test.

"Charlotte." Gwen leans down, placing her palms on her jeans. Her voice cracks. "I can't believe you are home. And I apologize for what I said. I'm just worried about my girls. The same way you are scared for Theo."

"Yes, I know." She sips her water. "I'm sorry for all this."

Gwen blinks. "Truly, this is all my fault. I'm not good at explaining what I mean sometimes."

"A lot of the time," Jimi interjects, his mouth full of food.

Elizabeth isn't sure what to say. Does Gwen really blame herself for what happened to Charlotte, all these years later?

"I don't expect you to forgive me."

Elizabeth hasn't seen Gwen since she was twelve. And clearly, Gwen doesn't remember her. "Please don't say that."

Gwen folds her hands in her lap. She sniffs, tears rolling down her cheeks.

"Why don't we let that go? I hardly remember that night anyway," Elizabeth says, after a long, uncomfortable pause.

"You have no idea how much we have missed you. I can't wait to catch up. To do all the sisterly things we never did."

Her throat burns from the onion and garlic. "Okay, Gwen. I'd like that."

"It's not your fault a monster is after us all," she says. "It's mine."

This is a punch to the gut. The clock ticks.

Gwen puts her fingers to her neck. "Mom says you still have your half of the necklace."

"It's in the room. Where it is safe." The greasy chicken rises in her throat.

"It was so sweet of you to pick the necklace out and share it with me. I didn't appreciate you enough."

Charlotte picked out the necklaces. This is good information to have. Elizabeth sighs. She is becoming an expert liar.

"Mom always knew you'd come home." Tears glisten in her eyes. "I'm so happy you're back." She pulls her into a tight embrace. "You never met my husband. And my kids. Cora is Theo's age. They're cousins."

"Cousins," Elizabeth repeats.

"Yes, of course." Her voice rises a couple of octaves to keep pace with the loud conversation around the table. "They'll be best friends." She motions toward Jimi. "Come here and talk with Elizabeth."

Jimi trudges toward her, his scuffed boots clunking against the floor. A beat of anxiety skips across her chest. He stares at the ground, hair in his face, shoving his hands in his pockets. He drags a chair around and plunks himself down on it.

Cracking his knuckles, he leans close. His icy-blue eyes are a lighter shade of blue than his sisters'. Elizabeth cringes. His proximity releases a threatening aura. She rocks on her heels. The room is cramped, stuffy, suffocating. He exudes suspicion. Does he know she isn't who she claims to be?

"Hey," he says laconically.

"Jimi!" Gwen speaks in a low hiss, embarrassed. "Talk to your sister."

Elizabeth draws a shaky breath. "Are you in college now?"

He smirks. "Naw, that wasn't exactly my thing."

Gwen faces him. "Yeah, well, that was a huge mistake. One day you will regret it, when you get older. Everyone should have a college education to fall back on. In case the whole starving artist thing happens to you."

"Whatever, Gwen. You probably didn't expect to come home to this, eh?" He tilts his chin toward Elizabeth.

Blanketed by silence, Jimi and Gwen exchange a glance. They speak in a wordless language, but the message is clear: she is an outsider.

"Well," Gwen says, with a smile, "I suppose we should get to the party."

Party? Myra is clearing the table, and she tells Herb to get a photo album out. Jesus Christ. Elizabeth is dizzy with the people, the pressure, the heavy pile of lies she'll need to remember. "Theo," she calls. "Please." Her head aches.

"What's wrong?" Myra draws her lips into a frown.

"I just . . . I'm very tired. Theo is getting overstimulated—"

"No, I'm not, Mommy. This is fun." He clutches her hand. "I want to keep playing."

"That's okay," says Myra, her tone warm and pleasant. "You've had such a time. Such a terrible time." She shakes her head. "If you'd prefer to be alone, that's okay." Myra places a shaky hand on Elizabeth's shoulder.

"It isn't that. I'm just not used to all this noise."

Myra reaches for her, as if she is afraid that if she holds too tight, Elizabeth will run. If her grip is too loose, she'll slip through Myra's fingers and into the ocean, like she did that summer night.

Elizabeth inhales the scent of her lavender shampoo and thinks of her mother. Though Mom also smelled vaguely of the bleach she used for cleaning, that combination of bleach and lavender wafts through her mind. She rests her head on Myra's shoulder and pretends, for a moment, that her mom is alive. That she and Theo could have returned home to a real family. She knows this is not to be, that she cannot contort herself into the piece they're missing and fit inside the puzzle. Yet still, a voice in her head says, *Why not? Who can it hurt?* Because right now, her presence seems to benefit everyone. The line between truth and imagination is so fuzzy and faint she's not sure it exists.

"I love you." Myra's eyes are bright and clear.

Elizabeth tries to smile. She can hardly breathe. Lies. It won't be long till she believes them herself. How did she get into this? How will she get out?

Focus. Breathe.

"Are you all right?" Myra says, but her voice sounds distant, muffled.

"I just need to sit down," she says, and starts walking toward the room.

"You look pale. Let's head back to the table and sit down. Get some water."

She begins to protest, but her legs feel numb, unstable. The painting. Peter knows where she is. There is nowhere to run. She can't run anymore. Maybe the police can find more, at the cabin.

A rush of heat spreads through her body. She is very ill. This lie will consume her.

"Are you okay?" Myra asks.

"Mommy?" Theo says, panicked, as if he's about to cry. "Mommy?"

Elizabeth is dizzy and shaky, an imposter who can't get free of any of it. Her legs tremble beneath her. She reaches for the nearby coffee table and misses. Her vision fades to a crackly black, like a fuzzy old television. Her knees buckle and she careens to the ground, her head smashing into the coffee table.

CHAPTER THIRTEEN

ELIZABETH

She wakes in a strange bed. Her head is muddled and sore. Something grips at her arm tightly; the tender bruises sting her flesh. Where is she?

Peter.

"Theo!" she screams, her voice a gritty stream of panic. "Theo!"

She can smell the woods. The melted snow drips from his boots as he thunders into the cabin. The repugnant cadence of his voice and the scent of cut birch on his skin, hot from the warmth of the truck, closes in on her . . . he closes in on her . . .

"Theo!"

A bright, fluorescent light floods the room. Disoriented, she gazes around. She wears a blue cotton gown. She recognizes the bleep of the heart monitor, the stark smell of bleach. It is like the room her mother died in.

The doctor and nurse rush in with the light. "Is everything okay?"

Elizabeth squints at the woman's name tag. "Dr. Smith? Why am I here? And where is my son?"

"Your parents brought you in—"

"Parents?" Elizabeth blinks.

"I've heard the story. It's just amazing. Unbelievable. Missing for twenty years . . . wow." The doctor clicks a pen as she speaks. "We are so glad you're home."

"Doctor," she repeats, remembering that she is impersonating a missing girl. She needs to get on the phone with Alice. She will get her out of this mess. After they tell her where Theo is. "Where is my *son*?"

"He's just fine. Waiting for you." She takes a pair of reading glasses out of her front coat pocket and puts them on. "You're a bit dehydrated. And stressed. That's why you fainted."

Stressed is a mild word to describe Elizabeth's condition.

"I really would like to see my son now. Please." She pulls her legs from under the starchy sheet and swings them to the side. As she stands, a sticker rips from her chest, setting off some kind of alarm. Her movement yanks at the IV in her hand. She nearly trips on the blood pressure monitor beside her bed.

"Whoa. You have to stay in bed. We'll get you out of here before long, but you're getting fluids for dehydration, and the nurse will have to remove the IV."

She inspects her stinging hand. "What the hell? I want to leave. You can't make me stay here." Tethered to the bed, a sudden flash of anger strikes her. Stuck. Stuck. Stuck. She doesn't want to be *stuck* anymore.

Her head is muddled; she sinks back into the bed.

"I promise," says Dr. Smith, who fails to understand her soothing tone is ratcheting Elizabeth's anxiety up more, "that you'll be out of here soon. I've been told you prefer to be called Elizabeth?"

She nods, speechless.

Poor Dr. Smith, who really believes Elizabeth is Charlotte Barkley, smiles at her as if she is a newly found puppy. She feels like she might throw up.

"The police want to ask you a few more questions, just to make sure there isn't something you've forgotten."

Police? What will she tell the police now?

"Then you'll bring Theo to me?" Her throat is so scratchy. She reaches for the pink plastic pitcher of water on the hospital tray.

"Of course." Dr. Smith takes the pitcher and pours her a cup of water. "Drink as much as you can. Remember—"

"I'm dehydrated. Got it."

"All right then. I'll send Detective Marlow in, if that's okay with you," says the doctor, as if this is a choice.

Elizabeth squeezes her eyes shut. "I suppose."

What on earth was she thinking, coming back to Rocky Shores? And the Barkley Inn, of all places? She has lost her mind. That's the only explanation she can come up with. And now, Peter is back. He's after her. Slashing paintings. What has she done?

The door screeches open. The two cops fill the room with their presence. Sweat runs down her temples despite the chilly room. She is encroached upon, like the three of them are stuffed in a tin can.

"Hello, Elizabeth," says Detective Marlow, extending her hand.

Detective Schumer smiles. "I'm glad to see you're okay."

"Thank you." Marlow and Schumer were all over the news after Charlotte's disappearance. She can hardly swallow. They are almost as excited as Myra and Herb, and she is about to shatter their hope.

She considers this. Elizabeth and Theo exist in no one's world outside of the Barkley family.

And Peter's.

So what if the cops go up to the cabin and find his rotting body? So what if they go up there and find him alive? He's had her there, a veritable prisoner, for years. She has spoken to no one but Mrs. Hart from the area. What's the difference between six years and twenty? Between Elizabeth Lark and Charlotte Barkley?

This is wrong—she knows it is. But she thinks of Theo. This is his chance to live like a normal child, with family, friends—hell, even cousins. People do worse for their children. Everyone says, "I would do anything . . . anything . . . for my child."

She would do anything for Theo.

Elizabeth can be Charlotte Barkley.

No one will believe a word out of Peter's mouth. He won't be able to hurt them again. She won't have to go on the run, destitute, with a kid.

The plan forms quickly in her mind, details spilling together and connecting within moments.

"I remember where the cabin is."

She can't pass up this opportunity.

"Have some water first. Take a few breaths," Schumer says.

Elizabeth waves her hand. Now or never. "No, no. This is how it happened. He has kept me there all this time. Since that night on the beach." She clears her throat, tries to sit up straight. "I poisoned him and stole his truck. I thought he might be dead. I couldn't tell you that, because I was afraid of getting in trouble . . . but he's here. He's found us."

Sarah says, "It's okay, Elizabeth. You aren't in any trouble. Can you show us where?"

"Yes," she says, jutting her chin out.

"And that's where you've been all this time? Where Theo was born?"

"Yes, that's right," she says, because it is true.

Well, mostly true.

"Seeing where the two of you lived will help us gather more information about Peter. Maybe even catch him, if he's still there. I understand this will be difficult for you." Detective Marlow says this softly, like she expects this to be a slow, drawn-out process. The detective's eyes are a pale shade of green.

Elizabeth will make this painless. Rip the IV out, so to speak.

"Yes," she says.

She will take the police straight to him.

CHAPTER FOURTEEN

ELIZABETH

Elizabeth leans on the patrol car's window, shrinking as far away from Detective Marlow as possible. Buckled in a booster seat in the back, Theo seems pensive, quiet. Elizabeth wonders if it was a mistake to bring him here. She turns and says, "All right, buddy?"

He is concentrating on the iPad they borrowed from Gwen. "You should have let me stay with Cora and Savannah," he says. "That would have been fun." He doesn't look up from the iPad. She can see how tightly he's gripping onto it. He is crouched into a tense little ball beside the window, brown curls tumbling over his face so she can't read his expression.

"Hey, we're a team, remember? We stick together."

"That's why I don't get why we're coming here," he says. "You said once we escaped, we'd never go back."

"I'm sorry. At least it's a pretty day out." He is so wise, so logical. There's no point in explaining why she'd bring him back here, to where this man is. Because she shouldn't have done it. "You can play with the girls later."

She looks out the window. The sun pokes out from the clouds, and the coastal drizzle has stopped for now. She concentrates on the hum of the tires rolling over wet asphalt and the occasional splash of water as they hit a puddle. The road is flanked with thin-trunked fir trees, and windmills blow on gently sloped hills. They pass rows of small businesses with pink and yellow houses stacked haphazardly between them. Elizabeth is fond of the different colors and heights of the buildings. Many small businesses, such as art stores and tourist shops and even doctor's offices, are held in eclectic residential homes. They drive by her mother's favorite craft store, where they sell a variety of different fabrics and threads, from hemp to silk, to Egyptian cotton, out of a tall eggplant-colored home with Victorian windows and an ornate balcony. Maybe the owners live there, upstairs. She would love Rocky Shores if not for her history here.

They travel a few miles in silence, with many more to go, before Detective Marlow flips on the radio. "Do you mind?" she asks. "A little music calms me down when I'm nervous."

"It's fine," Elizabeth says. She sneaks a sideways glance at the detective, who hums along to the radio while tapping the steering wheel. Her skin is mapped with a light web of lines, and freckles splatter the bridge of her nose. She doesn't look much older than Elizabeth remembers. Maybe it is the effervescent relief that bubbles off her. Charlotte Barkley is home, after all this time.

Everyone in Rocky Shores and beyond searched for the little girl. Who would snatch a small child from the beach? No one, most people agreed. Charlotte must have drowned because her sister was lost in some teenage drama with her boyfriend.

"Your mother has been at that inn for so long. She was sure you were—well, somewhere out there."

"Detective Marlow—"

"Please, call me Sarah. Your family became a part of mine, through the years." Her lips turn up. Elizabeth's stomach aches.

She has to admit the truth. This lie will rip her to shreds.

"Sarah, I can't do this. I'm sorry, I'm just not—"

"I know this is hard. But we have to find him."

Elizabeth thinks a moment. What if by doing this she is actually helping? No one cared when Elizabeth went missing. There was no one left to care. But if Peter took another woman, out of anger directed at her, it would be her fault.

"You were one of the lead detectives when . . . when I disappeared, right?"

Sarah pauses for a beat. "Yes. This is Rocky Shores, and I was a young detective. I was just itching to save the world. Everyone thought you were gone. Hell, the department didn't think there was anything left to investigate. Besides a search for a body—" The words tumble out before she can stop them. "God, I am so sorry. I shouldn't have said that." Sarah rubs her forehead. "That was inappropriate."

Elizabeth turns around. "Theo?"

"What?" he says, clearly invested in his game.

"What are you playing?"

"A card game Savannah showed me."

Elizabeth returns her attention to Sarah. "The story is taking my mind off this." She gestures to the road ahead.

"I guess . . . well, it was your mother. She was convinced you were out there, and so I was convinced of it too. Now, I can't tell you if your mother had some psychic ability or if her insistence—and my god, she insisted—that you were out there was her way of coping. But here we are." Sarah smiles and shrugs.

Elizabeth remembers Peter slapping her son across the face, the scarlet color that erupted on his cheek. She can see Theo's glossy eyes, his trembling lower lip. Worse than this, Elizabeth could do nothing to protect him. She takes a slow, measured breath. This is for the best. Maybe she isn't Charlotte Barkley, but she *is* removing a dangerous man from society.

Peter will be caught. Her worries will be gone. Myra's grief will dissipate.

If only her chest would stop aching.

The altitude rises, and the air becomes crisp and cold. The smell of pine and birch and winter waft into the vehicle. She puts her ear against the window. As they twist and turn, the pain in her chest mounts. The pressure in her ears builds. A familiar bird shrills, like a whistle with tiny bells inside it, and a high-pitched shriek as its call ends. The trees go thick and dense, uncleared except for the road they approach. She presses her face against the glass and watches snakes of ice on the asphalt, thick as rubber cement. Flakes of snow hit the windshield in little rhythmic splats followed by the screech of the wipers.

"Careful, it's icy." She turns to her son. "Hold on tight."

"We're okay," says Sarah. "We're coming up to it soon, right?"

They have been driving for hours, except for a bathroom break for Theo. Sarah had offered to stop for lunch, but Elizabeth refused. She didn't want to change her mind again. They had bought a couple of gas-station sandwiches and hit the road.

"Yes," she whispers. "Slow down."

They crawl down a one-way road, where gnarled trees loom so close to the vehicle that branches nearly scrape the doors.

"Stop!"

The clearing is just ahead of them.

"Turn here."

Sarah grips the steering wheel. They travel the path of packed snow as the flakes come down faster and harder, like wet socks knocking against the window. A crushed velvet curtain snuffs out the day. Her heartbeat drums thinly.

They arrive. The cabin is smaller and sadder than Elizabeth remembered. A recent storm has dumped so much snow on the roof that it sags. The windows look like they were carved with an X-Acto knife. It could be a child's playhouse. A senseless shame rolls through her. This is her house. She is embarrassed that strangers will barrel through it, horrified at how they lived.

Stop, it has nothing to do with you. And yet, for some unfathomable reason, it does.

Elizabeth sinks into her seat, looks away. Cop cars and emergency vehicles surround the building.

Theo leans forward and grips her hand. "He's here, isn't he? What do we do? He'll want us back."

"We won't let that happen," Sarah says. "The police are here to handle Peter."

Theo starts to cry. Elizabeth climbs into the backseat and lets him rest his head in her lap. "We're leaving soon. I promise." She should have left him with Myra.

"Stay here, okay?" A gust of icy air pours in the door, and Sarah gets out of the car, flicking on her two-way radio. She runs toward the other cops and FBI agents. Their footprints and tire tracks leave gray patches in the thick snow. They trample through her home, digging through her belongings, unearthing their secrets. What are they saying about Theo's conception? They will certainly ask personal questions about things she does not want to talk about. Not now. Not ever.

She puts her face in her hands. Elizabeth can't look, can't look, can't look.

Theo is very upset. Her son is hysterical now, waiting for Sarah to come out. She holds him close. "Mommy is here, Mommy is here," she says, thumping his back gently as if he were a newborn being shushed to sleep. Elizabeth imagines her own mother. She thinks of her warm embrace, even after a twelve-hour day at the diner. Of the smell of lard on her scratchy brown uniform. Elizabeth misses the smell, and the trailer house up on the hill, not far from where Charlotte disappeared. Her mother. She misses her mother.

The heater blows dry, hot air, and she can't tolerate it.

She wants to yell, wants to cry, for herself, for Myra Barkley, for Theo. But she holds it back in her throat, acerbic and toxic. She doesn't cry. Not in front of Peter. And when she trained herself not to cry, to be strong, to protect her child, all there was left was this feeling. The air is siphoned from her lungs. It is physical.

Like drowning. It's like she is drowning in her own mucous, like her mother did. She hears footsteps crunch through the snow, voices grow closer. Sarah knocks on the window.

"I need to get away from here." Her throat is dry.

"Elizabeth. They're bringing him out now. He's inside the cabin." Sarah extends her hand and tries to pat her shoulder. Elizabeth flinches.

"What do you mean?" Her head is so muddled. "You caught him?"

"No, I mean, he's dead." She speaks softly, maybe because she wants to shelter Theo from this news.

"You're saying I *killed* him? I gave him half a bottle of pills. He was used to high doses. That's why I gave him so much. I didn't expect to kill him. Holy shit, no."

"What?" Theo says, wide-eyed. "How can he be dead?"

She draws him into her arms, unable to speak. These cops have forced their way into the dumpy cabin she's lived in for so long, and she wants to scream, *"Get out of my home!"* They invade into her private pain, into the blinding shame of captivity. How many people find themselves trapped with a psychopath and a five-year-old child? How stupid she has been, to be so stuck here with him.

Now she's stuck with Myra Barkley.

"The bed is unmade, and the empty bottles are in the house. Along with"—she clears her throat—"him."

"How?"

She thinks of the truck. The one Alice got rid of. She needs to get Alice on the phone.

"It's okay. We understand you had no choice. The police understand. Hell, what you did was brave—"

It was murder, she thinks. She killed a man. Her son's father. A monster, a psychopath, yes. But she's no different from him. Maybe she's worse. He didn't kill anyone. There had to have been a better way. Alice had a *plan.* If she hadn't deviated from it, they wouldn't be here right now. She covers Theo's eyes with her palm. "Don't look," she whispers.

Three EMTs trudge out of the cabin, wind blowing their hair, pushing a stretcher with a body bag on it.

Her husband's body. A scream sticks in her throat. She pulls her son into her chest. "I need to leave, Sarah." She cannot breathe. "Please."

"We are heading back to the inn," says Sarah, "and the FBI officers will handle investigating this . . . house."

She thinks for a moment. There are things in that house, papers that reveal her true identity—the cops cannot see them. "Wait," she says, and leans her palms on the dash. "No, we can't leave. I need to go inside. I need to get my things."

"Are you sure?" Sarah looks dubious.

Elizabeth should have run. She's going to jail. If she can't get into that cabin, it's all over. Theo will go to some foster home, and she will go to prison.

But if Peter is dead . . . Numbly, she tells Theo, "Stay with Sarah."

"But Mommy . . ." He grasps her coat.

"I'll just be a minute." Salty tears sting her eyes. "Play your game. Look at the iPad," she says, shoving the tablet into his hands.

She gets out of the car. "I need my stuff," she tells Sarah. "I can't stay at that inn. Everyone is in danger, all because of me."

She is in deeper than the dumping snow. "Peter may be dead, but someone else is coming for us. I don't know Peter's friends, who he works with. But if something happens, that's on me. Don't you understand?"

"You are safe, Elizabeth. And so is Theo."

No, I am an imposter. And we are anything but safe.

"I need to get into my house."

"Let's go," she says. "I'll go in with you."

"No. I want to go alone. This is insane."

"Are you sure? There's nothing here you really need. It's technically a crime scene—"

"I thought you said it wasn't a crime! That it was self-defense."

"I meant the kidnapping, holding you hostage." She takes Elizabeth by the shoulders, looks at her directly in the eye. "We are investigating him, not you."

"Let me go," she whispers.

Sarah sighs. "All right. But fifteen minutes. That's it. They're taking Peter to the morgue."

The morgue. She shouldn't care. But she shudders, puts her finger to her lips. "Shh," she says, looking pointedly at her son. Elizabeth doesn't want to explain what a morgue is now. "Fifteen minutes."

She trudges toward the door, cold air burning her lungs. The branches of fir trees crackle in the wind. Elizabeth tells herself that this sound is familiar. Nothing is here but the trees protecting themselves from the howling wind. The forest looms all around the property, the smell of frozen pine needles filling her nose. The air is pure, though the memories it incites are not.

They have left.

Peter is dead.

One last errand.

This is not me. This is Peter's doing.

Her fingers are numb. She tries the lamp; the electricity is disconnected. *Move more quickly,* she tells herself. Get in and get out. Her chest goes wild. Thud, thud. She cannot breathe the dank, acrid scent. Peter's smell, mingled with death, wafts to her nose; the sweat and oil from his greasy clothes make her cough. Bile comes up in her throat, but she swallows it. Old habits.

Her breath is shallow. She cannot drink even one sip of this place. Elizabeth takes four steps to the bedroom, dark from the thick curtains pulled tight. *No, no,* she thinks. But she acts, dazed, and avoids looking at the bed, rumpled and dirty.

The cops have tossed open drawers and rifled through their clothing, but she goes to the closet. Most of the contents are on the floor, but in a hidden corner a square is cut through the carpet. You can't see it without a good deal of light. The cops must have missed it. Elizabeth yanks the wood open and digs for a cold metal safe. She recalls Peter storing documents there.

"In case we have to run," he'd said, though she has never seen its contents.

But if the police find the documents, evidence of her real identity, this lie is over. And she'll go to prison.

She lifts the safe and drops it beside her. It hits the ground with a thud. The top screeches open. A few papers scatter. Mounds and mounds of documents are stuffed in the little safe. Elizabeth sifts through them. Her birth certificate. Her old Oregon state driver's license.

Her Social Security card.

This is what she is looking for. Elizabeth presses the documents to her chest. The trees bristle with the bitter wind. Droplets of sweat slide down her shirt despite her cold, blue fingers. Vapor from her breath hangs in the dim light. She squishes her toes inside her boots.

Sarah is approaching the house. It hasn't been fifteen minutes, dammit.

"Elizabeth?" Sarah calls. "Almost done?"

"Wait." Elizabeth freezes. "Wait a minute. Go watch Theo." She continues to sift through the documents.

What is all this?

"Let's go," Sarah says, footsteps growing closer. "It's cold in here. Theo is at the car with an officer." Her voice grows closer.

"Just a minute, Sarah! I need a minute."

An old ID of Peter's from Oregon State is buried in the thick pile. "Holy crap," she whispers. "What is this?" She squints, heart in her stomach. It's a guy's driver's license. "Who is Patrick J. Henderson?" She stares for a moment. Her jaw drops open. She slaps her hand over her gaping mouth. "He has another birth certificate," she whispers to herself.

"All right. Can I come in?"

"I'll be right out!" she yells, frustrated. "I want to get some of my things. Check on Theo. Please."

Elizabeth keeps digging. Maybe she shouldn't. But a warning, something deep and powerful that she cannot ignore, tells her there is more to see. Something vital. She must know the man she married.

Next, his Peter Briggs birth certificate. She tosses that aside. Maybe there are ten more birth certificates. Maybe none of them are real.

Her fingers reach for the bottom until she hits something small and metal in the corner. Snow splats against the thin roof. Wind smacks against the walls like it could crush them.

"A storm's coming. Let's go," Sarah says. She is hovering right outside the door.

Elizabeth slides the item out of the box. She opens her palm and lets the slinky chain fall onto her other hand. It coils like a poisonous snake. Her chest pounds. She can't breathe.

She inspects the necklace.

It can't be, just can't be.

The cracked heart is engraved with Gwen's initials. *GB.* Gwen's lost piece of the necklace was tucked in Peter's safe. She will match it with the other half in her purse, but the truth is obvious.

Peter is not Peter, at all. He is a monster beyond all comprehension. But how does this connect with her? This can't be a coincidence. Can it?

Elizabeth flips around and scans the cabin. Frozen, she trembles. It is silent. Vomit rises from the pit of her stomach like acid. She sputters and coughs, expecting to choke on her own blood.

She remembers the taste of blood after he punched her. The moment he made it clear he was her captor. How she and Theo were trapped in these cold, cold woods.

A flash of the magnanimous Douglas fir tree in front of the cabin cements itself in her mind. She can see the canopy of branches, smell its fragrant needles. Bright wildflowers would sprout in all directions each spring. It was her hope, her focus, what kept her alive.

She plants her feet on the ground, spreading her toes like talons gripping the earth. They are so cold they crack like ice.

Peter is gone forever. They have left.

She is the forest, with fragrant flowers blooming and stretching around her. Life grows beneath her branches. In the winter, the plants are dormant. But in the spring, they begin again.

She gathers the documents, shoves them in her bag.

"What are you doing?" Sarah comes up behind her.

"Looking for something."

"Let's go, Elizabeth. This is enough. This is too traumatizing."

Elizabeth brings herself to her feet, the documents and necklace folded safely in her bag.

Where the hell did Peter get Gwen's half of the necklace? How did Gwen know Peter? She is in the midst of something bigger than she ever imagined.

Elizabeth grips the door handle. She and Theo ride in the backseat together this time. The squad car travels through the wild. She wants to scream. There's no way out. Someone else is tormenting Myra at the inn, someone who wants to get to her and Theo. It's caught in the folds of the Barkley family. Even if Gwen didn't kill her sister, she had some contact with Elizabeth's dead husband. She clenches Theo's hand, she meets his eyes. "We are fine. Everything is fine."

But the questions ring in her mind like bass drum, unending, unyielding. Her head is a lump of lead on her shoulders, so heavy she can hardly hold it up.

Who the fuck is Patrick Henderson? And how had she ended up in the middle of it all?

CHAPTER FIFTEEN

GWEN

Gwen holds the brush, trying to steady her shaking hands. She paints a stripe of bubblegum pink polish down the middle of Savannah's little fingernail. "Like a tiger stripe," she whispers.

"What's wrong, Mommy?"

She adds a tiny dot of polish on each side of her daughter's nail. "Do this part carefully," she continues, tears gathering in the corners of her eyes. "Nice and soft, or it will get on your skin."

"Are you crying?"

Gwen swallows hard. "No, I'm just thinking."

Savannah avoids her mother's eyes. "I like this color."

"It's a lovely choice." She moves to the little pinkie, and says, "Now, we're doing more of a baby kitten stripe."

"Little cats can still scratch," Savannah says, shaking her head. "Like when Jenny's baby brother pulled the new kitten's tail. He got a big red scratch and screamed and screamed."

"Yes." Gwen finishes painting the nail and turns her head. "Yes, they can if they get hurt."

Savannah splays her fingers in the air for Gwen to see. The little half moon–shaped tips remind her of Charlotte's. "I used to do Aunt Charlotte's nails. When she was very little."

"Is that why you're crying?"

Gwen inhales slowly. "When Grandma and Grandpa were busy, during summer usually, we would do each other's hair and nails. She was . . . five or six, I think? Cora's age."

"You let a kid do your nails?" Savannah smirks. "You won't let me touch yours."

Gwen laughs. "I guess I did. And they were a big sticky mess."

Her daughter's wide grin sends a swell of tenderness through her. "You can paint mine today, if you want. I like the pink on you."

Savannah nods solemnly. "Don't worry. I'll start with the tiger stripe."

*　*　*

Tonight, the whole family is meeting for dinner. Gwen's stomach pinches at the thought of sitting in a crowded restaurant. She is ashamed of her anxiety. The evening will be a thousand times worse for Elizabeth. And then she is livid at her mother for this whole stupid idea.

Just stop, she tells herself. *Don't be so damned selfish all the time.* She inhales deeply, but the children are giving Gwen a migraine. They screech from the backseat of the car, arguing over one thing and another. It is murderous. She fights tears. This is her sister's night. "Girls, please."

Savannah kicks her seat. "Cora won't stop looking at me!"

"Look out the window, then. Both of you." Kevin turns to Gwen and says, "Did you try some ibuprofen?"

Gwen took two Percocet, actually. "Yes, I took something for it," she replies.

"Good. I'm sure it will kick in soon. I want us to have a nice dinner, babe. Ease some of this guilt you carry about Charlotte."

She sighs. "Her name is Elizabeth now, apparently."

He taps the steering wheel lightly and says, "Well, it's what she's used to. C'mon, Gwen, we're going out for a quick bite. The beauty of restaurant meals with family is you can literally eat and run."

"We may have to. My mother is going insane again, and I don't think I can take it. Why should Char—Elizabeth even want to be here? Mom is so paranoid she's going to disappear again that Charlotte can't even go on a walk with her son without permission." She pauses. "And now, she *is* a grown woman."

"Eh, your mom's just scared. Doesn't this feel weird? I mean, of course, for me, she is a stranger. The girl whose ghost lived only in Myra's mind."

"It is weird," she agrees. "She was eight. Now she is twenty-eight. I think we're all going to have to accept that she really isn't our Charlotte. She grew up in that cabin. She's an adult with her own kid."

"It's a miracle," says Kevin, shaking his head. "This almost never happens."

Gwen sighs. "I know the statistics. I've lived them, Kevin. And yes, I am thrilled. But in many ways, Charlotte *did* die. Eight-year old Charlotte is gone. Grown-up Elizabeth is here now. I guess no one thinks about this stuff when they dream of a missing loved one coming home."

"It's complicated," he says, drumming his fingertips on the steering wheel.

"You aren't the one who lost her." She bites her cheek. Gwen is being mean, yet she cannot help herself. People grate on her. It's an itch she can't scratch.

The screeching abates. Finally. She cranes her neck toward the backseat. The girls are absorbed in their tablets. She has allowed far too much screen time the past two weeks, but at least they are quiet. Kevin turns on a classic rock song and hums along.

Kevin is wearing the blue polo shirt she picked out for him for Christmas. He's sporting the watch she bought him for his birthday too. She remembers this vividly because she thought he'd like the opalescent color of the dial. He'd seemed unimpressed. When she pushed him about it, he admitted that he didn't get the point of watches. You could get the time from your cell phone.

"I thought you didn't like watches," she says, pointing at the gift he didn't appreciate just two months prior.

"I changed my mind." He smiles.

"No." She shakes her head. "You're placating me."

"What? I am not placating you, Gwen. If that were true, I'd have worn the thing when you bought it—"

"Oh, I get it. You're trying to be nice, then. Because Charlotte's home and you think I'm going nuts like my mother. Right?"

"Chill out. I meant nothing of the sort." His eyes widen. "You're just looking for a fight."

He's right. "Fine. I'm sorry."

"Food will help your headache, hon," Kevin says.

She slumps back in her seat. The Ripe Tomato is a family-owned restaurant in town. It will be stuffed with her parents' friends, to welcome Charlotte home.

"I hope they don't overstimulate Elizabeth and Theo again," she says. "They've been through terrible trauma. My mother doesn't gather that they're not used to loud noises and crowds."

"Maybe it will be a short dinner," says Kevin hopefully.

They pull into the parking lot. Gwen puckers her lips and spreads on a thick layer of gloss. "Ready, kids?"

"I wanna see the little boy again," says Savannah. "He's my cousin, right?"

"That's right," Kevin says.

"He has the biggest curls," Savannah tells Cora. "Maybe he'll let us play with them."

"No," Gwen says absentmindedly. "Don't ask him that."

Gwen never found the heart necklace. The smell of food is nauseating. She smooths her slim black dress. *Good posture exudes confidence,* she tells herself, pulling her belly in and straightening her spine.

The Saturday night crowd fills every corner of the boxy little restaurant. The tablecloths are made from unrolled sheets of paper. The table boasts a giant bottle of Chianti beside a basket of crayons. *A clever centerpiece,* Gwen muses. Distract the children while you drink. Theo is perched on his knees, absorbed in his creation. The girls huddle next to him. He doesn't seem bothered or overwhelmed. The three children chatter as he passes the crayons.

Gwen meanders toward the Chianti. She pours a glass to the brim and gulps half. She glances around before refilling it. No one notices. They loiter around Elizabeth. Except Dad. He sits a few feet away, immersed in the conversation, but not speaking. Nothing atypical there. When she was young, her father's soft-spoken demeanor had confounded her. She thought he was angry or pensive when, truthfully, he was listening. Gwen wishes she could be that kind of mother, but she can't stop herself from prattling on when she's nervous. Charlotte is home, and her father relaxes beside her, drinking in his youngest daughter's words along with his wine.

She surrenders Kevin to her mother, who gabs nonstop. This is clearly where Gwen developed the habit. Gwen's stomach swims. No amount of wine or deep breaths or primal screaming will relax the coil of anxiety inside her. This could be a permanent state of being.

Gwen needs to come clean about the necklace, but she isn't sure how. Poor Elizabeth stares at her feet. She is overwhelmed and everyone is oblivious to it. Gwen approaches her table, gut swimming.

"Hey there," Gwen says, pulling a seat out. "Are you okay here?" She waves around the crowded restaurant. "They have good cannelloni."

Elizabeth smiles, and suddenly Gwen realizes that her sister has never been to an Italian restaurant. "I'm sorry. I shouldn't have said that."

"Said what?" Elizabeth seems confused. "How are the kids?"

Relieved at the change of subject, Gwen launches into a discussion about her girls' extracurricular activities and how sports are so good for building self-esteem. "We really need to sign Theo up for something. Soccer? He looks like he'd be good at soccer."

Elizabeth stares at her blankly. "Well . . . okay."

Gwen is an idiot. "I talk too much when I'm nervous. It's just—" Her voice cracks. She can't contain the grief welling in her chest. The pain has lingered, sometimes dormant, other times explosive. "I am so sorry I lost you that night. I let him take you away. Shit. I wouldn't blame you if you never forgive me."

"You were a teenager. A kid yourself." Elizabeth sighs and rests her bony arm on Gwen's shoulder. Her voice trails off; she stares off in the distance. "Theo likes card games. He does tricks with them, kind of like a magician. Peter brought home a deck of cards and a game of checkers once. He had calm moments. Anyway, Theo will probably show you. He's been saying he wants to be a magician for years now. Silly, I know. But it was his hope, for when we got out."

"That's amazing. He's so smart." Gwen strokes her sister's cheek without thinking, and Elizabeth pulls back abruptly. Her jaw tightens, and a glint of anger—barely perceptible, but there—flickers in her eyes. She recoils and rubs her face as if it has been burned.

"I didn't mean to startle you," Gwen says.

Elizabeth gazes at her with glossy eyes. "I don't like to be touched unless I know it's coming."

Oddly, Gwen can identify with this. "Me neither." She pauses. "But you've been through so much more. I'm sorry." Her voice drops to a whisper.

Cocking her head to one side, Elizabeth studies Gwen's neck. "You didn't find it yet? Your half of the heart?"

"Not yet." She feels her cheeks color. "I don't know where it could've gone."

"Well, it will probably turn up soon." Elizabeth stands, turning away from her, and waves at the children, who are still coloring.

"Wait." Gwen swallows. "Theo is fine. He's right there. You can see him with your own eyes. Can we talk for a minute? I'll get us a glass of wine."

Elizabeth slides back into her chair, but she continues to focus intently on the children. "Okay."

Gwen marches toward the crayon table and pours two glasses of Chianti. Heading back to Elizabeth briskly, the wine sloshes onto her hand. Without thinking, she wipes her hand on her dress. That'll stain. She takes a breath. "Here you go." She plunks the glass down in front of Elizabeth.

"What did you want to discuss?" Elizabeth says, and sips her wine.

"I just wanted to catch up." She stumbles over her words. *That sounded stupid.* "I mean . . . you don't have to tell me anything. That isn't what I meant."

"Sorry, I just like to keep my eye on him."

Gwen's skin prickles. Is there something under the surface of the comment? Or is she being paranoid? She takes a long, slow sip of wine. "The other moms say I hover too much. That Savannah and Cora don't get enough freedom." She pauses for a beat. "But I didn't watch you that evening. And I don't want to make that mistake again. You know?"

"I do," Elizabeth says curtly. "And this is the first time I've been in a large enough place that I've had to hover. You know?"

"Yes."

"Anyway, I'm going to see how they're doing. I hope you find the necklace." She offers a soft smile, but Gwen can see that Elizabeth is anything but soft. She loves Theo; she is traumatized, of course. But she is strong. And suspicious. She is watching. Every moment of every day, her eyes are narrow, her back is straight. Gwen recognizes this kind of trauma; it is dangerous, in a sense, because a person clinging to survival cannot fully be trusted. Fear is more complex than people think. Elizabeth is not as meek and quiet as she seems.

If she were to so much as *think* Theo was in danger, Elizabeth would act unpredictably. And Gwen prefers life to be very, very predictable. Maybe it's her anxiety, or the three glasses of wine she has drunk. But an involuntary thought slides through her brain. *What if Elizabeth Lark* isn't *Charlotte? What if Jimi is right?*

No, dammit. She *has* to be. The poor woman has her hackles up, but she's been imprisoned for twenty years. Can't expect her to trust the sister who lost her. She can see Charlotte perched alone on that rock, shivering although the night was warm, begging to go home. Even now, she is obsessed with Gwen's piece of the necklace. This is unsettling.

Gwen realizes that in some ways, she needs this woman to be Charlotte as much as her mother does. Maybe more.

CHAPTER SIXTEEN

ELIZABETH

Elizabeth waits till Theo is in a deep sleep. She opens her bag and retrieves the thick stack of documents from the cabin. And Gwen's necklace. She switches on the green lamp, illuminating the desk in the dark room. Elizabeth holds the necklace in the palm of her hand. The shimmery silver catches in the soft incandescent light. She stretches it out beside Charlotte's piece and inspects it more closely. Charlotte's heart is rusty and tarnished, the silver cloudy from riding in Elizabeth's pocket or purse the last two decades. These cheap trinkets are easily damaged, don't hold up well when exposed to water.

Gwen's is shiny and new; it hasn't been worn much. She picks it up by the end of the chain. The heart slips off and plunks onto the desk. She peers at the clasp. The chain is broken. With her head in her palms, she stares at both coils of silver.

The night of Charlotte's disappearance is still so vivid. She supposes this is why she came back. Not to impersonate Charlotte, but because in some strange way, she identifies with the little girl.

The trailer park was just a couple of miles from the beach, but people pretended it wasn't there. No one wanted to believe people like Elizabeth and her mother existed. A trailer park brought down real estate values, chased away the tourists.

Elizabeth was used to the jokes, the days she sat alone in the cafeteria with her free lunch, scarfing it as quickly as she could because it might be her only meal that day. She didn't bother her mother about the children's whispers or the hunger pains that plagued her. This was not all the time. She wouldn't want to give the impression her overworked mother didn't provide for her. Mom did what she could. On payday she filled the cart at the store with food, and they rationed it slowly, hoping it would last two whole weeks. Inevitably, the last few days were as sparse as the dead grass in the yard.

On the evenings Mom got off work early, they settled on the couch together to watch game shows. Elizabeth's mother entered all the game shows. Someday she would be on that stage, she said. She would win lots of money and they'd have their very own washer and dryer. They would never visit that boring laundromat again.

Too many times, Elizabeth looked out the window, where the popular girls sauntered by, sneering and making jokes about the neighborhood. Unfortunately for Elizabeth, there was a convenience store with a large selection of cheap booze and porn nearby. The potbellied manager didn't card, so it attracted teenagers.

Her own father spent half his meager paycheck at the place. That is, until he left.

"We're better off," her mom had said, dragging his rust-colored, cigarette-stained chair to the trash. Even the Salvation Army wouldn't take it. But it was where her father had parked, beer in hand, holding the remote. Just to make sure they knew who was in charge.

They were better off. A million Top Ramen dinners would never hurt them as much as living with him.

One night, Elizabeth got tired of waiting in her shoebox of a bedroom for her mother to return from work. She squeezed her eyes shut, hoping to fall into a dreamless sleep. But it was a fruitless effort; she could never sleep till her mother's key turned in the lock. The clock read 10:02 PM. The local diner her mom worked at remained open all night, designed for travelers on the road. It was the last stop for food for fifty miles. During the tourist season, her mom often got extra hours she couldn't afford to refuse.

Elizabeth climbed out of bed and paced the shag carpet. Sometimes, the familiar cadence of her feet dancing on each creaky floorboard lured her heavy eyelids down. And she'd get back into bed, finally able to sleep.

After a long time—Elizabeth's mother had gotten many hours, it turned out—she kneeled by the open window and let the noises outside accompany her. The inky night was punctuated by a bright moon, and she could hear crows calling, owls hooting in the distance. Maybe she even heard a seagull's call, miles away, down at the bay.

Finally she got up and pulled on a pair of jeans. Maybe the brisk air would lift the heaviness in her chest. Fill up the little holes that riddled her heart. Elizabeth headed down from the trailer park, stepping over the cracks in the asphalt, and onto the sandy pavement that led to the water. The sea filled her nostrils with salt.

Then she smelled something burning. Was there a fire? As she got closer, she spied dark puffs of smoke billowing up from the water. Curious, she dug her heels into the hillside, half climbing, half sliding into a shelter of weathered rocks. Teenagers yelled over the rush of the tide. A full moon cast an incandescent glow on the choppy sea. She hid behind the boulders, watching the party.

A little cove sat far back from the sea; a bonfire crackled. Elizabeth knew this hideout. Sometimes she burrowed herself there, watching the younger kids traipse along the beach with their parents. But she'd never been here at night, when stars dotted the sky and older kids paraded about, laughing, with big cans of beer in their hands. The smell was sharp, like rotten bread to Elizabeth, and all too familiar. She shielded her nose and watched the scene unfold. The heels of her shoes sunk into the wet sand. Little gusts of wind blew her hair back. Squinting, she caught a glimpse of the Barkley girls. This surprised her. The Barkley Inn was not far. The bay hooked around to the ocean; one could walk there in ten or fifteen minutes. How had they convinced Myra Barkley to let them hang out here at night? Of course, at twelve, Elizabeth knew little of these matters. But it occurred to her that booze and cigarettes were forbidden, even for teenagers.

Gwen Barkley flopped into the sand, laughing. "Look at the sky. The moon is so . . . shimmery."

The dark-haired boy spread out beside her. "You crack me up, girl." He punched her arm playfully. "Lightweight."

The friends languished on the sand beside the roaring fire. The tide ebbed and flowed predictably; calm radiated from the party. No one, that evening on the beach, knew that life could switch rhythm on you, could sweep you off your feet and knock you breathless and lost. A melancholy stab of envy struck her deep in her ribs, and she wished for that life.

Oh, she wished for that life.

Except something curdled in Elizabeth's stomach. She looked to her left, where the youngest Barkley girl perched on her knees, drawing in the sand with a stick. Charlotte Barkley couldn't have been more than seven or eight. A cold wave trickled through Elizabeth's veins, straight through her fingers, into her toes. Was Charlotte supposed to have a babysitter? Elizabeth wondered why the little girl was sitting alone. Charlotte pulled herself to her feet, and called, "Gwennie, can't we go home? I'm tired."

"Stop whining, Charlotte. We'll go back soon."

"I'm telling Mama. You're supposed to be watching me."

"You better not."

Elizabeth squeezed her knees to her chest. Smoke rippled into the atmosphere. The voices melted into one another; the tide overcame their conversations. Elizabeth wanted to run home—she *would* run home. She was going to be in big trouble if her mother found out she was all the way down here in the dark, and her mother would be home soon. What time was it?

Goose bumps erupt on her flesh as she thinks back to that night. How she wishes she'd checked on the little girl, made sure Gwen was watching.

The truth is, she wanted the necklace. Elizabeth was entranced by the necklace. She feels sick, thinking about this.

Charlotte whispered something under her breath and ripped a chain from her neck. She tossed it in the sand and plodded away, head angled down. Elizabeth was compelled to get a closer look. Gwen and her friends were farther down on the beach, hunkered beneath the little cove. She wanted to see what Charlotte had thrown in the sand. The teenagers were preoccupied with their party, too busy even to check on Charlotte. She would be quick about it. Curiosity got the best of her. She tiptoed toward the sand. The moon illuminated something shiny. She picked it up from the sand. The necklace. A rush of anxiety coursed through her bones. Elizabeth could be seen here, at the Barkley girl's party. And her mother would be home soon. Shoving the chain into her pocket, she climbed the steep path to the road.

She remembers how the ocean hurled waves against her shore; the night was inky. The little girl wouldn't have tossed the necklace into the sand if she needed it, right? She walked for a few minutes before she saw a truck squeal away from the dirt path. The truck took off down the road, headlights off. It kicked sand into her eyes as it flew by. Where was it going so fast?

Elizabeth shrugged and inspected the necklace. "Best Friends Forever" was engraved in the metal. It was prettier than anything she'd ever owned. Her eyes trailed to the cloud of sand left by the speeding vehicle. She ran her fingers along the jagged edge of the heart and continued to walk.

If only she had told someone, if only she had followed, if only she had screamed for Gwen.

If only, if only, if only.

She didn't tell the police about the truck, the heart, all that she'd witnessed. When news hit that Charlotte had gone missing, Elizabeth had been terrified to come forward with the necklace. It would mean admitting she'd snuck out that night, that she'd stolen the child's jewelry right out of the sand. If anyone knew she had *both* pieces now, they'd dig deeper and discover her true identity. She puts her face in her hands, trying not to cry. Even if Gwen is guilty of hurting Charlotte, how the hell is Peter involved? She can't imagine Gwen and Peter in the same hemisphere, let alone in on a crime. He is not the sort of man Gwen would be caught dead with.

She shudders and pushes the necklaces aside. Next, the pile of IDs. There are several, including her real Social Security card, passport, and expired Oregon State driver's license. He must have had fake ones made for her too, because there are others bearing her photo and a different name. "In case we have to get out of dodge," he'd said. She glances at the necklaces again. He'd promised to never let her go, to kill her if she tried to take Theo away. He had dangled the threat in her face like a grenade. Peter was a predator; she didn't doubt this.

Still, he'd played a role in Charlotte's disappearance, and it shreds her insides. He didn't have to hold them at that cabin. Plenty of dangerous men silently terrorize their wives and children in suburban homes. She shakes her head, bites the inside of her mouth till it bleeds.

She wants to push the thought away, but it echoes over and over: *He knew Gwen.* Somehow. Maybe he was a guest at the inn at some point and stole it from her. But considering its role in a high-profile missing child case, this is far-fetched. No rational person would want to get mixed up in that, over a cheap necklace. She slams her fist on the table. He wouldn't have saved that necklace unless he had something to do with her disappearance.

She tries to remember the day she met Peter. His connection to the town. It's all so blurry.

She had just buried her mother. It was a simple service. Her mom didn't want an extravagant funeral, just her ashes spread over the side of a glorious mountain. Elizabeth remembers ash and bone flowing from the urn onto purple and yellow wildflowers. "I never did get to skydive," her mother had said, and she'd smiled weakly. It was one of those bucket list items they could never afford.

Her mother had wanted a party. It was the height of summer, during one of the few hot Oregon days a year. Elizabeth didn't have a lot of friends, but her mother did. She invited the whole crew from the last diner where her mom had waitressed, and some of her loyal clients. Elizabeth tries to think of any connection her mother might have had with the Barkleys at the time of her death, but she hadn't worked for the Barkleys in many years. She's not sure the Barkleys even knew her mother had died.

When people left, and the distraction of the guests and their toasts to her mother dwindled, she found herself alone in an empty house. She was caught between sweet nostalgia and sour memories of the illness, when she got in the car and left. The house was so quiet. Even the blip of the machines and the company of the hospice nurses was gone.

Was Peter at the party? They didn't speak till she got to the bar, by herself, so no, he couldn't have been. Not unless he'd been stalking her covertly and followed her to The Keg House, which seems unlikely, even for Peter. Why? He said he had been driving through and decided to stop for a drink. She pinches her arm to remind herself that Peter was a pathological liar, an unreliable narrator of anything.

Her mind floats back to that evening at the bar. Rum and Coke for her; straight-up tequila for him. They had gone back to her house that night. Did she love him? She can't say if she did or she didn't. They dated for such a short time before he suggested the homestead. She hated being alone in that house. "I was so stupid," she murmurs to herself, thinking about how easily Peter sold her. He'd said his parents died when he was young, in a car crash. Elizabeth wonders if his parents are alive somewhere, if that was just another lie to isolate her. He said he was from Washington. She remembers this very clearly. He had wanted to start a homestead up Mount Rainier because he was from the area originally. That's where the accident was, on one of those slick mountain roads. She nods, sure of this now. Maybe, if one of the other IDs is real, she can locate someone—anyone—who knew him. Maybe even his family. That would be a start.

She peers at the IDs again. He'd had IDs for both Peter Briggs and Patrick J. Henderson.

Patrick Henderson's identification expired five years ago. It has a picture of a much younger Peter, and a Washington address. This, she might be able to use. All she needs is a computer. She can't take these to the police, not till she has more evidence, till she finds out more about the man she married.

Elizabeth draws a sharp breath; her eyes are drawn to Theo, curled up on the bed. In the morning, she'll take him to the library, where there are computers. It's a public place, as safe as she can possibly find.

*   *   *

The library isn't picky about the validity of Elizabeth's driver's license. She easily obtains a slick library card and signs her name on the back. She smiles at Theo. "We'll check out some books if you give me a few minutes to work, okay?"

"What are you doing?" he says, scrunching his face up. "I want to look at books now. Plus, they have toys in that little room." He points toward the kid's section, with a child-sized table, painted wood chairs, a kitchen set, and various costumes. "There are babies in there."

Elizabeth draws a sharp breath and considers this. He's right. There's a toddler playing while his mother flips through a book, looking up now and then to check on her daughter. Occasionally, the girl meanders toward her to show her a Lego creation or a doll. She remembers what Gwen said about helicopter parenting. The library is so open and bright. It's a weekday morning, so it isn't terribly busy, but the collision of voices is enough to set her on edge.

"Okay," Elizabeth finally says. She chooses a computer with a direct view into the playroom. "I'll be done soon." Gwen's expression hadn't betrayed anything when Elizabeth asked about the necklace. She sighs and enters the library card number to access the internet. Peter might be dead, but the painting slasher is out there. She shivers and glances up at Theo. He's wearing a chef's hat and holding a wooden pizza. *The kid's adaptable,* she thinks. He prances up to her, holding a deck of cards.

"Wanna see a trick?" he says.

"Sure."

He shuffles the cards, a sparkle in his eyes. A new trick. Then he quickly divides the cards between them, like a blackjack dealer.

"Damn, you're smart."

He launches into an explanation. This card is worth more than that. This hand is the winner. Elizabeth starts to get bored a few minutes later. But Theo's interest in games, in the world around him is impressive. He's been like this since he was a toddler, jabbering on, trailing after her with questions. *"What is the name of that flower? Do people on TV really live in big houses and drive cars in the city?"*

That one broke her.

She's afraid she isn't as strong as he is, that she will fail at caring for him now that their world isn't built around survival. That's the thing about people, Elizabeth knows. When you've got the privilege to be complacent, to let your guard down, you can get blindsided. She glances at Theo once more, sucks in a deep breath, and turns back to the computer.

"Why don't you go back and play for a minute? We're leaving soon."

"All right," he says, and dashes back to the kids' area. She hears him talking to a little girl about the cards.

Elizabeth starts by typing in "Patrick J. Henderson" and the address on the driver's license. It doesn't yield much, other than a Zillow listing for a house her husband may have rented in the distant past. And there are plenty of other Patrick J. Hendersons in the Pacific Northwest. Shit, this is getting her nowhere. She looks up, checks on Theo, and glances around the computer area, making sure no one can see what she's typing.

She wants to know more about the day Charlotte Barkley vanished, about what was reported to the media twenty years ago. Maybe Patrick Henderson's name will pop up. Or a photo—something. She sifts through many articles, all stating some variation of what she already knows. There are photos of the Barkley family, teary pleas from Myra. Pictures of little Charlotte. God, it's heartbreaking.

The problem is it's nothing new. And no mention of Patrick or Peter anywhere. Where did he get Gwen's half of the necklace? She's not leaving Rocky Shores till she gets the answer to this question.

Her vision is blurry from staring at the screen; she's begun to sweat from frustration. Theo comes back to the computer, whining that he's hungry and ready to leave. Her fingers are numb from typing; there's nothing left she can think of to search. She erases her search history and logs out of the computer.

"Please go clean up the toys, and then we'll head back," she tells Theo absentmindedly. Staring at the burner phone, she thinks hard about what to do next. She needs an address. Family. Someone from Peter's past who can point her in the right direction.

She dials Alice's number. "Hi, it's me."

"Girl," Alice says, breathless, "what the hell have you gotten yourself into?"

"It's a long story," she says, "but I need a favor."

"It always is . . . what do you need?"

"If I give you a Social Security number, can you get information on a person from that? Or a driver's license number?"

"I have no idea what kinda trouble you're into, but the police can investigate that stuff far better than I can."

"Alice. It's complicated. You know how helpful the police have been in the past—"

She scoffs. "All right. Give me the names and numbers, and I'll see what I can come up with. You really need to get out of there. But I can give it a shot."

"Thank you so much," she says, relieved.

"Uh-huh. I swear to god. You should just let me pick you up and get out of that town."

"Soon, Alice. I promise. I just want to know the man I married."

"Yeah, that's what they all say," she mumbles. "Give me twenty-four hours."

Elizabeth can't fail Charlotte Barkley. Charlotte didn't meander into the water alone. Maybe she drowned, but it was no accident.

CHAPTER SEVENTEEN

MYRA

Myra is working the front desk at the inn, checking in a new guest. She starts back for the lobby, when something catches her eye. The door to Elizabeth and Theo's room is open. She steps cautiously toward it. *Don't be silly,* she thinks. *There's nothing to worry about.* Everything has her on edge lately. Maybe she should take Gwen up on her offer to try yoga class.

She knocks on the hollow door. "Elizabeth?" she says.

No answer. She peers around the corner and shivers at the chill in the room. The window is open. Wind bellows through the screen.

She checks her watch. Theo and Elizabeth are still on their walk. It's just so strange she left the window open. As she takes a step into the room, her gaze trails to the nightstand just under the window. A shiny pocketknife, blade ejected, lies there, as if on display. She stumbles backward, into the hall, and runs into Schumer.

"Someone was here," she whispers. "Broke in the window and left a knife on the bedside table."

He rushes inside, tears open the closet door. "No one's here now. Might wanna consider evacuating. This is going to scare the crap out of the guests."

*   *   *

Myra shivers violently, though she can hardly feel it. A scream sticks in her throat.

Detective Marlow had said they'd be cautious. *"But don't get too worked up,"* she'd said. Myra scoffs. She is bitter and can't hide it. Her chest has broken out in angry red splotches.

"Don't worry Myra," they said. *"We've got it under control,"* they said.

Herb wraps a blanket around her shaking body. Police trample through Elizabeth's room. They tear it apart, dusting for fingerprints. Herb rubs her shoulders. "Myra?"

"Yes," she says, startled. "What?"

"Sarah wants to speak with us alone."

She follows Herb through the crowded lobby. Myra catches Kenneth's eye as he leans against the wall, arms folded across his chest. A detective sends him back to his room.

"I'm sorry," he says, as he trails down the hall. "This is awful."

Sarah ushers them outside, through the gravel. Icy water sloshes into Myra's crocs and awakens her senses. She concentrates on stepping around larger chunks of stone and grips Herb's hand. They move swiftly, past the whispers and craning necks, into the quiet of their home.

Myra slumps into a chair at the dining room table. Herb rakes his fingers through his silver hair. He looks at her. His wrinkles seem deeper, eyes more resigned. He shakes his head.

"I need you to listen to me," says Sarah, sitting across from Myra. "It's very possible Elizabeth is the one who slashed that painting. How else would she get the knife? It's so unlikely that someone would climb in the window and leave it there."

The room goes silent. The detective exchanges a glance with Herb. They are waiting for Myra to explode, burst into tears, lose her mind.

Instead, Myra laughs. She takes in their wide eyes, and she laughs from deep in her gut. She laughs and laughs till she can hardly breathe. "Do you really believe she'd be stupid enough to leave that knife sitting there for us all to see? And besides, what would ruining a painting accomplish? Even if she was some sort of . . . imposter. That doesn't even make sense. Don't you see? Plus, it's *our* pocketknife. Someone had to have taken it from our office. It's a weird coincidence. You must see that. How would he get into our office without anyone seeing?"

"We aren't saying Elizabeth Lark is not Charlotte. Not yet." Sarah speaks slowly. "What if she did damage the painting herself? And you did waive the fingerprinting and the DNA test."

White-hot rage threatens to boil from Myra's gut and out her mouth. She presses her lips into a straight line.

Sarah reaches for Myra's shoulders but stops in midair, as if she can feel the heat emanating from her. "Okay. Let's say someone stole the knife and left it in her room. God only knows. But we've got to do that DNA test."

Myra blows a scalding breath through her teeth. She can't stop trembling, can't look at Herb or Sarah.

"Have you checked the safe, Myra?" Herb asks tentatively.

"Of course not. She would never—"

"Because she and Theo were in the lobby when I dropped a couple of grand in cash in it—"

"Oh, Herb. Come on." The blood rushes to her cheeks.

Sarah puts her hand up as Herb begins to speak. "Stop," she mouths. "We should definitely check the safe," she says aloud.

"It's not just the money, Sarah. There's a gun in that safe. I keep it in case of an emergency."

"Go ahead and check the safe, darling." Her eyes go steely, hard.

At this moment, the screen door whines open, clacking against the door. Herb peeks into the front room. Maybe a storm is picking up. Myra's pulse quickens.

"That better not be some reporter," says Herb.

Elizabeth and Theo emerge from behind the door and step into the kitchen. She drops her bag and says, "What's going on over at the inn? The cops are everywhere." Theo clings to his mother's leg.

Myra rushes toward them.

Sarah puffs her chest out. "We found this in your room." She produces the pocketknife and sets it on the table. "Are you sure there's nothing you want to tell us?"

Elizabeth picks up the knife and twirls it under the light. It falls from her fingers and hits the table with a thud. "We have to go." Elizabeth speaks in a low, shaky voice. She grabs Theo's hand.

Myra recognizes the wild, panicked expression on Elizabeth's face, because she, too, has felt the weight of worry for a child: all Elizabeth wants is to protect Theo. "Someone stole that knife from our office, Herb."

Elizabeth ignores her. She steps out the door, dragging Theo behind her. "I'm going back to the inn to make a phone call." Tears stream down her cheeks. "Hurry up," she tells the boy. "It's time to go."

Myra rushes after them. "I can't do this again."

Elizabeth turns around, facing Myra. "Don't say I left you," she says. "I protected my son. And your family." Her hair tangles in the cold wind. Leaves rustle around them, and the ocean roars.

"You are part of this family." Myra's voice cracks.

"Myra—"

"Don't say it." She steps back as if preparing for a blow to the stomach. "We are your family."

Elizabeth tosses her hands toward the sky, raises her chin to whatever spiritual power she does or does not believe in. Myra doesn't have a clue what this woman—her daughter—believes in. "I'm sorry for this. Don't you see that? I would think you'd understand."

She should understand. Maybe it's selfish. But she can't stand here and let them walk away. She follows Elizabeth into the inn, down the hall to her room. Standing in the doorway, she watches Elizabeth toss her tawdry belongings into that duffel bag. "Can we talk for a few minutes, before you go?"

Elizabeth stares at her. "For just a minute."

Myra tries to memorize her face. Her eyes are drawn to Elizabeth's loose, torn clothing. To Theo's threadbare pants. He wears the red shoes Myra purchased for him. They wear none of the other clothes she got them. "Is it too late?"

Elizabeth shakes her head. "I don't have much choice."

A weight pulls Myra down. "I meant, is it too late for us to be a family again?"

Elizabeth sits on the bed and pulls her knees to her chest. "I've spent my life alone. And I have pondered what it would be like to come down from that cabin. To be free."

"You're free now. Safe. Things are hard, but they'd be worse all on your own."

Elizabeth focuses on Myra's face. "I can do hard things." She folds the clothing she and Herb bought, and neatly stacks little shirts and jeans on the bed. "C'mon, Theo."

"But, I'm your mother. Don't you like the things we picked out?" She stops, thinking. "Remember, we've paid for your brother and sister's education. We owe you some new clothes. A home to stay in, with heat and food." She bites her lip till it bleeds. "You are my child. And I'm nothing but a stranger to you."

"I don't want anyone to get hurt," Elizabeth says. "Peter is gonna haunt me from the grave."

"This isn't about him. I mean you and me. Give me a chance to try. You don't have to love me. But I gave birth to you." A crack runs through her, and it webs like naked tree branches in a frozen winter. "I remember."

Elizabeth tosses her duffel bag over her shoulder. "I'm sorry."

Myra leans close to Elizabeth. She embraces her, leaving space between them. "When you were a little girl, you used to say, 'I'll give you a dozen pansies and a marigold' when you wanted something." She says, softly, "I'll give you a dozen pansies and a marigold if you let us handle this. If you stay home."

Elizabeth hugs back. It is electric, this fleeting moment. Myra closes her eyes and breathes it all in. "I love you."

Elizabeth does not respond.

CHAPTER EIGHTEEN

MYRA

She stands on the porch, watching her shed through narrowed eyes. Water drips into the awning, dancing with the rusted steel in a slow, melodic beat. Night has fallen; the shed is a gray silhouette in the porch light. Her mind twists with haphazard thoughts strung together, swirling incomprehensibly. Tapping her foot is involuntary. It is after one AM. Herb says she needs to sleep, but she can't sleep until she checks her shed. This place was her comfort. It has gone cold; Peter Briggs stole her daughter, her ocean, her art.

Even in death, Peter Briggs has sent someone to hunt them.

Myra can hardly breathe as she descends down the step. Her mind travels in figure eights and circles, in straight lines and angles. She darts behind the house and hides in its shadow. The shed is pitch-black. She blows a thin stream of air from her lungs.

Stay calm.

She runs across the crunchy gravel, and she concentrates on her breath, on her feet as they hit the ground. Muddy water splashes onto her ankles. Still breathing hard, she lifts the heavy latch up. The windows are sealed shut. She hovers outside and listens to the rain plunk down, the wind bristle around her. Bats squeak in the distance; the whistle sends a bone-deep panic through her. Waking a bat in winter is bad luck.

A hibernating animal has warned her. She opens the door anyway.

Myra rushes inside, mouth dry and chest pounding. She pulls the cord to the hanging lightbulb. It illuminates the small space. She laughs at herself. The painting slasher isn't stupid enough to return here. Besides, she can't go back to the house till she's painted her angst out. Still, insomnia can drive even a sane person mad. She rubs her weary eyes. No one is here. *I'm losing my mind,* she thinks, and cracks the window.

All of her paintings of Charlotte come from scenarios she has dreamed of over the years. She hasn't had a subject on the little stool in her studio in forever. Not since Herb began pestering her to paint something or someone else besides Charlotte. He said it wasn't healthy to be stuck in the past. She said it kept her breathing, kept her in motion. Myra checks under the table, behind the paintings. She will not let this man control their lives.

She has memorized her adult daughter's face, excited to transfer it to the canvas. Her mind empties as she prepares the piece, swishing the stiff brush over the canvas in rich, thick strokes: sienna, white, red. She blends the colors with ease, ignoring the splatters of paint that flick against her cheeks and smear onto her apron. As she swipes the paint, her arm tires, but she loves the fatigue; the cramp in her hand is one unique to creation. She uses the thick brush to draw a basic outline. The details will come later. This is a process. It is methodical, soothing.

Myra prefers portraiture over other types of art. She enjoys watching the subjects, really watching them, through a series of photographs or in person. She knows how to capture a certain vulnerability in a hand, or a sparkle in the eye. There are dozens of pictures of her babies and Herb, of the family.

Painting was a way to bring subjects to life, and she was up for the challenge.

And after, Myra hoped to bring her daughter to life, when everyone thought she was dead.

She sweeps a wild blue color across the canvas, heavy-handed. She scrapes white over the blue. It sounds like a builder evening out mortar, rough and careless. Sweat pools on her forehead and she blinks away tears.

Myra drops the supplies with a bang. She slides to the cold floor and rests her head on bent knees. Loose hair cascades around her face. The scent of wet paint is pungent in the air despite the cracked window.

After Charlotte's disappearance, Myra considered all of the places her daughter might be.

In the first painting, Charlotte remains eight years old. Suspended in the air on a wooden swing, she wears a broad smile. A tangerine sea of California poppies surrounds her. The sun brightens her face. She pumps her strong legs, catapulting into the sapphire-colored sky. Charlotte has wandered to Southern California. The weather is warm. She is found by a kind farmer. He brings her home, where she joins his wife and other children. Charlotte cries, but the old man gives her a popsicle and calls the police. She is like a lost child at Disneyland, playing with Mickey and Donald and a slew of princesses while she waits for her parents.

Soon the news will make it to Rocky Shores, and she'll be sent home. For now, she swings with the couple's children. They dry her tears and keep her fed.

She is okay, Myra told herself. The couple will send her home soon.

In the next painting, Charlotte is eighteen years old. Her hair is clipped to her chin and dyed purple. A cigarette hangs from her lips, ribbons of smoke flirting with a cold November evening. Her legs and arms are thin and drawn to her chest. Her lips are painted, with a sharp brush, into a pensive expression.

She is okay, Myra told herself. Charlotte would have come home, if she could have, by now. She isn't safe or unsafe, but eventually she will be back. Charlotte remembers who she is, where they live. She couldn't have forgotten, right? Maybe that's what it is. She was far too young to remember the inn's location. Probably she is living somewhere with a couple who couldn't have children. They love her deeply, cherish her. Someday they will realize what they have done is wrong. You can't just take someone's daughter and claim her as your own.

My daughter has to be out there, she'd think. She could not believe what they had told her, that Charlotte had probably drowned.

A rap on the door breaks her thoughts. She peers through the small window. The pale moonlight is muted by old dust smeared on the glass.

"Who's there?" Myra clenches the palette knife in her fist.

"It's me. Elizabeth."

Her heart skips in her chest. She gets up and opens the door, breathless. "It's okay. I just thought . . . I don't know what," she says, and drops the knife from her sweaty palm.

"Sorry I scared you." Elizabeth shifts on her feet.

She freezes. "It's very late."

"I haven't been sleeping well," Elizabeth says.

A hint of unease courses through her. "Does Herb know I'm out here?"

"He doesn't know you're awake, if that's what you're asking." Elizabeth raises her eyebrows.

"What's that supposed to mean?" Myra asks cautiously.

Elizabeth shoves her hands in her pockets. She looks around the corner. Her lower lip trembles.

"Come in," Myra says, dropping a handful of brushes into a coffee mug filled with cold water. "It's all fine. See? It's just me and my art."

Elizabeth points to the painting of the little girl on the swing. "Is this me?"

Myra nods.

"And this is Gwen?" she asks, pointing at the portrait of the angsty teen.

Myra doesn't want to sound crazy. "Yes, it is. Not a very good rendition, I suppose."

Elizabeth slides down beside Myra on the floor and crosses her legs. She doesn't seem to suspect the lie. "Can I see the others? You're really talented, Myra."

"Okay. Let me show you this one I did when your grandmother was still alive." She flips through the canvases and pulls out one from the very back. Setting it beside the light, she glances at Elizabeth. "This is it."

Bernadette was seventy years old when Myra painted her, capturing the gleam in her eye and the beauty in her thick-knuckled hand. It was the first and only time Myra understood her mother as a human, and not the mother who found baking and sewing joyless. Bernadette taught her daughter to be fearless and tough, and Myra didn't quite appreciate this until she listened, really listened, during those last days of her mother's life.

You have to listen while you paint a person, Myra discovered. You have to listen to capture a whole life in your teeth and usher it softly to a piece of canvas. And then, with empathy in your heart, you cajole the blob of color into the layers that make a person's life.

"She looks so soulful," says Elizabeth. "You must have had a very unique childhood."

"Unique is one word to describe it," says Myra, laughing. "I didn't appreciate her enough. Kids grow up with the belief that their parents are above regular humans—or that they should be. I wanted her to be one of those 1960s moms, when she was a free-spirited woman who spoke her mind. I was proud of her and embarrassed all at the same time."

Elizabeth smiles pensively. "I think that's normal."

"Someday, Theo will find out his mama is just another person, trying to make her way through a difficult world. I long for the day when Gwen understands. Her two perfect girls might grow up and pull something unexpected on her." She wipes a tear from the corner of her eye and says, "All that therapy she gets and the books she reads won't prevent her children from coming into their own."

"Gwen loves you," Elizabeth says.

"I don't know, honey. The mother–daughter relationship comes effortlessly for some people. That's not been my experience," she says.

Elizabeth shifts on her feet. "The painting that was slashed. It's very different from the rest. The style is different. Did you make it for someone else?"

Myra pauses for a moment. "I guess I just like babies. New beginnings. So, I thought I'd try something new."

"It seems incomplete, yet not. Somehow. It's indescribable."

Myra thinks about this. "You're right." She laughs. "Clearly, I'm not Van Gogh."

"I think it's lovely," she says. "Maybe you could show me sometime."

"I'd like that," says Myra. Hope swells in her chest.

Elizabeth laughs nervously. "Okay. Though I doubt I'm any good."

"Eh? Good, great—whatever. It's fun. Want to try?"

There is a want in the breathless beat, a need curled inside of her question. Elizabeth had said *sometime*, not at one AM. Myra can't ever remember having anxiety like this. She wants to scream at someone, anyone who might listen. She is a bomb hidden in the shrubbery on a safe and tended road. With all the curves that have been thrown at her lately, her sanity feels precarious. How can she take this rejection from her own daughter? When Charlotte was a little girl, she wanted to use her mother's paints. Desperately. And Myra made her use the cheap, washable watercolors. She should have let her daughter use the paints when she cared to. Because now, she has to beg this stranger to spend time with her, and it shreds her insides.

Just say no. Say you hate me. Say you wish you'd never come home.

"I guess so. For a little while."

"Are you sure?" Maybe Elizabeth senses her desperation. Heat prickles her cheeks.

Elizabeth laughs—she really does—and says, "I'd love to paint with you."

Myra swallows this heavy, heavy lump, and it lands in the pit of her stomach, nauseating as cold meat. "Here, try these." She picks out several colors and squirts them on a palette. She can't let Elizabeth see that she is nervous.

"I'm not good at this at all," Elizabeth says, painting a giant orange stroke across the canvas. "But this is amazingly fun. This is better than any therapy."

"Someone finally sees! Your father is certain all the medications and the therapy are what cured me. But I needed a thing. Do you know what I mean?" She's rambling now. "I guess maybe you don't. But someday, after you feel more secure in this world, I guarantee, you will want a thing of your own."

"I get it. No one can take this from you." Elizabeth stares at Myra. "That is brilliant." She pauses. Myra resists the urge to fill the blank spot. "When he took me to the woods, I had this spot under a tree. Even in the cold, dead winter, it was covered in this thick, frozen moss. In the spring, wildflowers bloomed. So many—dozens and dozens—in pink and purple, blue and yellow. They were my thing." Tears drip down her cheeks.

With a paint-stained thumb, Myra wipes them away.

Elizabeth stiffens, but not too much. "It's time to go in, Myra. Herb is going to be worried if you stay awake all night. Lack of sleep is very bad for you, right?"

"Can you not mention it to him? That we were out here so late?"

Elizabeth pauses. "I guess so. But you have to sleep now, okay?"

"Promise." Myra swishes the brushes in water and wipes them on a paper towel. Elizabeth gathers the tubes of paint. "Just leave the paintings to dry," Myra says. "We'll get to them tomorrow."

They finish wiping the counters and step toward the door. Elizabeth swings it open, and a cold gust of wind rushes inside. Myra turns to take a final look at her shed, to make sure everything is in order.

"Wait." Something peeks out from underneath her stool.

"What?" Elizabeth freezes. "What is it?"

Myra marches toward the stool and pushes it hard. The wheels screech as it rolls backward.

"Nothing." Myra sucks a breath. "I just have the strangest feeling when I come out here. It's like I'm being watched."

Myra meets Elizabeth's eyes.

She shudders. "Yes. I feel that too."

CHAPTER NINETEEN

MYRA

It's a bit past noon and the restaurant is packed. Myra slinks inside and requests a table in the back. She ties a lacy scarf around her hair and scans the menu. The lunch crowd buzzes around her. The palpable energy of patrons mixing alcohol and office politics makes her head pound. She searches the room for a familiar face or group, but the only person she sees is Paul, a sad alcoholic who switches between various bars and liquor stores in an attempt to conceal his addiction. He's stayed at the inn once or twice, probably because his family had grown weary of him. Myra doesn't care what his reasons are; she tries not to get involved in the guests' problems. Paul shows no interest in her either. He slurps his drink, oblivious to Myra or anyone else.

Myra spies Michael Calgary first. The waiter leads him toward the table.

"Michael Calgary." He offers his hand. Myra takes it. It's as limp as a dead fish, but she decides to reserve judgment. There are other private investigators in line for interviews if this one doesn't work out. The problem is, she'd prefer not to involve Herb just yet. He thinks all PIs are crackpots because of a few bad hiring decisions Myra had made right after Charlotte's disappearance, which really isn't fair. So, she'll scope the man out first.

Mr. Calgary wears slacks and a jacket fresh off JC Penney's sale rack. She clucks her tongue. "Have a seat."

The waitress comes before he can reply. She snaps a piece of gum. "Know what you want?"

"Iced tea, please."

"Whiskey," says the private investigator. "On the rocks."

Bold move for a job interview. She hopes he doesn't expect this to be easy. "Make mine a Long Island iced tea," she says, with a smile.

The waitress scribbles this on her notepad. "Did you check out the lunch menu?"

"I haven't decided if I want lunch." Myra narrows her eyes, focusing on Michael.

"We'll let you know in a few." Michael waves the waitress off like an irritating fly.

"Suit yourself," she says. "Be back with the drinks." She saunters into the crowd and toward the bar.

"All right, Michael. I've been down this road before, hired a few PIs and psychics since my daughter's disappearance."

"There's a big difference between a psychic medium and a professional investigator, Mrs. Barkley."

"*Ms.* Barkley, please. Or Myra. Your choice. It's not 1950." She laces her fingers together. "Now, the point is, I am experienced in the art of detecting bullshit. Do you understand what I mean?"

Michael cracks his knuckles. A thick wedding band encircles his ring finger. He removes wire-rimmed glasses and wipes them with a paper napkin. "Look, Ms. Barkley. I am so sorry for the nightmare you've lived through. I just want to get a better idea of what exactly you want investigated, now that Charlotte is home."

"Yes, Charlotte." Myra smiles at the sound of her daughter's name. "You're familiar with her case, then."

Michael clears his throat, watching as the waitress approaches with their order. He is silent, waiting till she plunks the glasses on the table.

Myra sips her drink. The cold splash of liquor slides down her throat, and warmth spreads in her belly. She sucks an ice cube, absentmindedly stirring the tea.

Michael slams the whiskey in one deep gulp. "All right. So, Charlotte is home. And she killed her own kidnapper. It's quite a sensational case—all over the news." He pauses. "Do they plan to release his identity?"

"This conversation is confidential, right?" she says warily.

He nods, watching her curiously. "You've got my word."

"They have not identified the body. The name he gave my daughter is fake, obviously. Beyond that, his DNA is not in CODIS, which only means he's never been arrested. Dental records cannot be confirmed with no starting point, as his identity cannot be traced to a job, friends, or even a vehicle. So, we're lost."

"And you want me to figure out who the guy was? 'Cause, if I'm being honest, Ms. Barkley, I don't see the point of it. The man's dead. You've got your girl."

"It's not quite as simple as that. My family is still being targeted. Harassed. A person broke into my studio and slashed my painting." Her voice cracks. She takes another long sip of tea. "I need to ensure my family's safety. That this nightmare is really over. The person who slashed the painting left a knife on Elizabeth's bedside table. The police think she slashed the painting herself." She lowers her voice, and says, "That she could be an imposter."

He cocks his head to the side. "And you're sure she's not?"

"Mr. Calgary." Tears well in her eyes, but she blinks them away. "My daughter is home. And someone has been in my shed. The police say nothing's there. I have security cameras. It looks like the feed was looped because nothing shows."

"And you replaced the cameras? No strange activity the day the knife turned up?"

"Yes, of course we replaced them. New passwords, everything. But we don't have cameras in the rooms. That's horribly illegal. So, I can't say who left the knife in the room."

"Hmm." He leans back in his chair, calls the waitress over. "Want lunch, Myra?"

"So you believe me?" She takes a shaky breath. Finally. Someone gets it.

"Yes," he says, stroking his chin. "Tell me more about this painting."

"The painting was slashed in broad daylight," she says.

"Because the person knew no one was out there to see."

She shakes her head, thinking. "I had a feeling—"

"I don't take stock in feelings, don't believe in intuition. None of it. I deal in pragmatic matters, Ms. Barkley." He pauses. "I suggest we put a tail on your daughter and any suspicious vehicles coming or going from your property."

Her throat is suddenly very dry. "What do you mean? You want to follow Elizabeth?"

"It's for her own safety," he says.

Something about this doesn't sit right with Myra. "No, I don't want to go that far. She's already skittish. It could push her away."

"Suit yourself," he says. "Let's take a look at your security system. What do the cops say about that?"

"Very little," she says with a grimace.

He grins. "First, I wanna take a look around this shed. Check the cameras to see exactly how they did this. Is there a chance someone found out the password? Do you have a password that's too common? That would be the easiest way."

"Not sure. The cameras have been there a long time."

"All right. We'll start there, then."

She nods. And next, she's got to tell Herb.

CHAPTER TWENTY

MYRA

Herb seems reticent Saturday afternoon as they stand in the parking lot, waiting for Michael Calgary to arrive. Myra is too exhausted to drill him with the usual questions: *What's wrong? Are you mad? Sorry, I didn't tell you about the private investigator, but I told you so, I've been saying it for years.* She doesn't say it because she's not sorry at all. Gwen would call this a non-apology. And it would be. Staring straight ahead, she points at Michael's black SUV as he drives up. "Here he is."

"Good." Herb stuffs his hands in his pockets, kicks a pebble into a brackish puddle. A thick fog settles between them. Myra feels the urge to rescue him from his embarrassment.

But she waits.

"I'm sorry," he says, and clears his throat. "I said the police were doing their job. Over and over, I told you that. I did it because I hoped—oh lord, I hoped—that if we handed over the wheel, they'd find her. Truth is, I pushed you away from your instincts."

"Herb, you couldn't have known. Besides, you were right; most of the psychic mediums and a lot of the private investigators are searching for a buck. You're a natural skeptic. I didn't take it personally." She shakes her head. "I never considered that we were in danger at the inn. That Gwen and Jimi were at risk."

"I belittled you," he says. "In trying to protect you, that's what I did. It was chauvinistic. You can take care of yourself." He nods to himself.

Michael opens the car door and waves. "Be right up. Gotta get my equipment from the back."

Myra turns to Herb and says, "Apology accepted."

He gives her that wry grin, and she feels warm inside.

Michael darts around the puddles, his shoes crunching on the gravel. He wears a red Poncho over his shirt. "Michael Calgary," he says, extending his hand. "You must be Herb. Good to meet you."

"Likewise." He points at the house. "Let's talk inside."

"First, I want to take a look around the shed, where the painting was stolen."

"How much is this costing us?" Herb asks.

Myra elbows him hard and tells him with her eyes, in no uncertain terms, to shut the hell up. He receives the message.

"Never mind," he says. "It's not even about the money. I just want to make sure you're the real deal. But if my wife trusts you, I'm on board."

"Oh, Herb. Men try so hard to be pragmatic." He claps his hands, draws them together as if he's praying. "I get it, I really do. It's a protective mechanism. But you ain't a dog, Herb. And your wife doesn't need a guardian."

Myra tries to contain her smile. "All right then. Let's go."

They walk behind the house and to the shed. Fingers trembling, she shoves the latch to the door open.

She flicks on the interior light. Everything is in order.

"I want to take a look at the camera system. You said it was somehow circumvented, right? Did the cops know how?" Michael says.

"No, just that the feed skipped."

"Where is it located?"

"Hidden in this light fixture," she says.

Herb gets a flashlight and a screwdriver from the drawer where her tools are kept. He holds it up to the light. "I hid them better, after the incident with the painting." He goes back inside and turns off the light switch. The soft halogen glow flickers and disappears.

"You hold the flashlight." He unscrews the light fixture and removes the cover. Inside is the camera. "See that LED light?"

"So what?" Myra rubs her shoulders. "Cameras have lights, right?"

"Not exactly," Michael says. "If an LED light is on, that means someone is watching the feed. Wave hello." Michael sticks his middle finger up. "And goodbye." He smashes the camera with the screwdriver.

"What the hell was that?" Herb says, wide-eyed. "Are you saying someone is . . . on the other side of that camera?"

"Yup. Let's get in my car," he says, and leads them to the black SUV in front of the house. He clicks the key fob to open the car. Myra and Herb slide in the back while Michael gets in the driver's seat. He turns the motor on and pushes another button. The backseat windows fade to black.

She grasps Herb's cold hand.

Michael shifts slightly in his seat so he can see them in the rearview mirror, but he does not turn his head or twist his body. He taps the steering wheel, turns the radio on. Myra draws her lips into a deep frown.

"I can't tell you if the girl is your daughter—not yet anyway. But I can say she did not hack those cameras. Unless she's a real piece of work, trained in sophisticated hacking. And we know she's been living in a hellhole in the mountains with that prick. Definitely not a high-tech situation."

Blowing out a slow stream of air, Myra says, "I knew it. And she didn't plant that knife either."

Michael flicks his hand. "God knows."

Myra shivers. The thought of this man watching her sends a chill straight through the marrow of her bones. "Oh shit." She exchanges a glance with Herb, whose face is as white as a fish belly.

"You think Peter Briggs set them up?"

"Maybe. Or the painting slasher."

"Still, it makes no sense. He stole her off the beach two decades ago. Why spy on us fifteen years later?"

Michael twists his lips. "But the boy is five, right?"

"Yes," Herb says, shaking his knee.

"Here's my theory," Michael says. "Maybe Briggs chose to keep track of you after the boy was born. She escaped recently. He might've been afraid she'd take his son." He pauses. "Are you following me?"

They nod.

"Okay, so she's getting more anxious to get out because of her son. Briggs knows the first place she'd go, if she escaped, was home to you. And she did," he points out. "So, he installed the cameras to watch you. And if she came home, he'd wait for the right moment, when she was away from y'all and the cops, to get her back."

"Holy shit," Herb says under his breath.

"Only, this isn't a typical situation. Briggs is dead. Someone else is still watching your camera feed."

"Which means your theory is wrong," Myra says.

Michael shrugs. "Not necessarily. However, this will take a bit more work than I previously suspected."

Herb bangs his head against the back of the seat.

"First things first. We disable your system completely. And for good measure, smash every camera on the property."

"What? How?" Herb says.

Michael opens the glovebox and pulls out a gun. "Like this. Are you going to join me?"

Herb clears his throat. "Can I just e-mail you a layout of where the cameras are located, and you can . . . ah . . . remove them for us?"

"For a fee," Michael says laconically.

"No problem," Myra says, and sinks back into her seat. "You just do your thing."

Herb stares at the sky.

CHAPTER TWENTY-ONE

ELIZABETH

The inn is brimming with people, packed with unfamiliar faces, and it makes Elizabeth claustrophobic. She tries to be calm, but her chest hurts and palpitates and drops straight to her stomach. The walls, layered with decades of different paint colors, collapse in on her. Bells hang from the door handle, and each time someone enters, they clatter like old copper pans.

She stays in the room most of the time, begging Theo to stay with her, but he gets bored in there. He likes Myra, likes Gwen's girls when they drop by; he seems to crave people, noise. The isolation has affected them differently. Elizabeth supposes he feels safer in a room full of people than when they were alone in that cold, dark cabin. Theo has been showing the girls his magic tricks. They've set up a puppet show. He revels in their excitement.

Someone pads up behind her. She whirls around, startled.

Theo stands there. "I'm sorry I scared you."

"It's okay," she says, though her voice trembles. She holds her stomach, memories darting through her mind. The painting slasher is someone Peter knew, someone who is angry, someone who is connected to that night on the beach with Charlotte.

Elizabeth remembers when she took Theo to the Harts. She had paid for that in bruises and fractured bones. Theo is smart, clever. But she can't let her guard down. She has to protect him.

He acts as if this is over. She hopes, for Theo, it is. But in Elizabeth's mind, Peter is always hiding around the corner, even from deep in a pauper's grave.

"I want to play with Savannah. She's in the living area," he says plainly.

Before she can answer, he prances off. "Okay, I guess," she calls after him. "Don't leave the living area."

That morning sticks in her mind . . . because that day she had tried to make him feel like she knew what she was doing, reassured him. And she'd failed. What if she fails him again?

"We're getting out, Theo. I promise you," she had said, meeting his eyes. "This time, I have a plan. A foolproof plan."

"What is it? 'Cause if he catches us, we'll be in big, big trouble."

"We won't get caught."

"Are you sure? He follows us everywhere." Theo turned away from her. With her eyes, she traced the curve of his neck and his head, which settled like a globe onto his shoulders. He gazed at the ground, as if the weight of his head was too much, or perhaps it was the thickness of sorrow in the air. A sort of vulnerability lived in his bumpy spine, and it moved her, filled her with tenderness.

He was lovely and too big and too small all at once.

"Theo. Please look at me." She swallowed the lump in her throat.

He faced her, lower lip quivering. "Okay."

She blinks. "Look, Daddy is somewhere around here. He took the truck, but he didn't turn off the water. So, we can't leave, not yet."

He bit his lip. "Stop calling him Daddy. He's not my daddy."

"You won't miss him at all when we're gone?"

"No," he said, glowering. "He makes everything hard."

Elizabeth took a slow breath. "I will fix it. We're taking a walk. You like the homesteaders, right? They're just a couple of miles away. Last week, I heard Daddy—I mean Peter—talking about them on the phone. How the farm the Harts have built is too close. I heard him whisper something about them finding out about us if they saw the inside of the cabin."

"They have animals," he said, wandering into the bedroom, "and we're gonna find out about them?"

"Yes, my brilliant boy. That's exactly what we are going to do. We're only stopping by to see the animals. To say hello. He wouldn't even mind that. Remember, if we stick to ourselves like hermits, that will make people suspicious. That's the last thing he wants." She paused. "I've washed our clothes and shoes." Elizabeth thought for a moment, nervous about what Theo could accidentally reveal. "You don't have to say anything. Just say hello. Or play, right at the edge of their farm. By the goats—"

"Let's just tell those people how he's got us trapped up here. They can help us, right?"

Elizabeth cleared her throat, considering how she could explain how much she needed him to keep the secret, without instilling even more fear into her son. And she knew, children are not good at keeping secrets. "Theo, if we do that . . ." Her eyes were wet with tears. "You have to let me talk. I understand that you're so desperate to see people. That you believe they can save us. But it's not so simple, okay?" She dried her eyes with the back of her sleeve. "Now, the first thing we need to do is get cleaned up. The water is on. And we must hurry if we're going to be back by tonight."

"Okay," he said. "You're sure, right?"

"Please, trust me on this one." She tousled his hair and crouched down to his level. "Now, let's get our coats and shoes. Wash your face and hands."

Elizabeth readied her son quickly; there was no time to spare. Her breath was fast, heart pounding. She tied his shoes, wishing they had boots. How long was the trip down there? A mile, maybe two?

They rushed out the door, into swirling wind. She pulled his hood over his head. "Keep your hands in your pockets," she said, teeth chattering.

He did not complain, only followed. But she couldn't take her focus off his wet, icy shoes. With each step, the warning bells in her head intensified. This was a mistake, a terrible idea. Daylight broke, with the moon pale against the dusky blue sky. The air smelled thick and wintery, like snow. A deer moaned in the distance.

She stopped. "I don't think we can make it."

"If we turn around, it's even farther. We're more than half-way," he whined, pointing at the large farm just past a clearing. "It's right there, Mommy."

"No. We're going to freeze out here." Her feet were like ice; Theo's tiny toes could be frostbitten. What was she thinking, bringing him out here?

"Let's go. Really, it isn't far."

She grasped his hand, focused on the path ahead as they trudged toward the farm. *Faster, faster,* she thought. They didn't have much time before they got frostbite. The path was thick with slush seeping into their ratty shoes. Snowflakes flicked at their faces, becoming heavier as they moved. *Keep walking.* Her chest pounded as they approached. What would they say? They were soaked, freezing.

The dark brown farm sat in the middle of a large clearing. Boxy metal structures were hidden behind it, with a snow-blanketed pasture for horses, though none were out of the shed. Smoke puffed from the chimney. Elizabeth and Theo exchanged a glance. "Follow me," she said.

"It's so quiet here," he whispered.

The house was surrounded by a wire fence. She wondered if it was electric. Maybe they were afraid their livestock would be stolen, but there weren't many people around these parts. Or it could've been designed to keep the animals in. She had never seen such a large barn on private property. They must have had cows. It occurred to her that she knew nothing about the Harts.

The powder-blue sky shifted to gray, though sunlight could still penetrate the clouds, dappling the snowy path. "Let's walk around. One of the other doors probably leads inside." There were lots of entrances. Elizabeth thought it seemed more like a compound than a homestead.

"This is creepy," Theo said. "Almost like no one lives here."

"It can't be as bad as where we're at," she said, through clenched teeth. "No choice but to find out. I hope they're home. I need to use a telephone."

"What? If you call the police, he'll find us. You aren't calling the cops, are you?"

"Theo—"

The door behind the fencing opened slowly, creaking on its hinges. A woman, wearing jeans and rubber boots to her knees, stepped outside. "Hello?"

Elizabeth took a deep breath. "Hello," she said. "My son and I live in the cabin up the hill. We seem to have lost power. I was wondering if we could use your phone to call my husband."

The woman ushered them inside. "Sorry, I'm taking care of the horses. They need to be blanketed in this weather." She furrowed her brow. "It's not safe out there. A lotta you people come up here, right in the wilderness, and fail to put a generator on your property. You could freeze to death."

"I know. We really should," Elizabeth said.

"There are safety precautions you have to take if you wanna live off grid."

Ah. So that was the Hart's story. They were survivalists. Elizabeth could work with this. She sighed. "Yes, exactly. We really aren't doing this right."

Mrs. Hart eyed her curiously. "Right. Fredrick can give your man some advice."

"No," Elizabeth said too loudly. "I mean, that's okay. We don't mean to trouble you. The phone?"

Mrs. Hart invited them inside and gave them towels to dry off. "Not smart. You and the boy could die in these temps. Gotta do something about your electricity. I bet you don't have a cellar either."

Elizabeth shook her head.

"Well, here's the phone," she said, and clucked her tongue. "And the computer." Mrs. Hart arranged the laptop on the table and opened a search engine for her. "Now, make sure you find a local business. They understand the weather here. And you'll have to explain the setup of your home."

"You're so right, Mrs. Hart. In fact, I should get someone out here today." She looked at the phone. A pay-as-you-go. The Harts must be paranoid, conspiracy theorists. This was a benefit to Elizabeth. They definitely didn't want any trouble, didn't want to be traced here in case the shit hit the fan.

Mrs. Hart still seemed incredulous. "Oh dear. You really don't know what you're doing, do you? The two of you are soaked. Where are your boots?" She sighed. "I'll get the boy some clothes. You want coffee? And cocoa for the boy?"

"Sure," she said, and squeezed Theo's knee.

Mrs. Hart disappeared down the hall.

"Shh," she told Theo. "Just thank her for the cocoa and be quiet." She started tapping on the keyboard. Found Alice's e-mail and sent her a message. Just as she was considering call-ing the police, the doorbell rang.

Elizabeth's heart dropped to her stomach. Resigned, she put her head in her palms. Theo groaned. They didn't have to wait for Mrs. Hart to open the door, to hear her speak to the visitor.

He'd found them. Just like before. She shoved the burner phone in her pocket. Later, she'd use it to find Alice.

* * *

Peter is dead, she reminds herself, but it does little to calm her down. The police pose as guests; they are shadowy figures sip-ping their coffee. They sleep with one eye open. Schumer takes a large bite of his Danish and scrolls through his laptop.

It's business as usual, and yet it's not.

If Peter were alive, he could smash through the door like a tsunami and sweep them all to their graves. And if someone is out there, someone who knows she is lying, she might be about to take her son on a new and equally dangerous journey. And Alice hasn't gotten back to her yet.

Stop thinking.

Myra works the front desk. The inn is an entirely different place than when Elizabeth was a child. She watches as Myra squints at the drivers' licenses and insists on credit cards. She says she knows a fake ID when she sees one, but unlike before, they have to turn guests away. The Barkleys are no longer the cash-accepting bed and breakfast they were; Myra probably feels guilty, because not all of the guests drifting through are running from the mob, the law, or a loan shark. Who knows which ones are just like Elizabeth? Sure, most are here to wit-ness Charlotte Barkley's remarkable reappearance. But some could be running for their lives.

Still, the inn is crowded. The voices competing with one another for volume are torturous.

She covers her ears with her palms.

"Morning, Elizabeth," Myra says. "How about lunch later?"

"I appreciate the offer. But I really can't handle the noise." She cranes her neck toward the living room.

Myra smiles, but she's obviously disappointed. "I think they're playing with a fire truck Gwen brought for him."

"I'm sorry about lunch." Elizabeth swallows.

"No, no. You take your time. That's what the therapist said." She smiles sadly. "You and Theo have been through more than I can imagine." She pats Elizabeth's shoulder and goes into the lobby.

Elizabeth looks out the window. The pier is empty, and the sky is streaked with gray clouds, but a semblance of calm settles over the beach. It is morning, when the ocean fog is so dense it is nearly opaque. She takes a deep breath, watching as a car approaches the inn. It's either Gwen or another guest passing through.

They're all just passing through, they say. In the dead of winter.

The headlights, hazy in the fog, are lower than the ones on Gwen's minivan. She is thoroughly exhausted. Maybe Myra will say they are out of rooms. The car crunches through the gravel, dipping up and down over the uneven parking lot. As it gets closer, a bright red convertible comes to view.

"Who is that?" Elizabeth says.

Myra sighs. "It's an old friend. Kenneth Callahan. He drives a very impractical car for Oregon. And Herb doesn't like him."

Elizabeth rolls her shoulders and imitates Gwen's yoga stretches. Kenneth has been to the Barkley Inn before. A lot of times, in fact. He could recognize her. Where will she go if he does? Elizabeth remembers him—rich, cocky, the type to make a scene. "Where did you say Theo was playing?" she says hoarsely.

"I don't know. Maybe by the couches? Oh, here he comes. Excuse me, sweetheart." She heads for the reservation desk.

Christ. She darts toward the couch and lets her black hair fall over her face. Crouching beside it, she pretends to be searching for something. The bells clash as Kenneth comes inside.

His stride is brisk and professional. "Good afternoon, Myra. Got a room?" Kenneth asks. He is Myra and Herb's age, approximately, but he seems youthful, put together. He wears a starched white shirt with pinstripes, and silver cufflinks. His pressed navy slacks brush the tops of shiny leather oxfords. His shoe polish smells like lemon dusting spray.

"Why do you need a room?" She rubs her temples. "You live three miles away. Don't you?"

He found out Charlotte is home, that's why. He's no different from the rest of these people. Except he is sophisticated. He's not caught up in emotion like Myra and Herb. What will she do when he recognizes her? She is the little girl whose mother scrubbed toilets till her hands were raw and chafed. Elizabeth was the three- or four-year-old child who hung around watching Mom sprinkling green Comet in the sinks and tubs and scrubbing them with Brillo pads.

"Adele and I are having issues. I'm moving out, just for a bit. Till we work stuff out."

"How long are you planning to stay?"

"I don't know." He shrugs. "Why does it matter? The stuff between you and me has long passed." A thickness fills his voice.

Wait a minute. What stuff between Myra and Kenneth? Elizabeth's ears perk up.

Myra says, "You heard, didn't you?"

"Heard what? Myra, I don't have time for this. My wife just left me."

He hasn't heard? How is that possible?

"Kenneth, Charlotte is home."

"What the—" He pauses. "Are you serious?"

"Let's have coffee, okay?" she says lightly. "Let's sit down, and you can tell me about Adele. And then I'll call her out to meet you. Briefly, though. She has anxiety. I have a grandson too."

Elizabeth stands up and heads toward the hallway. She picks up an Oregon travel guide and pretends to be engrossed in it.

"I think your news trumps mine." He clears his throat. "Herb must be over the moon. Holy shit—are you sure this time?"

She sighs. "I wish people would stop asking that."

"They don't want you to get hurt again. That's all."

Elizabeth meanders closer to the kitchen. She listens as they talk.

Myra waves him into the dining area. "I have coffee prepared." She plucks a mug off the shelf and fills it with steaming coffee. She slides into a chair at one of the round tables. "Nothing fancy," she says.

He sits beside her, warming his hands with the cup. "This is unbelievable. No wonder you're packed," he says, eyeing the guests. "What happened, exactly?"

"When you walked in, I was sure you'd heard." She leans on her elbows, waiting for him to speak. Finally, she says, "She escaped from the man who kidnapped her. Killed him."

He raises his eyebrows. "Are they certain this is her? People steal identities all the time. I work with very rich and powerful people who get conned—"

"Why are you doing this? We're happy. The police agree with us."

"I'm just saying, that even people who know what to look for can be victims of fraud or identity theft. It's become far too simple with the internet." He sips his coffee. "I'm only looking out for you."

"We have it handled. Police are all around us." She straightens in her seat. "Now, what's going on with you?"

"I guess Adele is fed up with it all." He gazes into his cup.

"I don't blame her. Some of us learn our lesson quicker than others."

He waves his hand, dismissing her comment. "This is shocking," Kenneth says. "About Charlotte."

"She prefers to be called Elizabeth. It's what that monster has called her since she was eight. Kenneth, I knew. I knew she was out there."

He avoids her eyes. "Have the police run DNA testing?"

"They offered. But it's her. Even Herb knows it." She paces toward the sink, crying. "I don't want to talk about it anymore."

"Charlotte was such a sweet child," he says, shaking his head. "It was such a terrible tragedy."

"She *is* a sweet woman. And a smart one," she says without turning around. "Do you want to meet her?"

Oh no. Elizabeth cannot talk to Myra's friend. She inches down the hall.

"Elizabeth? Could you come here for a minute?"

Anger flushes through her. This is her own fault, all because of one mistake she cannot seem to undo. "Sure," she says, stepping cautiously into the kitchen.

"This is my old friend Kenneth," Myra says. "We've known him since high school, so he was here when you disappeared. He was involved in the search."

She pushes her fist in her stomach and forces a smile. There must have been a hundred people combing the beach for Charlotte, passing out flyers, answering phone lines for tips. Memories fuse with images she has conjured. The Barkley girl's disappearance not only affected Rocky Shores but set the whole state on edge. Her stomach aches; she makes herself sick. How will she get out of this lie?

I tried to help too. Everyone did. Mom would kill me . . . kill me if she was alive to see what I've done.

Kenneth shakes his head, colt-brown eyes shining. "Oh yes. It was devastating. We are so, so glad you're home. Wow, you look, you look—"

"Come on, Kenneth. She doesn't need to be scrutinized right now."

Sweat drips down her neck. Her shirt sticks to her body. She's boiling hot. "I need to find Theo," she says.

"I was just going to say you look just the same," he says softly. His gaze is intense. "Just the same as when you were a little girl."

"I'm sorry, Myra. I'm just really worried about Theo with all these people around. I can't predict—"

"What might happen?" Kenneth frowns. "It's okay. The police are taking care of all that, right Myra?" he says kindly.

Myra shifts uncomfortably. "Of course."

Elizabeth feels dizzy and faint. She repeats, "I'm going to find Theo."

As if on cue, the siren from the toy fire truck howls toward them. She waves at Kenneth. "Nice to meet you," she says, walking toward the lounge.

"Come on, buddy," she says. "Let's go have a rest."

"I'm playing," he protests.

"Please, Theo. I'm tired. I'm just so very tired."

He pauses for a beat. "Okay, Mommy." Her son curls his fingers around her arm. "It's okay."

They walk down the corridor. As they approach the room, she relaxes. Do the police really have a handle on this?

Elizabeth ushers Theo into the hotel room and locks the door.

"Mommy?" Theo sits on the bed. "Is everything okay?"

"It's fine," she says. "I just need a nap."

He curls up to her on the bed. "Cuddle with me."

She flops beside him and rubs his back, staring at the popcorn ceiling above her.

CHAPTER TWENTY-TWO

MYRA

The house is quiet except for the whiz of Myra's nervous energy. She lies in bed, listening to the bitter wind. If Herb knew she was awake at two AM, he'd insist on calling the psychiatrist. Insomnia is both a cause and symptom of mania, she knows. But she can't sleep, knowing someone has been watching them, for years probably. She shivers; her own thoughts attack her. *What if they return?*

If so, she needs to be ready.

The house is dark and foreboding. Not even a sliver of moonlight penetrates the window. Herb snores gently, and she climbs out of bed. She tiptoes to the bathroom, where a change of clothes and running shoes await her. Slipping on her jeans and sweater, she listens for movement in the bedroom. She's safe. Herb is asleep. The evening is quiet, with only wind and rain punctuating the darkness.

Myra wanders into the kitchen and opens the cabinet. A pocketknife hides behind the dinner plates. She runs the cold knife against the sharpener, lost in the shriek of the blade against the stone.

She opens the door, wincing as it screeches. Myra skips toward her shed. Rain drips over her head. She unlatches the door and lets it whip open—it is an ominous warning. He will return. That knife was an invitation. Whoever slashed her painting, left the knife, and hacked the cameras has been on her property after Peter Briggs died—and is bound to return. She shivers in the cold. Her shirt is damp, and her long hair is plastered to her forehead. She fixes her braid and waits, sipping hot coffee from a thermos. Myra warms her hands.

"Where are you?" she asks, not expecting an answer.

She swings the door again, coaxing him to her space. "Come on. I'm right where the painting was." Her mind sharpens. She narrows her eyes and searches for the new cameras, the ones Michael tightened down with the best of security. Myra unlocks her phone, opens the security feed. If anyone drives up, comes for the shed, she will see them.

Still, a niggling fear lingers in the back of her mind. Won't the hacker be pissed off, once he discovers the cameras have been removed, disabled, blown to bits? That could send him into a tailspin, invite more problems. She shoves away her doubts. Cold sweat drips down her neck. She feels violated; this room is the only place she has that is hers and hers alone. This sends a flash of anger through her.

This is my studio.

She reaches up and pulls the string. The room floods with a soft luminescent glow. She wants to hit something, someone. This life has not been fair.

Stop whining and do something!

Her eyes fill with tears that she blinks away, as always, she realizes. As she's been forced to do, and the rage inside her grows like a glowing monster. She looks at the tips of her fingers and envisions fire spewing from them. And she tries to fill her lungs with air, to cool her burning lungs. She can almost hear the flames crackling within her.

Breathe. Wait—what is that sound?

Something *is* crackling, and it isn't coming from her. She cranes her neck to the side, listens to the birds squawking outside.

This time, the volume increases, like static. She freezes, grips the knife in her palm. "What is that?" she says, this time out loud.

"Myra, hello," a voice bellows.

She glances around, trying to identify the source of the voice. "What the—who are you?"

"Someone who is really, really good at breaking into security systems," says a voice, low and hard, a whisper above the static. "You're in over your head. Don't you see that?"

Myra picks up her phone, taps in the security code. The screen is scrambled.

"That won't work."

She starts to dial the police.

"Neither will that."

Her phone won't unlock. What is she going to do? Gripping the knife, she says, "Where are you? What the hell have you done to my phone?"

Silence.

"Come out and face me." She presses the buttons on her phone. It's completely, hopelessly stuck. Frozen, as she is.

A car rolls up. Her eyes trail to the exit. She'll run. This is her only chance.

The car door opens. He shuffles around and slams it shut. His footsteps pound onto the ground to the rhythm of her heart. He ambles in the darkness, his footsteps growing closer and closer to her.

She runs for the door, tries to push it open.

It won't budge. The latch has been shut from the outside. She clenches the knife in her palm. Sweat pours down her neck. There is one window in here.

"That window is too small to climb out."

Christ. He can see every move she makes. He knows that she is trapped.

"Lack of sleep can make you crazy, Myra. You know you should be asleep."

The voice is coming from the cameras, she thinks. Her stomach swims. She pulls the knife from behind her back and flicks out the blade. It glints under the hanging lightbulb. Time slows. His words spill on and on.

She cannot take that *sound.*

She whips around in circles. Which way is he coming from?

The light flickers and burns out. She pounds on the rough pine door till her knuckles are scraped and bleeding. "Open up! What do you want from us?"

In the darkness, Myra backs up, gets under the desk. There was a tire iron here, long ago. Dammit, she hopes it's still there. With shaky hands, she feels around till her fingers reach the cold metal. She rushes hard and fast at the door. It doesn't budge. Myra drops the knife and jimmies the tire iron into the door frame. With all her might, she rips it open. Wood splinters, the door moves a few inches. She shoves it through the door a second time and pulls, screaming.

The door opens another half a foot. She slips her bloody hand outside and flips up what remains of the latch.

Myra bolts for the house, screaming. The car she heard is gone.

On the porch is a bouquet of flowers. A dozen purple pansies and a bright orange marigold lie there, lurid and taunting. She picks them up and sniffs the flowers. Her chest is heavy with tears she cannot shed. Myra peels the plastic wrap off and shreds each petal, leaving a blanket of orange and lavender in the dirt. She curls up on the ground and brings fistful after fistful of soft petals to her nose.

*   *   *

Myra wakes in her bed, propped up on pillows. She rubs her bleary eyes. Maybe last night was only a dream. Hushed voices emanate from the kitchen. She is groggy, medicated. Has she gone mad again?

There is a knock on the door, followed by Gwen's voice. This surprises her, somehow. "Mommy," she says, much like a little girl. "Are you okay?"

"Did you see it? Where the voice was coming from?" Myra hopes she doesn't sound crazy. Who is she kidding? Gwen is bound to think she's hallucinated the whole event.

Gwen shakes her head. "Yeah. Someone broke into the new security system you set up."

"What the hell? How?"

She sighs and sits on the bed. "Have you ever gotten on the wrong channel on a radio and overheard someone else's conversation? Or heard the neighbor's toddler crying on a baby monitor?"

Myra's skin breaks out in goose bumps. She shivers violently. "What does that have to do with the camera?"

"The newer security systems are set up so you can speak to a person on your network. It's complicated, but your hacker managed to circumvent even that." Gwen rubs her temples. Her eyes are so red. "I can't believe you were waiting around to kill the dude. It's . . . badass."

Myra smiles. "All I ever wanted was for you to be proud of me."

"I am," Gwen says. She tilts her head, confused. "I always was." She looks into her mother's eyes as if she has something more to say, but she stops herself.

"Where is Elizabeth?" she says.

"She's with the cops." Gwen clears her throat. "She's scared, like we all are."

Myra takes a sharp breath. "Is Detective Marlow out there?"

"Yeah. She's coming in soon. Just tell her what happened. Obviously that creep is stalking us, but we all have to work with the police. Okay, Mom?"

"Of course," she says, sinking back into her pillow. She is so very groggy.

"They gave you a sedative." Gwen blinks tears away, and continues, "They'd give it to anyone who went through what you did."

"I went out there last night because I knew he'd come back. He's got a thing about my paintings. I don't know why. But if he returned, he'd go to the shed."

"Why not try to grab Elizabeth? Why your paintings?"

"Oh, he'll come for her. But not till he terrifies us thoroughly. He's playing games."

Gwen rubs her arms, trembling. "The cops are surrounding the place. They have yellow tape around your shed. It's a crime scene."

"A crime scene?"

"Yes. But you've got to listen to me, Mom. Don't screw with that man. If he comes anywhere near this house, you call 911. Playing his games will not help them catch him."

"Oh Gwen. You can never understand what these twenty years have done to me. How I have changed. I can't let this go. Peter is dead, but whoever this other person is, he's involved. He knew Peter. Probably, Elizabeth pissed someone off by killing him. But I'm not gonna let him go down easily."

"What are you saying?" Gwen says, eyes wide.

"I want them caught. I want them to suffer."

"We all do," she whispers. "But we don't even know who we're dealing with. And you're going to get us all killed. Please be reasonable. Don't toy with this monster. We have her back. Now, the police will deal with him."

"Yes ma'am," Myra says, slumping into her pillow. "Whatever you say." Her daughter loves to insert her opinion on mental health issues. "You might see a therapist, but that doesn't make you an expert—"

"That's not what I was trying to say." Gwen glowers. She has a very specific scowl that can scald you if you aren't careful.

"Oh yes. Yes, it is. That is precisely what you were saying."

"You're right." Gwen's eyes turn steely. "I am very worried. You aren't sleeping. I really, really don't want to involve myself in this. But I hope to god this Elizabeth Lark is who she says she is. I won't be able to stand it if you go crazy. And Jimi is worried, Mom. He's freaking out, thinking you're getting sick again."

She waves her hand dismissively. "He thinks she's lying. Thinks I'm not smart enough to recognize my own daughter."

Gwen's mouth falls open. "Are you kidding me? Jimi doesn't think you're stupid. He's *worried*, because you have, in fact, mistaken perfect strangers for your daughter."

"Tell Jimi I can take care of myself. He's a good kid. But he wasn't here. Not like you and Dad and me . . . you know?"

Gwen's tone softens. "I know. When is the DNA test coming back?"

"Soon," she says, and twiddles with her braid.

"Don't tell me you're not getting it." She blinks. "I want her to be Charlotte too, you know. But I'm scared of what might happen to us if she isn't."

"I promise. Things will be fine," she says. "We've got it under control."

Gwen gathers her purse, a haughty expression on her face. "Really? I don't see any evidence that you're in control." She pauses, as if thinking. Finally, she says, "I have yoga."

"I thought that was yesterday," says Myra.

"My therapist suggested I double up on yoga. Stress relief." Gwen drops her cell phone in the purse and tosses it over her shoulder, marching toward the door. "Anyway, Elizabeth is waiting outside."

Myra brightens at this. "Well, why didn't you bring her in?" *My two girls,* Myra thinks.

"Because you're tired. And the police wanted one person in here at a time. Dad's worried you aren't sleeping enough. You know what can happen."

"That's enough." Myra clenches her jaw. "Just send her in. You act like I'm dying."

"For fuck's sake," Gwen says, walking into the hall. "I don't want to talk anymore. Everything turns into a fight with you." She waves Elizabeth inside and stomps away.

Elizabeth is pale, her skin sallow. "Hey, Myra," she says. "Rough night, eh?" Her face is tear-stained.

"Whoever this is will kill us all. And it's entirely my fault. Because it's got to do with Peter." Her voice rises several octaves. "And you can't get murdered over me. I am sure as hell not happy with you messing with him because next time, he will come for Theo. Do you understand what that would do to me?" She steadies her voice and says hoarsely, "Do you?"

Myra cowers in her bed. "Yes, I am fully aware what losing a child does to a person, Elizabeth. We missed an entire childhood together, and every time you talk to me, you treat me like a stranger. And I can't stand it. I hate that I am a stranger to my own daughter."

"Oh Myra. I can't do this anymore. You got trapped in that shed because of me." She chokes on her tears, wipes her nose with her hand. "I can't keep this up—"

Myra sits up and folds her daughter in her arms. "I love you. It's my job to protect you. Please stay."

Elizabeth climbs into the bed beside her mother and lies on her pillow. Curling her knees to her chest like when she was a toddler, she shuts her eyes and drifts to sleep. Myra listens to the rise and fall of her breath. She takes it in, lets it sink into her ears like a lullaby. Charlotte slept between her and Herb till she was three. Sprawled out between them, her head was often on Myra's pillow and her feet in Herb's face. He'd grumble that it was time for her to sleep in her own bed. She had agreed, but she sopped up the memory of her daughter's delicious and musky head. Secretly, she missed her when she moved into her own room. Charlotte was happy to have princess sheets, just like Gwen. She was ready, though Myra was not. *That's the way it is with children,* she thinks. At the time, she had never thought she and Herb would have their bed back, never thought she'd get a night's sleep without getting head-butted by a kid. But the years, well, the years went by too fast.

Gwen is the tambourine, the drums, the beat. Her clashing and clanging, her strength and her willfulness keep Myra going. But Charlotte was the stringed instrument, the one who plucked the family into harmony because she knew how to slow dance. Even as a very young child, she could do this. Together, her girls made music inside of her, deep and true.

Now, Myra watches her exhausted daughter sleep. She instinctively goes to stroke her hair. But she stops herself, a shaky hand hovering in the air. To touch her without permission would be a violation of sorts. She tucks her arm under the covers and falls into a dark and dreamy sleep.

CHAPTER TWENTY-THREE

ELIZABETH

The morning smells damp and hungover. She yawns and stretches her arms above her head, from side to side. She slips out of bed and rearranges the comforter over Theo's little body. He mumbles something in his sleep, and he flips over, curling up into a little lump. It is cold, as if someone forgot to turn up the heat. Elizabeth's eyes are red and swollen; the inn is so quiet she thinks, for a moment, that last night was a dream, just another one of her nightmares.

Elizabeth didn't arrive back to the hotel until early this morning. It comes back to her now—this woman who has arranged cameras, hired a private investigator, who ended up trapped in a shed because of her. All she knows to be true is slipping from her consciousness, blurring softly at the edges that were once sharp and defined.

Myra could be her friend; they could have the sort of relationship adult daughters have with their mothers. This loneliness she carries subsides in this house, within this family. Yes, they are odd. But the presence of warmth, even layered over secrets and grief, is something she's craved. Gwen does not care for Myra's parenting advice; they never shop together or talk on the phone. Elizabeth could do this. She could be the daughter Myra has always wanted.

Myra would do anything for Elizabeth. This fact sends an unexpected swell of joy through her, and then she admonishes herself. How dare she think like this? She corrects herself: Myra would do anything for Charlotte.

You are not Charlotte. You are nothing to them, nothing but the maid's kid.

She tells herself this in hopes of evoking some kind of shame, except this time it ignites a fire in her belly. Why shouldn't she and Theo be treated like human beings? Why shouldn't her sweet son have a grandmother to spoil him? She is lost and confused, because what she thought was moral and right keeps twisting on her. And it kills her, to think about walking away from this family who loves them.

Elizabeth remembers the warm summer day she and Peter packed their things and tied them to the bed of his truck with bungee cord. She had just lost her mother and was already four months pregnant with Theo. The plan was to live in the cabin, like camping, Peter had said, while they built the farm. The mice droppings would be worth it; the dank smell wouldn't continue into the snowy winter. She thought they'd watch the farm go up, brick by brick, slabs of wood slowly turning a flat foundation into their home.

That winter, she was still waiting for blueprints. She'd quit asking. All she thought about was keeping herself fed, so she could make enough milk for her son, and keeping him warm. She had wrapped newborn Theo in his blanket like an elastic bandage and held him beside an impotent space heater. Her heart would pound, waiting for the crackling whoosh of the heat, for the coils to turn poker-red. If the heater wouldn't start, she'd zip him inside her coat, hoping her body heat would be enough.

Her hands are freezing and numb. The lie is metastasizing inside her: it has scraped through her skin and stabbed at her flesh, swished through her blood and finally, it has sunk deep in her bones. It is a parasite devouring its host. Even Theo is burrowed within the Barkley family like a little mouse in a garden. He and Myra have forged a connection. He loves Gwen's daughters. How can she explain that Myra is not his grandmother? That she is a liar?

That Peter killed the girl she's pretending to be.

She's got to get back on the phone with Alice. See what she's found out about Patrick Henderson.

Keep investigating. Don't get distracted by Myra Barkley. We will leave, go with Alice to Washington. But not till I get to the truth. I owe her that.

Elizabeth rubs her eyes. She has only slept a few hours and is tempted to get back under the covers and sleep until her head screws itself back on straight. But a gnawing sensation grips her chest. She needs to see what the police are doing, what is going on at that shed.

She leaves Theo in bed, and pads out into the lobby, the wood floor cold beneath her bare feet. No one is sitting on the couches or in the dining area. Maybe they cleared out the inn last night. It is an early morning sort of quiet, with dappled light beneath the gray sky. Plover birds squawk in a lower pitch than usual. Even the tide makes a hushing sound as it ebbs and flows. She opens the cabinet and takes out a coffee cup.

"Good morning."

Elizabeth turns around. "God, Jimi. You scared the crap out of me!" She presses her palm to her chest. "Jesus. After last night." She takes a deep breath. "I suppose you heard about last night."

Jimi nods. He seems to be sweeping up the sawdust from the floor and shoving big fistfuls into a black garbage bag. Puffs of dust pop into the air as he pushes it deeper into the bag to make room for more. The sweet smell of pine infiltrates the room. He crouches down and sits on his heels. Sweat gathers at his temples, and he glowers and mutters under his breath.

"What are you doing?"

"Ma's pretty upset. She's been asking me to come by and get the floors cleaned up so she and my dad can start the remodel." He meanders into the kitchenette and takes a Coke out of the fridge.

She swallows hard and waves the dust out of her face. "Jimi, you don't have to do this." She sighs. "Your mom doesn't expect you to come over and start right this second. Besides, it's early. Guests are going to be coming out for breakfast."

"Surprised there aren't police lines around the place." He pops the tab of his soda open and takes a long swig. "After last night."

This is the closest thing she's had to a conversation with Jimi since she's been here. Myra is pretty tight-lipped about their relationship too. Either he's the laconic type or he hates her. Maybe both.

He slumps into a folding chair outside his workspace.

"Mom decided on the mahogany, I guess." He rocks back on the legs of the chair. The clacking irritates her, but she does her best to ignore it.

"It seems so." She pauses. "You don't like it?"

He taps his fingers on his black jeans absentmindedly. They are now coated with a layer of dust. "She's been set on keeping the sawdust forever. Even when Dad wanted it changed. Mom is kinda set in her ways." He chuckles. "Wants it the exact same as when my grandparents were alive."

Jimi has longish dark hair pulled into a low ponytail. His beard stubble looks like it has been stippled on with a paint sponge. Her mother had a short painting hobby and made little trees of the same texture. He wears a Nirvana T-shirt. Elizabeth thinks of him as an old soul. Quiet like Buddha. Brooding like Kurt Cobain.

"And what do you think?"

He twists his lips. "Doesn't matter what I think."

"I can relate. Want coffee?" Elizabeth's nerves are frazzled. She looks down at her own ratty sweats.

He tilts up the soda can. "I'm good." Jimi taps his foot and startles her. "Know what I think?"

She nods warily.

"I think you were terribly treated by that man," he says, nodding. "Yes, that is what I think. He probably deserves what he got."

"It's probably not something we should go into," Elizabeth says uncertainly. She takes a step back.

"Know what else I think?"

She does not speak.

"I think this is a much better situation for you." He gapes at her pointedly and clenches his jaw. A shiver runs through her.

"What does that—"

"But. You are not my sister." He folds his arms against his chest with furrowed eyebrows.

"Oh Jimi." Her lips curve upward slightly, though her voice quivers. "I think you've had a rough go of things. Invisible in the shadow of your dead sister."

"Stop," he whispers. "You know nothing about me."

"You're just twenty years old," she continues, "and you ought to accept that there is a whole lot of bad in this world you haven't experienced. And I hope you never do." She splays her fingers and presses them firmly against her jeans to stop the shaking.

He strokes his painted-on beard. "You better not hurt my mother," he says, pulling a pack of Marlboros out of his back pocket. "I'm going out for a smoke."

Elizabeth watches him stomp out the door. She can see his shiny eyes. This is wrong, all wrong.

She goes back to the hotel room and calls Alice's number. Again, she doesn't answer.

"What's wrong, Mommy?" Theo says, sitting up in bed.

"Nothing," she says. "Just trying to call Alice. I'm not getting through."

He swings his legs off the bed. Elizabeth notices that they are now long enough for his toes to touch the floor. "We're going back," he says.

She thinks for a moment. "You're a smart kid. And I want to be straight with you. I don't want to go back. But I *need* to figure out some things. Important things."

"About Daddy?" he says.

"Sort of."

"I want to stay here." He pauses for a beat. "Someone is still trying to hurt us. Or Myra, right? And we are leaving again. It's all his fault." He flops back on the bed.

"It's nothing for you to worry about, okay?" She leans down and envelops him in her arms. "But we might need to go meet Alice, just for a while. When I get a hold of her."

He shakes his head, purses his lips. "We're leaving the inn."

"Only if we have to, Theo." She smiles softly. "One step at a time."

"I don't want to leave. I don't want to go back," he says.

"We aren't leaving. We're visiting Alice. We can visit a friend, Theo."

"All right," he says warily. "If you say so."

Theo doesn't trust her. In his little-boy mind, Elizabeth should have been able to control all of this. She is here, and because of this, she is to blame. It's black and white thinking, the therapist says. He'll understand someday. It's just the way kids are, a symptom of trauma.

He loves her, and she is his safety, his security. Theo can be angry with her, because she'll never leave him. That's what they tell her anyway.

CHAPTER TWENTY-FOUR

MYRA

Myra wakes early the next morning, drenched in sweat. She is swept under, choking on saltwater; her nose stings, her throat closes. With the next frothy wave, she is tossed onto the dark shore. Each strand of her hair is coated in a layer of sand. Her body is scraped and bruised. She screams and screams because her arms are empty; Charlotte is gone.

The dream is always the same: she paces the shore, searching, as if a piece of her own body has gone missing. Except now, she wakes up, takes a breath, and reminds herself that the nightmare is over.

She swings her legs over the side of the bed and grounds her feet on the carpet, shaking. *Water,* she thinks. Myra steps into the bathroom and turns on the faucet. She splashes her face and fills a glass of water. Her sleep hygiene has suffered. *Go to bed earlier,* she tells herself. *Read a little before bed, then turn out the light.* She's got to get it together.

Myra can't get the stranger out of her mind. She replays the scenario again and again: trapped in that shed, the sound of his voice crackling through her own alarm system, his footsteps in the dark. The house is guarded by police and FBI. Still, she envisions him peeking at her through the window.

You are safe, they are safe, she is safe.

She sits on the edge of the bathtub, the familiar panic intense and unyielding. The racing thoughts are more focused than they used to be. She opens her emergency meds and gulps one down.

Check if he's in the shed. Check. Check. Check.

She steadies her breathing and climbs back into bed. Drowsily, she shoves her hand under the mattress, searching for the cold steel knife.

* * *

Myra feels like death, but Kenneth saunters out to breakfast with his usual flair. Myra suspects he is hiding something. He's been at the inn for days, showing no sign of leaving. She is also surprised he hasn't pulled her aside and pratted about Adele. Myra's known Kenneth since they were teenagers. Her stock answer is, "Kenneth, I'm not your damn therapist."

The man plods down the pier in expensive shoes one would not want lacquered in salt, allegedly mourning some problem he's having with Adele. Myra cannot, for the life of her, understand why he values her marital advice so much. Sure, plenty of the guests drop their secrets off with Myra and Herb, unburdening themselves as they travel through some grand epiphany. Their own little version of *Eat, Pray, Love.*

But Kenneth Callahan is nothing like the Barkleys. He spent his college days grooming himself for the corporate ladder. Myra knew they'd take this inn and make it a rustic, romantic sort of place that tourists loved. She had a vision for the Barkley Inn—to sculpt what her mother had started into something unforgettable. They'd stay right across the street from the bay, like always, because they slept best with the company of water. The dark, brooding sky is their home. Myra wanted to share it with others.

Kenneth knows the difference between working smart and working hard, but both have their merits, and Kenneth believes in hedging his bets toward the biggest chance of winning, so he does both. He believes in dressing for success—in higher education, in blood, sweat, and tears. Kenneth runs on all six cylinders all of the time. He avoids distractions like love and keeps hobbies to impress his colleagues. Having legitimate friends is less important to Kenneth than ensuring that people believe he does. His wife comes from money. His father-in-law got him his job, for Christ's sake. He wanted to start his own company selling aftermarket auto accessories. German cars are his love, after all. But there's never been time, especially since he has had to take over his father-in-law's various business ventures. There's nothing more boring in the world to Kenneth. He'd have taken his chances on a hotel in Vegas. He knows the law of large numbers and would make a fortune. Or maybe he'd open a strip mall. They're very lucrative. Adele is beautiful, classically so. Polished. He likes to have her on his arm. Ultimately, she goes with his reputation.

Kenneth Callahan chases money and women. That's all there is to know about him. Myra wonders how Adele can stand it.

Plenty of regulars burden her with their issues. Lots of people think Myra has a kind of wisdom, maybe because the Barkley place is almost as old as Rocky Shores. When Myra thinks back thirty years, to when she met Herb, it's hard to imagine being so young and naïve. Still, the memory makes her smile.

One evening, while serving another beer to a customer, a boy had caught her attention. Or rather, his voice did. He crooned a song with the richest, most melodious voice she had ever heard. When combined with the plucking of his fingers on his guitar, and the smell of incense and saltwater wafting through the room, it was exquisite. He packed up his guitar as the patrons trailed out, the restaurant suddenly empty. A shock of light hit the bar, and he stood in the smoky haze. He wiped the sweat from his face with a towel and looked up.

"Hey there." He smiled.

She felt her cheeks burn. "Hey." Her throat was suddenly very dry.

"I'm parched," he said. "Just dying after playing so long."

"Wanna lemonade?" she asked.

He slid into a chair, hands folded, with that wry grin she would come to know so well. "Only if you have one too."

She returned a moment later with their drinks and set the frosty glass in front of him. Herb Barkley. She knew who he was. Her parents had him on the performance roster.

"Your ma sure is nice to let me come and play," he said.

"She's a good mother," she replied. "A bit different."

"Different is good."

She shrugged, figuring that Herb would have little interaction with the patrons and staff, like most of the musicians who performed.

Except he made it clear he only had eyes for her. *Crazy,* she thinks, *how long ago that was, where we ended up.*

Because now, Herb thinks Myra is damaged and tender. Maybe he likes this, at least when it suits him. He is her protector; this is how he has coped with their loss. The boy with the guitar and the husky voice is gone, replaced with a placid old man. He was stripped of any dreams he had after Charlotte disappeared, maybe before. Marrying a woman with mental illness is taxing. His job as a musician ended after her first manic episode. Herb figures out hard things the way some men toil about changing lightbulbs and fixing broken fuses. He doesn't need to be important, to inflate his ego. No, it is all about security. Herb is Safety Man.

Maybe they're both just trying to get by in any way they can. Maybe life will finally get easier.

Charlotte saved them.

After Gwen's birth, Myra just felt numb. She couldn't believe how blank her mind was. The baby elicited no emotion in her whatsoever. She was not angry; she wasn't sad. This all-encompassing fatigue settled deep in her bones, so heavy her body felt pinned to the bed.

She starved this hunger and the emptiness satiated her. And in these black and lonely nights, she needed nothing because she felt nothing. Gwen's cries were subdued and distant. Herb's presence was like that of a wispy specter, vague and translucent.

She had wanted Gwen desperately, and now she did not. In this dichotomy, she could not make out anything but static. She felt fortunate to be so fertile; many of her friends had trouble getting pregnant. Except Gwen sapped Myra's energy. She was nonplussed by the experience of motherhood.

Herb said he no longer knew the woman he married. He changed diapers, soothed Gwen when she cried, bonded with his daughter. And he told Myra how very much she was missing.

Words, she thinks now, *are so powerful.* And Myra cut him too.

But when Gwen hit a year old, Myra snapped out of the depression. Herb only knew that his wife had returned. She bustled about, coming up with new ideas to market the hotel. People stopped by on their vacations because the Barkleys developed a reputation as the quaint, small-town place to stay. And she put money into it. She bought expensive art and furniture that had to be returned when the checks bounced. Herb was confounded by her behavior. She found him downright irritating.

"Your mother is a ridiculous hippie who hates me," he'd said.

"You're the reason we can't afford to take the hotel to the next level," she'd said. He wasn't making any money at his little coffee shop gigs. She'd made sure to remind him of it too.

Rage built inside her for no discernable reason; she'd go days without sleeping. Her thoughts raced, so much so that she would speak out loud, in long, jumbled sentences. People would ask, "What did you say? What are you talking about?"

Herb, too, would ask, "What are you talking about?"

Gwen was two when Herb left. The image of him, rolling his suitcases to the car, is stamped in her mind. She tried to capture the dust as it swirled up from his tires and suspended in the sunshine. She sneezed and sneezed, inhaling the particles of dirt that were left of her life.

Myra had just one friend in the world. Her name was Rosie.

Rosie didn't speak to her with raised eyebrows. She helped with Gwen.

And her presence at the inn exuded sanity.

Generally, folks avoid dark and creepy hotels in remote areas. They most definitely do not like innkeepers who speak incessantly, whose garish red lipstick is smeared on their teeth. Myra has movies like *Psycho* to thank for this prejudice.

Rosie said, "We need to get you psychiatric help. I have an uncle with this disease. He started a medication called lithium and he is doing so well now."

Rosie drove her to her primary care physician. And then to the psychiatrist. Rosie camped out beside Gwen's toddler bed while Myra was in the hospital. Myra was infuriated—with herself, with those who raised an eyebrow at her words. She has explained this to Gwen, to Herb, to the doctors—people say they understand, and maybe they're trying. But the pity in their eyes, the way they treated her, like both a child and a crazy woman to be feared, showed otherwise. This was worse when she was unstable—a brittle bipolar, the doctor had said with a shrug. No real hope of returning to normalcy. And she fought and she fought, through gnashed teeth, to prove the doctor wrong.

Rosie stayed when everyone left. She stayed when Herb left. Some people can handle so much, carry so much weight. It's a strength Myra didn't know she had until years later.

There were also those few embarrassing nights Myra spent with Kenneth Callahan.

Herb never found out about Kenneth. But Herb left his family for an entire year. He traveled across the Pacific Northwest to California, from bars to cheap venues, playing his stupid guitar. He wasn't secure in his own skin yet. He wanted to show her that he had talent. And if she didn't appreciate it, other people would.

When he came home, they both knew they had made mistakes. They loved each other. They had a daughter who didn't deserve this. He picked her up and folded Gwen into his arms, tears tumbling down his face. "I never thought I was this . . . man," he said. Ever so slowly, they rebuilt their relationship. He learned about bipolar disorder. Not entirely, but he understood there were reasons. She'd never intended to hurt him with her words, or the affair he still doesn't know about. Even as she thinks of that time now, she realizes that his anger toward her, the reason he left—she'd thought it was purposeful, when it hadn't been.

Besides, he was always her Herb. She had known this since she was seventeen years old.

Myra loves Herb more than ever. That's the thing about marriage, she thinks. It's a rollercoaster in its youth. It slides up and down and sideways and knocks you breathless and nauseous. But when the ride slows, you gather your bearings and realize that much of what was once so important just isn't.

Kenneth strolls on in about once every two years, but he is good at keeping the secret. He's probably sleeping with some woman he met on the road. That's why he's staying here, away from Adele. That's the irony of his little visits.

And so she listens to the details of the shallow life he has curated for himself, all the while wondering what he could have been if he'd followed his heart rather than his ego. Maybe all that plastic surgery sucked the gray matter from his brain.

She has enough issues. For shit's sake. Myra wishes he'd figure his shit out and go on home. As he saunters toward the pile of Danishes on the Formica counter, she concentrates on her to-do list. She taps the pen on her pad of paper, hoping the thwack thwack thwack annoys him enough that he'll grab his breakfast and meander back to his room.

"Myra?" He says this with a tinge of expectation.

"Yes, Kenneth?" She glances up at him and speaks cordially. "If you're ready to check out, I'll have Herb help you with your bags—"

"Are you okay?"

"I'm fine," she says. "Why would you think I'm not?"

"Well, the other night in the shed must have scared you. Anyone would be freaking out. It's only natural."

"I'm fine," she says in a more acerbic tone than she intended. "But thank you for your concern, Kenneth." She takes a breath. "Ready to check out, then?"

"Nope, I'm going to be here for a few days, I'm afraid."

Myra sighs. "Well, you're free to stay, of course. How long are we talking? It isn't as if the place is swamped. Other than busybodies poking into my personal life—"

"I'm thinking a week or two. Adele is not happy—"

"Kenneth, what the hell is going on? I'm serious. You know how it is, between Herb and you. I've got so much going on."

"Why doesn't Herb like me? I don't get it." He scrunches his eyes, incredulous, as if he's waiting for an answer to a deep mystery.

"You're very different people, that's all. And he never got over high school bullshit." She wrings her hands and chews the end of the pen, astounded at his stupidity.

"Does he know, Myra?" he whispers, wide-eyed.

"What?" Her eyebrows shoot up. "That was a million years ago. Quit bringing up old crap or you're gonna have to go, Kenneth. My daughter is home. Our family is healing."

"Okay." He waves his hand as if the question could dissipate at his will. "But, Myra."

"Kenneth, don't. Please don't. I told you Herb took her driving, didn't I? That we bought her a car? Things are going so well for us . . ." Her voice trails off.

He leans close to her. "I told her."

"Told her? Are you serious?" Myra's stomach aches. She twists her braid.

His eyes shine, lips curve into a frown. "I know you don't believe it. But I've changed. I needed to be honest with my wife. It was selfish of me to keep this from her."

"Oh god." Myra rubs her temples. "I guess she didn't take it well. Please don't tell me she's going to be over here contributing to the drama and taking my marriage under with yours. I can't handle one more thing, Kenneth."

She knows why he's here. And he's the selfish one. White-hot anger sears her ribs. Elizabeth and Herb will be home soon; her precious grandson is sleeping, his cheeks pink from the warm pillow. Here she is, with her adult daughter.

They are a family again. Kenneth needs to deal with his own problems.

"Myra, I'm not here to ruin things for you. I just thought you'd want to know."

Bullshit.

"Really?" She softens her tone. Myra will play along. Anything to get him to make up with his beautiful wife. "I think you should go home. You'll work it out."

Kenneth stands and faces the Danishes. "This has been a good talk."

Theo scuffles into the lobby, breaking her thoughts. The siren of his toy fire truck wails through the room, followed by a crash. "Let's discuss this later."

Kenneth sighs and looks at the ground. "All right." He takes his pastry and coffee mug, and heads to his room, moping.

Oh, for fuck's sake. She wants to scream. Maybe Adele really left this time. Maybe he's had a revelation of sorts. It's hard to tell with Kenneth. He has a tendency toward melodrama. Whatever it is, she needs him to get the hell out of this inn. And she has to make him think it's his idea.

She won't let Kenneth Callahan destroy her life. Not this time.

CHAPTER TWENTY-FIVE

GWEN

Jimi lives in a studio apartment over an antique motorcycle shop downtown, amid the other little shops in the bay. It's the weirdest location for an apartment, but Jimi knows the owner and puts in part-time hours at the store for cheap rent. She tosses her purse over her shoulder and gets out of her car. Silver clouds are feathered over the pale blue sky. She walks through chilly pockets of moisture. Large sailboats, adorned with names of women, are proudly docked in the marina. The sun cuts through the fog and leaves a light shimmer on the ocean.

The apartment is right at the top of the stairs. She bangs on the door. "Jimi, it's me. Open up." She checks her phone and grimaces. It's noon. Leaning against the stucco wall, she takes a tube of lipstick out of her purse. It's early, for Jimi. It'll take him a few minutes to get out of bed and open the door. Wait till he has children. They wake up at six on weekends. And they're bouncy and happy about it. Children are confounding at times.

She leans against the stucco wall, trembling. "Answer the door, Jimi! You can't leave cryptic messages on my phone at two AM and expect me to just stand here."

"Ugh, Gwen. Just forget it. Go away."

She pounds on the door again. "You said you had something to confess. I am freaking out. Tell me what it is."

No response. She taps her foot. "Come on."

Finally the door swings open. Jimi rakes his hand through his hair. He's shirtless, wearing baggy sweats.

"Jesus," she says. "Took you long enough." She steps over a pile of laundry and plops down on the couch. "Sit. We need to talk. Tell me what's going on. You're terrifying me, and I'm stressed enough."

"Well, good morning to you too, Gwen." He effuses his typical insouciance.

Gwen feels her hackles raise. "Afternoon, technically. It's lunchtime."

Jimi sits on the loveseat across from her and puts his feet up on the ottoman. "Can we just forget about that?" he mumbles. "I didn't mean it."

"You didn't mean it? You said you'd done something horrible. What is it?"

Her brother is going to become one of those permanent teenagers—she can see it now. He's twenty and about to lose his "baby of the family" pass. She grits her teeth, tries a silent primal scream, but it's not effective. The musty smell in his apartment intensifies her irritation. She resists the urge to start sorting the laundry on the couch. Thank god she and Kevin have girls.

"Maybe I should call you more often. You usually only subject yourself to my humble abode when you have something to lecture me about."

Gwen exhales. She bites her lip, avoids looking at the pile of dishes in the sink. It's going to take everything in her power not to wash them. "Honestly, I'm a bit worried about you. Tell me what the hell is going on. Since Charlotte came home—"

"Come on now. Are you still falling for this shit? Do you really believe it's her?"

She smooths her shirt. "I do."

He scoffs. "Right. I'm the only one in this family with any sense. You all believe her because you want her to be Charlotte. Well, I'm not falling for it— not till Mom gets that DNA test. Why not run the DNA? It's logical."

Gwen thinks for a minute. Jimi isn't wrong, exactly. "Mom doesn't want to demand proof because she's afraid it will drive Elizabeth away. She's skittish, you know?"

He crosses his arms against his chest and looks at the floor.

"What's wrong?" She holds her breath and waits. Maybe he's had some drunken epiphany about what an asshole he's been to Elizabeth. Maybe he feels guilty about how rude he's been and needs her advice. She hopes.

He shakes his head. "I might have done something bad."

"What?" Gwen says softly. "What *might* you have done?" Jimi is impulsive, always has been. And he can't even fake subtlety. "You said something to her, didn't you? Oh god, Mom is going to kill you if she bails town—"

"Well, yeah . . ."

Her chest palpitates. This family is going to give her a heart attack. Unrelenting stress alters your DNA, kills you young. "What, Jimi?"

He digs through the pile of laundry on the couch. "Why don't we go have coffee or something? I need fresh air for this." He retrieves a blue T-shirt and pulls it over his head. "Promise me you won't tell Mom."

She glares at him. "I will do nothing of the sort."

They leave the apartment and head down the stairs. The motorcycle shop seems to be closed. Two businesses over is a small café. The crowds are minimal, which is good, because if she has to kill her brother, there will be fewer witnesses.

"What do you want?" he says.

"Iced latte with no sweetener and almond milk."

He stands there, hands in his pockets.

"What?" she says.

"Do you have any money?" He shrugs.

She opens her wallet and hands him a twenty. "Hurry up and order." There is one family sitting across the café, right by the water. The two children, a boy and a girl, are eating organic muffins—probably. The four of them are wearing tennis outfits. The woman laughs heartily at whatever her husband has said. Her hair is all the way down her back. She wakes up early to straighten it, not one to let kids keep her from a beauty routine. Gwen simultaneously admires and hates her. Or maybe her children sleep in, which pisses Gwen off so much she shifts her thinking. Probably, these people make heart-shaped sandwiches and grapes for the kids' lunches. Then they pack them in forty-dollar bento boxes. The kids eat them with gratitude and never leave the boxes at school to be stolen. They don't allow plastics in their home—BPA causes cancer. The man carves their toys out of wood with a pocketknife.

On top of this, they both have careers they excel at. She's a doctor. He's a lawyer who occasionally models for Calvin Klein. She never misses a Pilates class.

Meanwhile, Gwen's family could be featured on a reality TV show. Motherfucker.

Jimi saunters toward her in his wrinkled shirt, carrying their coffee. He sets them on the table and hands her a fistful of cash and coins. "Here's your change."

She takes a sip of her latte. The beans are burnt to hell, and it definitely has sweetener. "All right," she says with a grimace. "What did you do?"

"Remember the knife they found in her room?" he says, head turned away from her.

"Yes," she says, her heart in her stomach. "What about it?"

"I put it there."

"*What?*" she hisses.

"I said, I planted the knife. I'm sorry—I really am." He takes a sip of his coffee after dropping this nuclear bomb on her head.

"Why?" Her eyes are close to popping out of her head. This is confounding. "Did you slash Mom's painting too?"

"No, no. Of course not. Don't hate me for this. I was panicking. I'm sorry." He bursts into tears. "I just wanted . . . I don't know—"

"You scared everyone. Jimi, I cannot even believe this. I can't. You need to accept that our sister is home." She sinks in her chair. "Charlotte is home."

He clenches his eyes shut. "Are you telling Mom?"

She considers this. "I don't know. Maybe not. I'm not sure it would help anything—not anymore. That's all over, luckily for you. You promise you did not slash that painting, Jimi?"

His jaw tightens. In a low voice, he says, "I am not that awful. I would never go that far."

Gwen nods. She tries to read the expression on his face. Which way is it people look when they're lying? Left or right? She can't remember.

"I'm serious." He sighs. "I just panicked. Thought it would make her leave. You know how Mom is. All the time, thinking random guests are Charlotte Barkley. And then it actually happens? It's rare."

"It's rare, yes. And it's a miracle. If she was lying, she *would* have bailed after you tried to frame her."

He nods. "It sounds terrible when you put it that way, Gwen."

She shrugs. It is terrible. What does he expect her to say? "All right, then. Thanks for the coffee. I'll call you tonight. I need to take a walk."

She dumps her coffee cup in the trash and heads to the parking lot. Gets in her car, turns on the ignition. The family that was sitting across from them is still there, laughing and chatting away. Gwen shifts her car into drive and heads for the beach.

Gwen slides down the grassy embankment, her hair smacking against her face from the wind. As soon as her feet hit soft sand, she begins to shiver. The cold marine layer sends goose bumps down her neck. She trudges toward the sun-weathered driftwood cove she and her friends hunkered behind, drinking and smoking weed and kissing. She runs her fingers along the eroded tree. Underneath, there is evidence of their parties— charred sections where plumes of campfire smoke darkened the thick, gray branches.

She remembers every contour of Jared's body, the way his left big toe curled to the right, the scent of his aftershave. He was her first love, and like all teenage firsts, everything was so damned vital. A little argument necessitated crocodile tears, raised voices. It required a girlfriend to comfort her, a cigarette to calm her shaky hands. Every event with Jared was momentous, larger than life. Gwen expended almost as much time picking a homecoming dress as she did later on Savannah's birth plan.

Images of her sister, flailing in that water, are emblazoned in her consciousness. The crackle of the cell phone, as she called her parents at the restaurant, cavorts through her dreams. She can hear each trill ring, feel the ground snatched from beneath her feet. Knocked breathless, she knew she was about to break her own mother's heart. Once someone cheerfully answered, "Giovanni's!" reality would sink its teeth into her flesh and never let go.

She thinks about the pickup truck Elizabeth arrived in. Most likely, she was taken in a similar truck with an ancient, growling engine. Why didn't she hear it drive up? She imagines her sister's screams, but Charlotte's little voice was no match for

Gwen's big emotions for Jared. Stupid Jared. She wouldn't think twice of him now, if not for that evening.

It's over. She has come to erase the memories.

But what if Elizabeth Lark is not Charlotte? What if Jimi is right?

Gwen takes a deep, cleansing breath. She sinks into the sand and lies her upper torso over her knees, stretching her fingertips as far as they'll go. Child's pose. Her clothes will be ruined; her hair will be a mess of salt and sand. She remembers her mother spraying her hair after a day at the beach. "You've got sand clear to the roots, Gwen. How'd you manage that?"

She zips her jacket to her chin and focuses on the sea, with its frothy waves ebbing and flowing, quiet and sharp at once. The clouds hover just over the offing, so close the water looks like it has been blended against the sky with a paint sponge.

She hates the ocean she used to love.

Someone calls from behind her. Gwen quickly pulls herself up, startled.

"Is that you, Gwen?"

Her mother.

"Gwen!"

She spins around, blinking stinging sand from her eyes. "God, Mom. You scared me. What are you doing here? Thought you'd be with Charlotte."

"Elizabeth." Myra swallows. "I came to watch the water. I do that sometimes."

"Well, you don't have to anymore, right?"

"Gwen, please. Can't we start over?"

"So," Gwen begins, "now that my sister has returned, I'm forgiven?"

"You've been forgiven. I do not blame you for this. I never have."

Mom doesn't lie well.

"Sure," she says, "but if you'll excuse me, the girls have soccer practice." Turning toward the embankment, she swears under her breath.

"Can we talk?"

Gwen almost pretends she doesn't hear.

"Please," yells Myra.

Gwen flips toward Myra and sighs. "What is there to talk about? I thought you'd be happy."

"I am happy." Tears drip down her nose, and Gwen has a sudden urge to wipe them away. "I just want a normal life. To have a relationship with you."

Myra's words are foreign. It hits her that this silver-haired woman is a stranger. Finally, she says, "Everything is fine, Mom."

Myra steps toward Gwen, and as the distance between them closes, a stream of sweat runs down Gwen's neck. Her stomach churns. And when Myra finally envelopes her in a hug, Gwen's anxiety cuts right to the bone. She fights hard not to cry; she will not let Myra make her cry.

Because Myra has never hugged Gwen so sweetly.

Gwen begins to walk toward the embankment, wagging her fingers goodbye.

"Come back here! Why do you think I blame you? You say this constantly. It's not about blame. I lost my little girl. Until now. Not your fault she was taken. Maybe I'm crazy. Maybe I was . . . obsessed. I admit that. But it was never about blame."

Gwen turns around and slides back down to the sand. "Right."

Neither speaks. The ocean rolls, and Gwen finds herself lost in it. She remembers when Savannah was born, how she'd breastfed around the clock, insistent her daughter never be given a bottle. Kevin offered to feed her, but Gwen was determined.

Maybe it was sheer stubbornness, but the raw determination to feed her new baby only at the breast came from a deep, internal need to get parenthood right. And by god, the La Leche League mothers had told her, if you give bottles, your supply will dwindle and dry up, and in the end that kid's gonna end up on chemical-laden formula.

Gwen would not fail at breastfeeding. Babies wake to feed every two hours, the books all said, and she could handle this.

But Savannah hadn't read those books, apparently, because she woke up every hour, sometimes every thirty minutes. Gwen remembers her frustration because she needed predictability and structure, and her baby didn't. And the La Leche League moms said, well, this is common. Cluster feeding. Growth spurts. Gwen grit her teeth, and kept her daughter attached to the breast for what seemed like twenty-four hours a day, handing her to Kevin now and then to change a diaper.

But dammit, this was not what she'd expected out of motherhood.

One evening, her eyes were so bleary and her brain so foggy she thought she was literally losing her mind. Just like Mom. And Kevin said, you need sleep. You need it Gwen. You cannot go on doing everything—you've got to give up control. Lie down, just for an hour. Really.

So, she did. She fell into a sleep so deep and dreamless she was almost comatose. For six hours she slept. When she woke, a surge of panic ran through her. It was horrifyingly similar to the night she'd lost Charlotte. That *feeling*—it had returned. She bolted up in bed. Her milk let down, soaking her shirt. In her head, Savannah was gone. She was just gone. The sense of missing her, that she should have been there, in the bassinet by the bed, was like missing her own arm.

Slowly, she remembered. *Kevin has Savannah. I was only napping.* And she could breathe again, feel her limbs.

That's when she understood. By losing Charlotte, she had done this to her mother.

"No," she says finally. "A part of you was . . . amputated. Taken away—"

"Gwen, that is not—"

"Dammit, let me talk!" She wipes a tear from her eye. "I'm serious. Let me talk. Every time I saw you waiting there at the desk, waiting for her, after my own children were born . . . the anger grew deeper because I could never forget. I cut off my own mother's arm."

They stare at the ocean together for a long while.

"You didn't," Mom finally says. "He did."

Gwen swallows hard. She nods, but the truth is, not everything can be erased; some things cannot be forgiven. And for that, she can't blame her mother. Not entirely.

CHAPTER TWENTY-SIX

MYRA

Michael Calgary's office is a tiny brick building wedged between two average-sized businesses, which make it appear even smaller. Several inches of snow hang over the edges of the flat roof. Her breath is as rough as the car engine, puffing white exhaust into the street. She opens the window and takes an unsteady breath. Vapor from her breath hangs in the fog before dissipating. The chill cools the sweat coiled around her neck like a noose.

Sarah has combed the area for anyone associated with Peter Briggs. She's called every trucking company in Washington. The biggest issue, as far as Myra can tell, is that Peter Briggs is not his real name. The companies have searched through every public record they have and cannot find evidence that he's used this identity with anyone but Elizabeth and Theo.

The police thought he was simply an evil man who kept her daughter hostage there in the wild because he could, because there was nowhere for her to go with his brute strength and her lack of resources.

They were wrong.

He was a smart, calculating psychopath, with friends who want her back. These people want to destroy her family, and Myra needs to know why.

She opens the car door. It scrapes against an embankment of snow turned to solid ice. "Ouch," she says, slipping through the small space between the car and the packed white hill. The cold slices through her light sweater. Michael's office is northeast, away from the ocean and into a wooded area, where the winters are harsher.

The office is quite dark, though the sky is clear, and an orangey pomegranate color emanates from the setting sun. Tall pines are tucked around the buildings that expand into the deep woods up the mountain. Michael clears his throat, stepping in the door. The walls are stained a dirty-beige color. A single lamp lights the place.

"Anyone here? Mr. Calgary?"

She hears shuffling in an office behind the reception area. A flood of incandescent light spreads through the lobby as the door widens. Michael steps out briskly. "Ms. Barkley." He smiles as if pleasantly surprised.

Myra sinks into a light green couch and sighs. "It's been a long drive."

"Icy out too." Michael reaches up high on a shelf and retrieves a decanter of some sort of liquor. He pours two glasses and slides one to Myra.

She squirms in her seat. The place is sleazy. It smells of stale smoke and ill-gotten cash. She wonders what exactly Michael does, besides setting up cameras and following people. She wants her money back.

Michael reaches into his front pocket for a cigarette. He rolls it between his fingers for a moment. "I'm sorry about the cameras. And what happened in the shed. It seems we're dealing with someone more sophisticated than we thought." Michael taps his foot. "Those cameras were locked down. They couldn't be hacked. I swear it."

"Well, they were," she says. "I was trapped in that shed." She rocks back and forth in her seat. "I thought he was going to kill me. And you were supposed to be solving our problem, not making it worse." His casual attitude is infuriating. She wants to spew obscenities at him, but she holds her tongue.

"There are no guarantees in life," he says.

"Stop with the fucking clichés, Michael." She grips the arms of the chair so hard she can hear her fingernails sinking into the faux leather. "Clearly, this person is smarter than you. I want my money back. Every dime."

"Hey." He holds his hands up. "I didn't guarantee anything."

She grimaces. "Look, you said yourself: this is a high-profile case. Do you want the world to know how impotent you are? How badly you've failed? Maybe you didn't make any guarantees. But you shouldn't have made things worse."

Michael snorts. "You have no idea what he was planning. It wasn't *my* cameras that turned the monster on you. But fine, you can have your money." He goes to his desk, slips open the drawer, and pulls out an envelope. It is so stuffed with cash, the flap gapes open. "Here," he says, counting out her money. "I'm sorry things didn't work out, Ms. Barkley."

"You have no idea what I would do for our kids." She puts the cash neatly inside her wallet. "I want him captured and sent away for life."

Michael lights the cigarette. He blows a thin ribbon of white smoke through pursed lips. "You couldn't make out a vehicle?"

"No," she says, and stands. She paces across the short room, twirling the end of her braid. "I couldn't make out a thing. He'd driven away by the time I was able to break through the latch."

"I feel you, Ms. Barkley, I really do." He changes tack. "That was very brave, hacking through a two-by-four. That had to have taken strength. If he comes back, you'd put a bullet in him, wouldn't you? For Charlotte?"

The familiar guilt twists inside her like a parasite eating her alive. "I can't do that. It's too far. I have a conscience."

"I ain't a therapist," Michael chortles. "I deal only in practical matters."

"So you've said."

"Let's start locally." He waves his arm around the room. "Everyone needs to make money. We just need to find out where and under what name."

"The cops have been after him for twenty years. I'm not sure who this other person is—or how you can possibly help."

"Are you *certain* this Elizabeth Lark isn't in on it?"

"I'm sure," she says, eyes burning. "She is my daughter, Mr. Calgary."

Michael pauses and takes a drag from his cigarette, "Well, you think about it. I can trail her. I can do some research into this cabin. You got DNA results coming?"

Myra shakes her head. "I've got to talk it over with Herb. He's got an issue with you right now."

"Suit yourself," he says. He slurps his drink and takes a business card from the desk. "I'm here, if you change your mind."

She heads for the door, toward the cold, inky night. An owl calls from somewhere in the woods. Trees creak in the wind. All else is silent.

Michael follows her and holds the door open. "Be in touch."

Myra turns. "I will." A shiver runs down his neck. She stomps over the ice as quickly as he can. She can't shake the chill glued to her lungs. The box of a place is freezing.

CHAPTER TWENTY-SEVEN

ELIZABETH

The restaurant is elegant, its high chandeliers adorned with pear-shaped crystals. The walls resemble the Sistine Chapel, painted with cherubs and angels. Elizabeth has always loved art, ever since she took an art history class in high school. Especially now, since she's visited Myra a few times in her studio and even used her brushes.

Charlotte wouldn't know anything about the Sistine Chapel.

The hum of polite chatter is comforting. No one seems to notice her. They sit in a darkened booth. Candles emit a soft light, and the clatter of dishes and drinks fill the room. Different foods intermingle in a cornucopia of smells.

Theo glances up at her. She spreads the cloth napkin on his lap. "See," she says, "It's just like we've seen on TV."

Myra nods. "You are such a well-mannered little boy. Why don't you color while we're waiting for the waiter?" She shows him the little section of the menu with puzzles and an elephant to color and takes the three crayons from their packages.

"Thank you," he says, scrawling on the paper.

Elizabeth gulps. "We've learned a lot from books . . . television." She takes a sip of water. Rests her hands on the ornate glass table, but she can almost hear her fingers trembling against it. Finally, she folds them together and places them in her lap. She emulates Myra's posture, one leg crossed gently over the other, no foot tapping.

Myra wears a flowery dress, and her silver hair is drawn into a long braid. The scent of her perfume burned Elizabeth's nose in the car, but here it wafts lightly through the air and smells pleasantly of fruit. Elizabeth's own mother never had the chance to dress up or visit real restaurants. Sometimes she brought home greasy burgers and fries from the various restaurants she worked for; they let waiters take home messed-up orders. They sat on the shag carpet, legs crisscross applesauce, eating limp fries and talking into the night. Her mother could do any job, it seemed to Elizabeth. It never occurred to her to be ashamed. Her mother's clients often gave them hefty bags stuffed with clothing their kids had outgrown. Sometimes holes gaped at the knees of the pants, but her mother could easily patch those. Mom shook her head and commented, "It's a shame they toss these jeans for a little hole in the knee. Easy enough to patch." Her mother said that resourcefulness would serve Elizabeth well. "Gratitude is good," she said. And if they ever won the lottery, they would not waste perfectly good clothes.

They wouldn't give poor children unsalvageable, ratty shirts and shoes either. Mom was too kind to say it out loud, but as Elizabeth grew older, she understood this. The pinched lips, the misty eyes—her mother was ashamed to be the recipient of these gifts. Mom believed in making the best of things.

"Do you like the new outfit? And your hair? It must be nice to be pampered." Myra smiles hopefully. Maybe she is afraid of Elizabeth's reaction.

Elizabeth steadies her voice. "It's all very lovely. Thank you, Myra." It *is* nice, but the soft blue jeans and the long, graceful sweater aren't really hers. Myra tries so hard to please her. Tries to fix the damage with new clothes and highlighted hair. Her mother would want her to be grateful. But she would also be so very disappointed with her. For once, Elizabeth is glad her mother is not alive to see her behavior.

Elizabeth Lark has saved and destroyed this family in one fell swoop. She takes another large sip of water and runs her tongue along the smooth, cold ice. It clicks when she sets the glass back on the white linen tablecloth.

"What are you ordering?" Myra puts her glasses on and opens the menu. "They say the steak is good." She scans the rest of the menu. "Yes, I think I'll order the filet mignon. It's not every day I get to take my youngest daughter for lunch." Her voice cracks a little.

"And Theo. Look at the choices on the kids' menu. Macaroni and cheese or a burger. What sounds best?" Elizabeth says.

He points at the picture of the burger.

"Good choice," Myra says. "Are you having the steak, Elizabeth? It really is wonderful . . . free range cattle and all that. Gwen says it's healthier . . ."

Elizabeth smiles and opens her menu. The steak is thirty-five dollars. Her eyes widen. She scans the other options. "I think I want something light," she says hoarsely. "This Cobb salad looks great." It's the least expensive item on the menu. Fifteen bucks. She closes the menu and smiles.

"You sure?" Myra furrows her eyebrows. "The doctor says you need protein and fats." She pauses. "I'm so sorry. I can't mother you like I did when you were young. Order what you like." Myra removes her glasses and cleans them with a soft gray cloth.

"I'll order steak if it makes you feel better." Elizabeth can hardly breathe.

"I never knew how hard this would be." Myra pauses. "What he took from us—"

"It will be okay," Elizabeth says briskly. There's nothing else to say. Anything else would deepen the lie.

"I want to get to know the woman you are now," says Myra, "like friends do."

Elizabeth thinks for a moment. "If I was a stranger, we would get to know each other, and it wouldn't be awkward because there wouldn't be all these expectations."

"Right," Myra says. "It wouldn't be so strange. What if we pretend that you're a woman who came to stay at the inn with her little boy? You could have been on vacation—"

"To be more realistic, I could have been this mama who needed help," Elizabeth offers.

"That makes sense. Lots of our guests are running from abusive boyfriends or legal problems." Myra's cheeks turn pink. "Anyway, let's say we hit it off. You and me. We become friends—"

"And Theo and I stay with you. You're very nice, and you offer me a job. Even lunch at a restaurant like this." Her chest fills with a tender sort of longing. She could be Myra's friend. Maybe they could have been, in a different time, a different life. "That will help, to think of it like that."

"Anyway." Myra clears her throat and smiles. "Let's have a nice lunch. You hardly remember us. I've acted completely unfair. Thinking you'd just float in the door and things would be like when you were little."

The air is thick and heavy. She looks at Myra, and something like love flutters in her stomach. This is the last emotion she should feel at this moment. None of this is real. With a sigh, she says, "You're right. Let's not think about that stuff."

Elizabeth orders the steak. It is delicious.

* * *

On the way into the restaurant, the persimmon-colored daylilies were lovely amid lush green ferns and ivy. On the way out, rain splatters and the plants have gone mopey and flat.

Myra, Elizabeth, and Theo pick up their stride, heading for the car. The scent of rain coalesces with the sweet flowers. Crystals of water crawl down the lacy fern leaves and over the trellis. Neither woman thought to bring an umbrella. Pacific Northwesterners don't bother for these little storms. Myra clicks the key remote, and they pile inside the car, stuffy with moisture. Myra tosses a hand towel to Elizabeth, who turns toward the back seat and dabs Theo's forehead.

"Geez." Myra shivers. "We ought to get back, I suppose."

"I'm fine," Elizabeth says. "I'm used to cold weather. A bit of rain is not so bad."

Myra dabs her face and neck. She turns on the engine and blasts the defroster. "Let's get going," she says. "I can't stand it when I can't see two feet in front of me. It makes me nervous."

The rain pelts the car like tiny pebbles on a tin roof, changing from cacophonous to gentle and back again. Elizabeth leans back in her seat. The ambient rain and briny smell of the ocean comfort her. She closes her eyes, and her body melts into the seat.

Except an eerie feeling creeps through her bones. She cannot place it. It's probably the PTSD the doctor told her about. Still, it's like eyes are boring into her skull.

She sits straight up and checks the back seat. Theo is humming, tapping his feet.

"What?" Myra is focused on the road. "Is something wrong?"

"Not exactly." The clouds rumble hungrily. They approach dark patches, where heavier rain awaits them, but that's not what is bothering her. "Make sure you stay in the middle lane. Don't wanna hydroplane."

"What the—" Myra looks in the rearview mirror. "Who is that?"

Elizabeth flips around. A car approaches, fast, engine revving like there is a brick smashed on the accelerator. Myra hits the gas. "They're coming up behind us quick."

"Slow down so they can pass. What an asshole."

Myra lets her foot off the pedal and opens the window. Wet wind surges in the car. She puts her arm outside, waving the car around them. It's a two-lane road. No cars are approaching from the other direction.

The car veers slightly to the left, boxing them in. It is mere feet behind them. The driver leans on the horn. Its bright headlights cut through the fog.

"Go!" Myra yells. "You know what they say about men in big trucks."

Elizabeth waves at the driver again. "Doesn't he see us?"

Myra stretches tall and looks to her left. "I swear he's trying to run us off the road. Wait a minute. It's him. It has to be."

"I hope not." Elizabeth scans the highway for an escape route. They are nowhere near a turnout, and the ditch is deep. "Theo, hold on tight." She reaches for his knee.

"Mommy, what's happening?" He starts to cry.

"Nothing," she says, heart in her throat. "It's okay, buddy."

The truck driver accelerates, grazing their bumper. Myra slams her foot on the gas. Water flies to each side, as if the sedan is surfing in the ocean. Elizabeth fishes her cell phone from her bag and dials 911. "There's a truck trying to run us off the 101 . . . No I have no idea where we are."

"We're gonna end up upside down in a ditch." Myra's voice is distant. She is wholly connected to the road.

The truck veers and skids behind them. Myra continues to drive steadily, and the truck's headlights fade. Myra's hair is pasted to her forehead. Mascara streaks down her cheeks. Her dress has slipped down, revealing a light brown bra with thick straps.

Elizabeth puts her head in her palms. Adrenaline pumps through her blood. "What the hell was that?" She exhales.

Myra shakes her head. "I don't know." She peers into the rearview mirror. "I can't see anything in this rain."

Elizabeth says dumbly, "All right." The rain has slowed to a light patter. Rays of gentle sunlight are silhouetted by the heather-gray clouds. "I should get back on the phone with the police. I called 911."

Myra twists her lips. "God that was scary." She clears her throat. "What have the police done for us, ever?" She taps the steering wheel. "Nothing. Absolutely nothing."

"Oh no—"

"No, it's true. That cabin you've been locked up in for twenty years?" Her voice inches up a decibel. "They didn't find it. You found your way down."

"Let's go back to the inn and call someone." She speaks as evenly as possible. The truth is, this is completely her fault. "Theo, hang tight."

He seems frozen in his seat. "Okay, Mommy."

Myra clenches her jaw. "At least the bastard isn't following us. Yet."

Elizabeth feels like she's breathing through a straw. Her teeth chatter. Tears sting her eyes. She gets her son from the back seat and bolts into the house, leaving Myra in a daze.

CHAPTER TWENTY-EIGHT

ELIZABETH

Elizabeth holds the crumpled photo of Peter in her palm, staring into his sea-green eyes. An unnatural shade of beauty, she thinks. His beard is thick, covering up the baby face she'd been so attracted to when they met. Here, she sees the whole of him, what he really was, and everything inside her screams *run*. Tears prick her eyelashes. Drawing her palms into tight fists, she thinks about Charlotte, wonders what her last moments were like.

Peter, what did you do?

She catches a glimpse of Theo in the kitchen with Gwen, who is helping him smear cream cheese on his bagel. Gwen invited them to have breakfast in the Barkley house, though they've been eating the continental breakfast at the hotel. She couldn't come up with a good reason to say no, and she doesn't want to arouse suspicion. After the incident in the car, the confrontation with Jimi—it's time to move on. But she can't run off yet. Not till she hears back from Alice.

Theo's bright voice rises high and low, a happy metronome she's never heard from him. The girls are in school; he is getting Gwen's undivided attention. Gently touching his shoulder, she crouches to his level. He laughs at whatever she is saying. Her smile is warm and nurturing.

The woman hides her secrets well. Gwen is more complicated than Elizabeth had originally believed. Loving toward children, defensive and irritable with adults. But what about the necklace? What the hell is she missing? Elizabeth can hardly stop herself from screaming. She returns her gaze to the photo as if it holds the answers she needs.

How did he get Gwen's necklace? She rakes a hand through her hair. Over and over, the question roils through her mind: What happened to Charlotte? It is unrelenting; it keeps her here against her better judgment.

A male voice startles her out of her thoughts. "Elizabeth?"

She jumps and swings her chair around. Jimi stands behind her, hands shoved in his pockets, head angled toward the ground. "What now? I don't want to discuss your theories about me. Take it up with your mom," she says.

"I wanted to apologize to you for how I've acted." His voice is raw and very young.

She avoids his watery eyes.

"That's very kind of you, but I don't need an apology." Elizabeth gulps. He shouldn't trust her. *Don't fall for this, Jimi,* she thinks. *Don't believe me.*

She doesn't want to be this crafty.

"And the knife. That was me too. I wanted to protect my mom. I didn't know—"

Holy shit. "That was you?"

"I'm so sorry," he says. And then he breaks. "You probably think I'm a terrible person. Maybe I am. But I promise, I was only trying to protect my mom. You have no idea what she's been like."

"Please, don't," she says, stumbling over her words. "No one broke into the hotel room?"

"Not that time," he says. "Charlotte. I am so very sorry."

Gwen stands off to the side, listening. She lifts her chin toward Jimi, arms crossed against her chest.

"I . . . don't know what to say." Elizabeth slumps into the chair. "We don't need to upset Myra more than she already is. Let's not tell her about this . . ." Her words are hollow in her ears. Jimi planted the fucking knife in her room?

Jimi cocks his head to one side, and says, sounding slightly confused, "You aren't pissed off?"

"No, I'm not pissed off," she says, glancing toward Gwen. She swallows the bitterness in her throat. It burns a hole in her gut. She feels betrayed, but who is she to speak about betrayal? Hot tears well in her eyes.

Gwen shakes her head. *"I know,"* she mouths.

He leans down to hug her. She resists the urge to recoil. Patting his back, she says dumbly, "Let's have a bagel."

Gwen whispers something into Theo's ear. He sits down with his plate and takes a big bite of the bagel.

"See, that wasn't so bad," she says, addressing Jimi.

He smiles sheepishly. "You forgive me?"

Elizabeth feels the blood rush to her cheeks, relaxes her fists. She forgets about the photo in her palm. "Really. Everything is okay."

"If you're sure." Gwen sounds dubious. "Now we can start again." She squeezes Jimi's shoulder. "I'm going to finish helping Theo." She turns to walk away, but then she stops sharply. "Wait a minute," she says, focusing on the photo in Elizabeth's palm. "Is that . . . I mean, was that him? Peter Briggs?"

Elizabeth nods.

"God, he looks like a boy I dated in high school." She shakes her head. "Jesus, I must be going crazy. For a second I thought he *was* my ex. All of this is getting to me."

Her ears perk up. Elizabeth says, as casually as possible, "What was his name?"

"Jared Henderson," she replies, a sort of wistfulness to her tone. "I've been thinking of him a lot lately, probably because he was with us that night you disappeared . . ."

"He was there?"

"Yes, he was there," She shakes her head. "Like I said, I must be losing my mind. Jared has been on my mind a lot, since you've been home. But that's not him." She inspects the photo more closely and shudders. "Are you okay?"

Elizabeth is up, heading for Theo. "I feel a little woozy from the coffee . . ."

"I don't think you should have that photo," Gwen says. "Talk to the therapist about it, but this doesn't seem healthy, you know?"

"Right," she says, staring at Gwen. "It probably isn't."

"I'm sorry," Jimi says again, stroking his chin. "I understand if you're mad. I've been an asshole."

"I'm not mad," she repeats.

This is enough. She needs to get to the room, to get Alice on the phone. *Patrick J. Henderson.* Maybe Jared was his middle name.

"Theo, come on. Let's go back to the room and change your clothes. Get dressed."

"But I'm not finished with my bagel," he says.

"You can bring it with you." She grasps his hand. "I'm not feeling well, and I can't leave you out here alone."

"I can watch him, Elizabeth," Gwen says.

"No, it's fine," she says absentmindedly, dragging Theo toward the door. There is no way she can trust this family. Out— they need to get out. She can investigate Jared from somewhere else.

"Well, okay . . ."

They trudge outside. The breeze is cool and damp on her face. Once they slip back into the hotel room, she draws her boy into her arms and inhales his scent. She runs her fingers across his cheek.

Her stomach flutters, thick emotion rising in her throat.

"Sit on the bed, Theo." She speaks in her most firm voice.

He flops on the bed. "What's wrong Mommy?"

"We're going for a little drive in the new car."

"Where to?"

"We're going on another adventure."

"No more adventures, Mommy." His face is crestfallen.

"Not a long one." She forces a smile. "Just to visit Alice."

She bends down to tie Theo's new red shoes, steels her mind. She throws her possessions in the duffle bag. Elizabeth scrawls a quick note. It's inadequate, she understands. And it's not over. She has to find whoever is working for Peter, on her own. It began with Jared. It must have. Gwen had been deeply intertwined with him. *She has to have more information than she's letting on.* Maybe she's messing with the cameras, trying to scare her away. Jimi could be part of it too. Especially since he planted that knife. He tried to make her look guilty of slashing that painting.

But why apologize at all? Her head is swimming. There are too many possibilities. Gwen and Jimi are trying to kill her or save her—and the truth is blurred, obscured.

She has to find out more about Jared. *"It's usually someone you know, someone close to the family. Stranger abductions are rare."* That's what Sarah Marlow said.

Jared was close to the family.

"Let's go." They get into the car and drive toward the crumbling yellow trailer, past the beach where her memories of that night hang thick and sorrowful.

Myra and Herb are loving parents. But Elizabeth's mother worked and fought and persevered with almost nothing at all.

She rushes inside her mother's home, tears streaming. Charlotte pulls at her. Like the girl is begging her to solve the mystery of the necklaces, to find her for Myra. Elizabeth is stitched into the fabric of the Barkley tragedy, through the man she married and the lies she told. Her mind races. Alice would know what to do, but she can't reach Alice.

They sit on the ragged carpet together, shivering in the cold. He is the boy she lives for, runs for, dissolves poison for. She sobs over his delicious head, and he pats her back in gentle little thumps, like she does for him.

"Oh, my mommy," he says, over and over. "My sweet mommy."

She finally rubs her eyes and begins to rise. "Button your coat," she says absentmindedly. She notices a thick stack of envelopes covered in dust. She almost ignores it, thinking it must be some tenant's mail.

Instead, she slides back to the floor and picks it up. Her name is written on a manila envelope at the bottom. "Something for me," she explains to Theo dryly. "They managed to leave a bill or two."

Theo shrugs again.

She slides her fingers underneath the flap, loosening the old glue, and slides out a stack of papers.

"What on earth is this?" She squints at a paper filled with many numbers. It will require much interpretation from someone more qualified than she is, but one thing is obvious.

It is a deed to the house. Signed to her mother. Behind it, is a will.

Mom *owned* this trailer? It occurs to Elizabeth that if she hadn't, it would have been foreclosed on by now. She wouldn't have used her own key to walk in the door.

But *how*? Someone had rented it out after she left too. At least for a short time.

She'd met Peter right after her mother died. Stage four pancreatic cancer. Even if it had been diagnosed earlier, before she came home from work writhing in pain, it would have been fatal. The mass of cancer infiltrated her pancreas and spread to her lungs, announcing its death sentence long before the fateful trip to the emergency room. She remembers stroking her mother's sweat-soaked forehead with a cool washcloth.

She paces, holding the deed in her hand. The envelope and the rest of its contents flutter to the ground. How much is this place worth? Probably nothing. It's practically in ruins. It might have been worth something had she known about this before she left for Washington. Even the smallest amount of money might have helped her get out of town.

There's no time to think. She dials Alice's number, holding her breath. *Answer, answer. Please.*

"Elizabeth," Alice says breathlessly. "I have looked everywhere. So many Patrick Hendersons in the world. I can't find any living relatives, if that's the real name. The driver's license is old. It's not enough to go on. I'm sorry girl. I tried—"

"I know, Alice. I need you to look for a Jared Henderson. Maybe a Patrick Jared Henderson. He would have grown up in Rocky Shores."

"All right," she says. "Getting online right now. I swear. Why can't you let this go?"

"Something is happening at that inn. I don't know how far it goes back, but it has to be years," Elizabeth says. "I need to know exactly what 'it' is, and how it relates to me."

"No, you really don't. The man is dead. You are impossible to deal with." Alice sighs. "Please. Let's just get out of here."

"Not yet. Because in that you're correct. I have been following along with endless bullshit my entire life. So, now, I am choosing to be impossible to deal with, because an eight-year -old child died."

"Fine. If you insist." Elizabeth hears Alice clacking on the keyboard. "Wait a minute," she says. "You think he went to school with Gwen?"

"If Jared is Peter, he must have. This is a tiny town. Rocky Shores High." She laughs. "Wait a minute. We'll just get a hold of the school. See if they have contact info."

"Christ, you're good," Alice says, breaking into a guffaw. "Hang up this phone. I'll pick you up at the bus stop—"

"Alice? Alice?"

The call drops.

CHAPTER TWENTY-NINE

MYRA

Myra grips the letter between her fingers so tightly it begins to tear. She reads and rereads, not sure what to believe. Has her daughter really left again? Did she come home only to disappear? She shuts her eyes and wills the words to dissipate, though the indelible black letters will be there no matter how many times she blinks. Herb rubs her shoulder ever so gently, knowing exactly how much space to give.

She wishes she understood selflessness like Herb does.

"I pushed her away," she says, tears streaming.

"No. You didn't. She was afraid." Herb instinctively puts his hand in his lap.

Sarah Marlow and Patrick Shuman sit quietly on the other couch. "Myra," Sarah finally says, "it looks like she left on her own."

Myra accepts this. Elizabeth has packed her duffle bag, made the bed. She left a note. But Myra does not want to hear the words from Detective Marlow's lips. She wants to scream at Sarah because this is her fault. The police let Peter Briggs remain in the wild for years. If not for Michael Calgary, they'd never have found out about those cameras.

The living room sags around them like a thick blanket, all over again. The ceiling hangs so low it could envelope her body. The walls engulf them. The dim lighting is not soft or relaxing. Shadows lurk around like slugs in the mud. She watches the detectives, who shake their heads with that syrupy sympathy they've had forever and ever. And now the pity is shameful; it has gone on for far too long.

"Yes." Her voice is hoarse, but she is going to be strong. For once in her life, they will not speak to her like a child. She breathes, slow and steady through her nostrils, sitting straight-backed, like a piano player. "Some asshole is still stalking us. I hope Elizabeth and Theo are free of him, at least."

"We're searching for him. The Feds have a multistate manhunt going on here—"

"He is in Oregon. Remember, he trapped me in the shed." She pauses and clears her throat. "She's been held in that cabin for most of her life. I think that was really what scared her away, the thought of being trapped again. And I don't disagree with her. I'd do it too if I could've protected her twenty years ago."

"Peter Briggs is dead. No one besides Elizabeth seems to have seen him in the area. No vehicles are registered in his name. We've asked every Washington-based trucking company for a missing employee, and again, nothing. The fingerprints don't match anyone in our database. Clearly, he operated under another name, but the fingerprints, the residual DNA—"

"Nothing," says Myra. "It's almost like he never existed, on paper."

"His blood is not in CODIS. He's never been convicted of a felony," Sarah says.

The detectives exchange a glance. Sarah drums her fingers on the coffee table. "She signed a waiver for the DNA testing. I checked with the lab. They can have those results quickly."

"What on earth are you *saying*?"

"Maybe Elizabeth is in on it with whoever is stalking you."

"Why would she agree to a DNA test if she was lying?" Myra's voice rises. She tells herself to slow down, that she must be rational. The cops must think she is capable. "I mean, why do you think she might?"

"Because she thought you weren't going through with the test. But the sample was still sent off. I think she might have gotten some clothes and a few meals in and bailed before the results came back. The lab is probably running it now, if the results aren't already in. We can get maternity and paternity results in a few days. We have the best available labs in the country. But she wasn't aware of that."

"It's been two weeks," Myra says.

"That's right," Sarah says softly. "The lab might have the results now."

Herb grasps her hand a little tighter. She smooths her fingers over his flannel shirt and twists the little plastic button on the cuff.

"Like I said, we were nearly murdered." Myra tries to sound calm. "Again."

"Why didn't you mention this incident in the car?" asks Schumer. A note of suspicion lingers in the question. "Why didn't you call us immediately?"

"Detective." Herb raises a hand. Schumer leans back and shuts up. Men listen to other men, she supposes. She purses her lips and makes no effort to conceal her irritation.

"Please don't patronize my wife. We are not criminals."

Sarah says, "I think of you like family. I am not the bad guy here."

"All right. Please get the results. And keep searching." Myra speaks in the slowest, most measured voice she can muster. The colors in the living room are so muted. Hues of gray and mucky brown drape the furniture like specters. The shrinking walls remind her of turbid rainwater.

"My husband and I need a little time right now." She motions them toward the door. "Please."

The detectives follow her, clearly relieved by her collected manner. Sarah speaks more formally than Myra remembers. Maybe the detective is weary of this same old case that will live beyond them all.

"It's okay, Sarah. It's okay," she says. "This is a bad day for us. That's all."

Sarah smooths her ginger hair. "I know it is." She sighs. "You're strong, Myra. So much more than you give yourself credit for." She lifts her chin toward Herb. "I'll give you time. And we have not given up. I promise you."

Wind knocks the front door open and slices against her body. A shiver of aliveness scatters through her brain. The images will come back, they will always come back. That visceral fear, so primal it emanates from her brain stem, splinters through her bones—it will come back.

So much, she has yearned for Charlotte. So much, she has longed. Elizabeth Lark *has* to be Charlotte.

Herb takes her in his arms, and he says, "Let's just see what the test says."

She rests her head on his chest, even though he's just a couple of inches taller than her. He holds her so very tight. He is her Herb. No matter what happens, he will be her Herb. They sink into the couch. The exhaustion consumes him too.

Herb's voice is throaty and raw. "Even if she is our daughter, we don't own her." His voice cracks. "She grew up without us. And she can choose to move on."

"They will be safe," she whispers. "The important thing is, they will be safe."

They sit quietly in front of the window. They listen to the rain fall and the wind howl. The fire crackles and rises like a dragon's breath licking the chimney. Myra can't go back to the inn tonight. Jimi will take care of the guests.

"We have survived so much. If we can survive this, we can make it through anything." Herb folds his arms against his chest. "We can survive anything, Myra."

CHAPTER THIRTY

ELIZABETH

The tenebrous night is crushing. Elizabeth and Alice travel through a lush, wooded area, away from the seashore. She digs her fingers into her seat as the car rolls slowly. It is deliberate and foreboding, as if someone, somewhere is warning her. It is disorienting. She turns her head in all directions; she feels his gaze crawling down her neck. He is nestled in the thick patches of forest, nocturnal and waiting. He is an owl, still and quiet, talons twisted around a tree branch, watching her with luminous eyes that cut through the blackness.

The tears in her eyelashes feel like frozen butterflies splayed against her skin. The hairs inside her cochlea are on high alert. Rain plunks on the ground in an ever-changing rhythm; its beat picks up, harder and faster, until it comes at them sideways.

It's as if he's sitting beside her. The sweat and whisky that seep from their sheets flood her nostrils. The rhythm of his voice manipulates her emotions like music; thick and sweet when he wanted her to believe his lies, raw and barking when she refused. Elizabeth gulps the sharp mountain air.

Peter is dead.

They have left.

This trepidation is only in her imagination.

She has dragged others into the riptide with her. The Barkleys are stuck at that inn, their names plastered on the door, asleep with the lights out.

"So, what do you have?" Elizabeth asks.

"I called the school, pretended to be a cop, and got the parents' address. If the Hendersons still live there, you'll be able to knock on their door and ask about when they last saw him. But I could get in so much trouble for this, Elizabeth."

"But you make fake IDs all the time, Alice. Deal with dangerous men on a regular basis."

"Not quite this dangerous. This is out of my scope. I'm not a cop."

"Sorry," she says, staring at her seat. "I didn't expect any of this to happen either. If you want to be free of this, I understand—"

Alice waves her hand. "Absolutely not. Besides, I never did tell you my story. It isn't what you'd think."

"And what would I think?"

"Oh, you know," she says, waving her hand dismissively, "abused wife gets free and goes on a mission to help others. That isn't how I ended up here at all."

"I never assumed that," she says.

"Well, you're unique in that," she says. "I went to law school and worked in family practice. I discovered that we couldn't help women with violent partners with a little piece of paper. I discovered that the system fails. Too many women die at the hands of their abusers right after they leave. Stuff like that is hard to deal with day in and day out without a solid solution."

"So, you started taking people into your home. Changing lives by risking your own."

"The point of my history is not to brag. The point is, I'm an attorney. I can find people who don't wanna be found. Track down their families. Uncover lies. I've done it for a living. And that's what I've done with our Patrick Jared here."

Elizabeth relaxes, ever so slightly, and squeezes Theo into her arms. "What did you find out about him? Besides where his parents lived?"

"The man had no convictions that I can see, but he hadn't used that identification in years, since he was in his mid-twenties. Also, criminal convictions prior to age eighteen are sealed, most of the time. You can't even get a job without ID."

Elizabeth nods. "He has had help, even dead. Somehow."

They drive toward the rich part of town.

"Are we almost there?" Elizabeth says, chewing on her fingernail. The hills wind higher; the homes get larger and farther apart. Even the air smells rich, thick with the scent of dewy plants. The road is quiet except for the occasional elegant car driving by them at the speed limit. They pass a big white house with a luscious, manicured lawn, trimmed ivy, and clipped red rose bushes around the porch, as if the thorns are a form of protection. The house screams, *I am strong and stately and larger than you.* It probably scares off the robbers. A senator lives there. Yes, these homes are for important people.

She inhales the scent of cut, wet grass and fresh flowers.

"We're here," says Alice, in a low, even tone. She pats Elizabeth on the shoulder. "It's gonna be okay."

"What do I do with Theo?" she says.

"You leave him out here with me," Alice says.

Elizabeth goes silent.

"I want to come with you Mommy," Theo says.

"No," she murmurs. "I can't let you do that."

Alice speaks first. "If you aren't out in ten minutes, I'll take Theo and drive straight to the police station."

"Got it," she says.

The house is tall, with a more modest yard than the neighbors'. It is painted a neutral shade of brown and has clean white shutters. A swing hangs on the wraparound porch.

Reluctantly, she gives Theo a kiss. "Listen to Alice, okay?"

"Okay," he says, eyes shining. "You'll come back, right?"

"Of course I will. It's safer for you here, though. I'll be right back," she whispers, holding his hand.

"Now, listen, before you go in. Look professional," Alice says, "like you've got a job to do and they can't say no. Do not reveal any prior relationship with him, or the fact he's dead. That's for the police to do."

"Okay," Elizabeth says uncertainly. She lets go of Theo's fingers and turns around. He has to stay here. *Be logical*, she thinks.

Large columns loom on either side of them. Bushes around the property are carved as sharp as ice sculptures.

Straightening her posture, she raps three times at one of the large double doors. She's sure they've got cameras. A flood of light bathes her. Elizabeth is horribly exposed, conspicuous.

A man answers, opening the door wide. He wears slacks and a navy-blue pullover vest. "Can I help you?"

"Yes, sir. Perhaps you can," she says. Her voice is sharp, confident. Somewhere along the drive, she pulled herself together. Elizabeth flashes a badge, then quickly shoves it back in her purse. "Detective Smith. I'm looking for Jared Henderson."

"Looking for him?" The man's face turns a pasty color. They've definitely got the right place. He must be Peter's father. "Why would you think he'd be here?" he asks cautiously.

A voice echoes from beyond the door. She cranes her neck and sees Mrs. Henderson approaching. "John? Who is it?" She draws her light blue sweater around her waist.

Henderson clenches his jaw and turns to his wife. He says in a low voice, "The police. Looking for Jared."

She says, "We haven't seen Jared in, gosh, twenty years. I don't know what kind of trouble he's in, Detective, but we want no part of it."

"He's our son, Mary," whispers John.

"Whatever then." She throws her hands up. "Come in. Has he—is he—oh god, just sit on the couch."

She leads her through a foyer adorned with paintings. Perhaps a Manet? A Winslow Homer? No, she decides. A local artist. The table in the entryway boasts a bouquet of white roses.

There is one photo in the room adorned with art. A black and white photo hangs on the wall, depicting the Hendersons with a young boy. Peter. Her breath catches in her throat. She glances around the home. Nothing else. No recent photos. The kitchen is elegant, with stainless steel appliances, two ovens, two dishwashers.

"Lots of space here for just the two of you," she comments.

"Detective, sit." She motions toward a leather sectional. John and Mary perch on the loveseat across from her. Mary leans forward, cupping her cheeks in her palms. They must be around Herb and Myra's age, but they have a regal air. She wears makeup. He is clean-shaven.

"Yes, we bought the house before Jared was born. We hoped to have a gaggle of children running around. Grandchildren, the whole package." She laughs bitterly. "Oh well. Fantasies die hard."

The couple exchange a glance. "Jared turned out to have issues. And the doctors aren't sure if they are biological." John Henderson clears his throat. "We could have another child with the same problem, or the new baby could have been endangered by him."

"Problem?" Elizabeth waits.

"Please," she whispers hoarsely, "before we continue with this—is our son alive?"

"That I don't know." She lies smoothly. "The police are investigating an incident. I can't reveal specific details."

John rises and goes into the kitchen. "Wine, Mary?" He opens a bottle and pours half of it into a goblet-sized glass. Maybe Peter's parents were alcoholics. There has to be a reason.

She desperately needs a reason.

"No, thanks, sweetheart," she replies. And to Elizabeth, "Do you really want the story? Before you tell us what Jared did this time, I think you should hear our side of it. It's always the parents, they say—"

"Please. Tell your story." She stiffens.

Mary picks absentmindedly at her shiny red nails. John slumps into one of the barstools around the giant island in the kitchen. He gulps his wine.

"We were so ecstatic to have our boy. Like I said, we wanted children so badly. I was twenty-five, and it happened even more quickly than we expected. John is the CEO of a big company. I was so happy to quit my boring job and be a stay-at-home mommy." She smiles at the memory. "We were over the moon."

"Except Jared was off kilter from a year old. Different from our friends' smiley, happy babies that cooed at their parents from a young age. At first we thought it was developmental, because he had this temper. Meltdowns. But you know, we thought he had sensory issues. Maybe he was overstimulated too easily," says John, staring into the distance. "It's not uncommon."

"We accepted that there might be issues," Mary continues. "I still planned to become pregnant when he was three. It seemed like the perfect timing. They say so in all the books." She shakes her head.

"He did end up speaking, walking, all of those things on time. The doctor said it was normal for first-time parents to worry. That he was just on his own path. Tantrums were normal. He said to try not to compare him to other kids," says John.

Mary furrows her brow. "I wanted to believe the doctor. But I had this strange feeling. Something was off. Jared's tantrums were . . . different. Something told me we should wait. There was something calculated about him. Like . . . I can't even describe it . . . he was manipulating us."

John and Mary exchange a glance.

"When he was six, we began to question everything the pediatrician said. We knew we were right. Our son was not like other children," John says.

"What happened?" Elizabeth thinks of Theo. Her throat is parched and dry.

"Our six-year-old tried to strangle my sister's infant. Our niece." Her eyes fill with tears. She meanders into the kitchen. Her husband pours the other half bottle of wine into a similar goblet. "Could've been an accident. Maybe he was playing too rough. But we waited on the next baby. Jared clearly needed some love and attention." She scoffs, takes a slow sip of her wine and plunks the glass back on the table.

"Things got progressively worse," says John. "We didn't realize this could happen with a child. We did everything for that boy. Played with him nonstop. Mary was such a good mother. I tried so hard to do dad things—toss the ball around in the yard. We put him in sports . . ."

"But he was kicked out of every activity," Mary finished. "Violent with other kids. Tortured our family cat. You can't understand what this was like. I'd given up everything to mother this boy. But I was an outcast. The other mothers whispered about me."

"Teachers thought it was our fault," adds John. "That something was happening at home."

"I had one friend left in the world." Mary smiles weakly. "Our housekeeper, Rosie. She was the sweetest woman. Brought her toddler over. A cute little girl. Jared was eight or nine by then. "

Elizabeth freezes. She can't think, can't speak. Rosie was Elizabeth's mother. Mom was their maid. Colors spin in her vision. She's hallucinating—she must be. This can't be real. She flattens her palm against the couch, trying to stay grounded.

"Rosie and I were folding laundry when we heard her daughter scream. I had never heard anything so heart-wrenching. Her little voice . . . I knew it had something to do with Jared." She sips her wine. "We ran for the playroom. Rosie's daughter was wailing, holding her cheek. You could already see the bruise forming. She was barely old enough to talk, but she pointed at this heavy toy truck on the floor."

Elizabeth was too young to remember this. Did Peter, though? Did he remember this when they met? She feels like a lemon is stuck in her throat, and no matter how she tries to swallow it down, as she always did with Peter, she can't do it. She thinks of Theo in the car, and she has to get out.

"I'll never forget the scene. Rosie was comforting her daughter, asking what happened."

She stands to leave.

"And there was Jared, leaning against the wall, so casually, with that smug grin."

She stares at the door. He had abused her since she was a toddler.

"Are you all right, ma'am?" Mary says, gazing at Elizabeth.

No, she thinks. *No, I'm not anywhere near all right. And your grandson is in my car.*

Instead, she says thickly, "I'm fine. That's just such a sad story." She sits back in the chair.

"Never saw Rosie or her daughter again. I paid her double in hopes she wouldn't get the police involved." Tears stream down her cheeks. "You cannot imagine what it was like to live with him."

Elizabeth can imagine.

Mary takes a slow, deep breath, "At thirteen years old, our son was diagnosed with psychopathy."

Elizabeth listens intently. Could this really happen to anyone? Any parent? What if . . . did Mary say this could be genetic? Not her Theo. He has never been violent in his life. She pushes the thought away. It's intensifying her panic.

"That's right. We were told our son was born hopelessly without a conscience. That he enjoyed hurting others. He was dangerous. We had him committed for experimental treatments. Nothing worked."

"We didn't believe them at first. We had to try. He was our child." John shakes his head. "We tried every imaginable treatment. Every medication."

"Of course you did," she says.

"I'll never forget what one of the doctors told us." Mary starts to cry. "They'd show the patients photos of people expressing different emotions. This doctor, he told me to be careful around my son—"

"Mary, don't." John brushes the hair out of her eyes, tenderly tucks it behind her ear. "Let's not talk about this."

"No," she says, grimacing. "No. I want to tell this detective the truth about him." She turns her attention back to Elizabeth. "They showed Jared a photo of someone who was afraid. They asked him to name the emotion. And he said, 'That's how a person looks just before they die.' I was repulsed by this child I gave birth to," she whispers.

"Oh my god," Elizabeth says.

"I can't accuse him of stupidity. He's manipulative, cunning. Whatever he's done, I hope you catch him soon." Mary purses her lips.

"I haven't seen him since that night, years ago. The last thing we could accept," John says. "Till that night, I'd have done anything for my boy."

"How do you mean?" she asks, though she isn't sure she wants to know. "What was this final straw?"

"My own child tried to murder me." Mary's words are choked and bitter. "He came in while we were sleeping and pulled a knife on me. Held it to my throat, just like that." Her face hardens. She holds her index finger to her neck. "You wanna know my crime? Why he tried to stab his own mother?" Her voice rises. "Because I refused to let him take my car. I locked it up that night. Told him a teenage boy didn't need to be out all hours of the night on a school day."

"So you kicked him out?"

"That's not the end," says John. "When I socked him, he threatened to call the police on *us*. At this point, I would've gone to jail to get away from this kid."

"Pretty much," Mary says. "He ran to his bedroom and *lit a cigarette*."

The cigarette burn was self-inflicted. All these years, Elizabeth had believed Peter had been abused. Her stomach roils. She cannot stay here one more moment.

"Wait. This is just how manipulative he is," John says. "He burned his *own back* and threatened to turn us in to the police for child abuse."

"Well," Mary says, smoothing her shirt, "he didn't call the police. He left. That was twenty years ago, and we haven't seen him since. So whatever he's done, we can't locate him. I'm sorry to say, we can't help you find him."

"We were scared, helpless. If I could go back in time, I'd have called you all in. But we were afraid. Afraid of our own child. Hell, we thought he'd make us out to be monsters with his threats and manipulation. We had treatment records, stuff like that. But this kid could manipulate anyone into believing his lies." John's eyes are wet, glossy.

These parents can't help her. They are victims too. He'd victimized people his entire life.

Elizabeth turns toward the door, ready to leave.

"Wait. I have one more question." Her voice trembles. "Did Jared have friends at all? Anyone we might contact who might know where he is?" She chokes on the last bit.

"I think he had a girlfriend. What was her name, Mary?"

"Hmm. I can't remember. I'm sorry. We discouraged that relationship, so he didn't speak about her much."

Gwen Barkley, she thinks. Her name is Gwen Barkley.

CHAPTER THIRTY-ONE

MYRA

The police station breathes a strange kind of grief today, one of eerie quiet. This sadness knows she has arrived to claim it, to take it home for the rest of her life, and the structure itself, with its desolate gray walls and utilitarian architecture, folds her in its arms to bid her condolences.

The blood test is in.

She paces the waiting room for thirty minutes, then sixty. The front desk clerk informs her, almost coldly, that Detective Marlow is in a meeting. It isn't good news. But why not just tell her? She's got a right to the truth.

Myra wanted Elizabeth to be hers. Scarlet blossoms through her cheeks. She sinks in a neutral chair. The station is designed to be soothing, and yet not cheery. Not optimistic. It works for the guilty and it works for the victims because they are both imprisoned here. In this way, they are one and the same.

Ninety minutes later, Sarah calls her through a narrow corridor to a small office. The entire station falls to a hush. Cops and civilians alike await Myra's future. They sit watchfully, wondering, what will happen to that woman next? Where will the mother of the missing girl wind up now?

Where will Myra end up now?

"Sit down," says Sarah, slumping into her chair with a long sigh. "We've gotta talk."

An odd feeling slinks through Myra's stomach, something new, something different. She is afraid to speak. Heat runs up her neck. Sarah's face is pale; her eyes swallowed by dark, puffy circles.

"What the hell is going on? Just tell me the truth. If she isn't my daughter—"

"No." Sarah shakes her head. "No. This time I need *you* to tell the truth. It doesn't have to leave this room, but I think you owe me that much."

"What are you talking about?" The breath is siphoned from Myra's lungs.

"In all of my career, I've never encountered such a thing. I don't even know what to make of this." Sarah paces the length of the small, bland office. Raking her fingers through her hair, she says, "This complicates matters."

Myra has never seen Sarah Marlow this disturbed. Not ever. The hint of anger in the detective's voice is unsettling. "Why are you talking to me like this, Sarah? No matter what those results say, I am not the enemy."

"Elizabeth is not Charlotte," Sarah says.

"Oh god—"

"No, her DNA does not match the samples we collected twenty years ago."

Tears sting Myra's eyes. Why did she set herself up for this? She removes her glasses and wipes the fog off them with her shirt. "I guess I should have known this was a possibility. Herb is going to be devastated. Why did she pretend to be our daughter? She's an imposter, right?"

Sarah sighs. "Stop. It's not that simple."

"What do you mean by that?" Myra stares at the metal desk and shakes her head. "Why?"

"Well, you tell me why, Myra." Sarah narrows her eyes.

"Sarah. What are you talking about?"

She could never brace herself adequately for what was coming. For the rest of her life, when she returns her thoughts to this moment, that same tidal wave of fresh shock will roll through her.

"Elizabeth Lark—or whatever her name is—*is* your daughter. Not Herb's, mind you. But she's yours, and I don't know what the fuck is going on here, but I feel duped." Sarah walks over to the coffee table. She pours hot water from the cooler into a Styrofoam cup.

Myra can only stare. "What?"

"I do want to clarify that she is not Charlotte. Again. Just in case you don't understand."

She understands.

Sarah dumps a few tablespoons of instant coffee into the water and stirs it with a plastic spoon. "You tell me, girl. I'm waiting for it."

Myra's head spins and spins, the dizziness pierced with moments of truth, and still, this doesn't make sense. She cannot speak for several moments.

She is blinded by a memory she hasn't thought of in years. Breathless, she cannot speak. Sarah is nothing but a blur of red hair and green eyes and pale skin whipped to a nauseating shade of mud.

*   *   *

Herb was in Los Angeles, running with the boys in the bands, performing at random bars because he thought he'd make it big.

"I'll be back to you, baby," he'd said. "I can't go on if I don't *know*."

"Know what?"

"Know if I have what it takes. To be a star. And as soon as I do, I'll be back."

Then he walked out the door and left her and Gwen in the quiet aftermath of what Herb needed to *know*. And yes, she was angry. Oh, so very livid. Her veins pulsed with this need to get back at him. Who knew if he'd even return? Deep inside, Myra felt he would come home. But she told herself, she would not let his sorry ass back in her parents' inn. "This is *my* business, Herb. Don't forget that." She'd said this viciously, aiming to hurt him.

Myra was also sick. Neither of them knew that her reckless spending and sudden impulsiveness had nothing to do with Herb or Gwen or the inn; it was the onset of mania.

The only person she had left was Rosie. She listened when Myra cried. Fed Gwen homemade meals and read her bedtime stories. She gave baths and sang songs. Many times, Myra watched her and thought, *She is a better mother than I am. Gwen deserves a real mom like that.* Not the flighty woman Myra had become. Rosie, with her long dark hair and soft eyes, understood. There were lots of smart people in the world, lots of musicians, lots of artists. And Myra had decided that creative types were mostly pretentious assholes, as Herb had turned out to be. But very few individuals truly understood *people*.

Rosie knew people.

Kenneth Callahan was the married man who waltzed in every so often with his handsome smile and bright white teeth. He wanted her. Oh, Myra understood well enough he would head on home to Adele, that he was stopping at other small inns and big hotels to screw the owners or the guests, whatever was convenient for him at the time, but she didn't mind. She was enraged, and sex with Kenneth was the biggest revenge she could get.

She clears her throat. "Long ago, I gave a baby up for adoption. Herb and I were separated."

"I never intended to get pregnant, Sarah," she continues, "and I did not know Elizabeth wasn't Charlotte." Myra's voice breaks. "I didn't know she was the child I gave away. Elizabeth Lark has to be a fake name."

"I'm guessing Herb doesn't know?"

She shakes her head. "I was very pregnant when I found out. Gwen was four."

"So, Elizabeth is older than Charlotte?"

"By four years, yes. Rosie and her husband were newly married and wanted a child desperately. She couldn't conceive. They were a good couple, or so it seemed. What the hell was I thinking? It was a terrible choice, made out of desperation and convenience." Myra takes a tissue from the box on Sarah's desk and wipes her face. Her eyes are swollen, and her head pounds.

"Did Rosie tell Elizabeth? She must have. The coincidence is just too great."

Myra blows her nose and continues, "Well, the baby was born. Gwen was so little. I really did plan on keeping her. I did. She was so beautiful and could have been Gwen's twin as an infant."

Myra floats back to that time. Her mind was so frazzled. Thoughts ran through her head, twirling and short-circuiting at lightning speed. Herb had been an extension of her very existence, and suddenly he was gone. A guest would come in with an interesting story, and she'd get halfway to his office to gab about it before realizing he wasn't there.

"Anyway, Herb called. He said he made a huge mistake and he wanted to come home. I still don't know why I did it, Sarah. Maybe it was the mania. Maybe I'm a coward. Probably both. But Rosie was doing well. I convinced myself giving her Elizabeth was the best gift I could give. And it wouldn't have been so bad. I mean, people give up babies for adoption, right?"

"True." Sarah throws her hands up. "But you had an obligation to tell the police this when Charlotte went missing, Myra."

Myra takes a deep, painful breath. "The bad part, the piece that I will be ashamed of for the rest of my life, came later."

Sarah leans on her elbows, an expectant look on her face.

"I did tell Kenneth, who, not surprisingly, wanted nothing to do with his baby. He didn't want to contribute financially, and he is filthy rich. The man has an ungodly amount of money. He still shows up at my inn, but of course I can't start shit with him and stir up this old secret in front of Herb."

"Good lord. Your life is a soap opera." Sarah fills her cup and drops another mounded spoonful of instant coffee in the steamy water.

"On top of it all, he's back at the inn. Wants his child's contact info. He says he *told* his wife about her. He'd never have done that if he wasn't having some kind of midlife crisis."

Sarah's eyes widen. "But you didn't have it," she says.

She sighs. "No. I haven't seen her since she was little. Or spoken with Rosie."

"What is the bad part?" Sarah sips her coffee.

"Well, I gave her what I could. Then, within a year or two, her husband was drinking. I should have told Herb the truth and taken them in—they spent a lot of time at the inn. I wanted to give her more hours, at least. By this time Elizabeth was one hundred percent her child. Legally, and even more so, emotionally. I liked watching the little girl play, but the way she interacted with Rosie—well, Rosie was her mama."

"What about the guy that raised Elizabeth? Her father."

"He was an alcoholic. He left. She did not grow up with an alcoholic father. I swear I wouldn't do that to my baby. I gave Rosie extra money. I bought the mobile home. Tried to get Gwen to play with her at the inn. Gwen must've had a sense of it. She didn't want much to do with Elizabeth. Didn't want to play with a little kid, she said."

"She had a point, Myra. Elizabeth must remember her mother working at the inn. Are you positive she didn't know her identity?"

"I don't know. Why did I do it, Sarah?"

Sarah goes silent for a moment and leans onto her metal desk, banging her palm rhythmically against the surface. The hollow sound reverberates through the boxy, windowless office.

Myra can't take it. She wants to run and run, far away from it all, but she can't go anywhere. Not this time. The judgment is thick and palpable.

Sarah finally speaks. "I never wanted children. Drew and I agreed. I've got a dangerous job. But on top of that, I just did not want a baby. That was my choice."

"Where are you going with this?" asks Myra, confused.

"You didn't want a baby." Sarah speaks firmly.

"Herb is going to find out." Myra's stomach flips. "He's going to divorce me."

"Your marital stuff is a different matter here. And it's got nothing to do with the law. But you gave up a kid for adoption. You can feel whatever guilt you want. But I think you're chock full of guilt. There just isn't room for more of it."

"I left her." She shakes her head. "I did."

Sarah purses her lips. "Can you keep a secret?"

Myra nods. She is a little flattered that Sarah would tell her a secret. It's almost like friendship, and Myra hasn't had a friend in so long.

"I had an abortion at eighteen." Sarah clears her throat and continues, "and I don't feel guilty. It was not rape. My parents were not ogres who would have killed me. I did not want a baby. It's as simple as that."

"This is different."

"No. It really is not. You did not want a baby. For whatever reason."

Myra thinks about this. "It wasn't that exactly. I wanted my marriage more. I wanted my family together. Herb would have left. My health was deteriorating. Rosie *did* want a baby. I sent checks. I tried, but I should have tried harder. I was wrong, Sarah. Don't you see?"

"No. Your reasons were your reasons. Simple as that."

"Herb is going to find out," Myra says numbly.

"Probably," Sarah says with a sigh. "We've gotta find her now, Myra. This is some kind of revenge. Where is Rosie now?"

"We haven't seen her since Elizabeth was little. She quit after Charlotte was born. I couldn't do much to get her to come back. She was probably pissed because this was right around the time her husband left."

"Elizabeth might be pissed too. But this is wrong, what she's doing."

Myra is sobbing now. Shame bubbles to the surface. "I never tried to find my little girl or contact Rosie after that. I guess I thought it'd be easier on everyone. And she had the land and trailer."

"Elizabeth's no victim. Briggs may have been abusive, but I bet she killed him in cold blood. And now she's out for revenge. Pulling shit with the cameras. You were hanging out with her at the shed. It makes sense."

"There's no reason she'd do that."

"Maybe Rosie told her. Jealousy?"

"If it was jealousy, why wouldn't she do this years ago? None of it makes sense."

"No, it doesn't. But this *has* to be connected. If she doesn't know you're her mother—"

"Perhaps she found out. And she wanted to reconnect. Except I jumped to conclusions and went on like I do, and she couldn't find a way out."

"I have no clue about that," says Sarah, stroking her chin. "But we have to deepen this investigation. Now. So, the truth about Elizabeth is going to become public. Do you understand what I'm saying?"

"I'll tell Herb," she whispers. Her marriage slips through her fingers like wet clay. They spent years molding and chiseling and waiting for their young selves to form, and now she squishes it in her fingers. Soft clay on a wheel is delicate. He will leave, and she cannot blame him. She chews her cuticle until blood drips down her thumb. Myra is not a stupid woman.

Charlotte is not coming home. She never was.

CHAPTER THIRTY-TWO

MYRA

Myra clacks up the stairs, onto the tiny pier. She listens to the seagulls' honk and the sway of the wind intermingle with the rush of the tide. It's probably her imagination, but the pier is less vibrant than usual. Losing two children will do that to a person, take the color and sap it from everything. Most people find life in the ocean in summer, when the sun glimmers over the water and the sand is like crushed gold. They want to buy saltwater taffy and ice cream and do all of the tourist things. It is her job to sell the beachside vacation—of course it is. She hands out directions to the wider, sandier shores and the little shops along her own road; she loves how people gobble up the stories she has about nearby independent bookstores and poetry readings. Local bands play at coffee shops, and she reminds them that the Pacific Northwest makes the very best coffee. She says all of this because she truly loves Rocky Shores and the people in it, including her guests.

But, to Myra and Herb the real richness of the sea is the vulnerability of deep gray clouds and rain that turns the sand muddy and brown. This is the heart of the rural Oregon Coast. This is part of why they've stayed—yes, she's been waiting for

Charlotte. But she also held onto this inn because it is home. She reaches out her palm for the cold splats of rain, but none come. Myra leans with her back to the ocean and pulls out her cell phone. The thought of calling Herb makes her feel empty. And afraid. Marlow had said the police search would move faster with the information. That maybe, just maybe, they'd find Elizabeth and Theo.

She sighs and decides Sarah is right. What can she do from here? What can she do from anywhere? Michael Calgary can't help them now. How would she even begin? She paces down the pier, listening to the sound of her shoes as they hit the deck. She rubs her temples and thinks about how Herb will take this, how it will go.

Her stomach aches. She cannot remember the last time she ate.

She gazes across the street at their inn. The place they've made and shared a life together. And right across the Washington border was this man. He might be dead, but he works with someone who won't stop till he destroys them all. She wants to cry from the insidiousness of it all, but she holds back. Part of this is on her.

A shadowy figure crosses the highway. The figure grows closer, and she recognizes that it is Herb. He has probably come to take her home, to insist she has dinner. She needs to keep her strength up, he'll say. She needs to be strong.

His unwavering support is about to end.

She waves and pulls her sweater against her body. Her hair blows back in the wind.

"Hey there," she yells as he approaches.

Her husband shuffles toward him, hands stuffed in his pockets. She focuses squarely on the wooden planks. Myra will avoid his eyes as she tells him; she will take the cowardly route. What's done is done, and she might as well say it, let it all fall apart.

She can see from his face how the news ricochets through his brain, how it cracks back and forth like a pinball not quite hitting its target. And she stares at the frothy sea as it laps around the posts that hold up the pier. Because she wishes she had something sturdy like that to hold herself up as she breaks his heart.

"Elizabeth is my daughter," she says—and as these words tumble out of her mouth, she feels the shock of a truth she never intended to tell burning her tongue, and knows that the intensity is so much worse for Herb . . .

She is not yours, nor is she Charlotte. This marriage that we've fought so hard for is a lie.

He is sixty years old, not an inchoate little boy. And as she watches him spread to a thin and watery layer on the ground, Myra sinks with him. She has broken him and wants to cut herself with the cold, biting wind—she holds her cheeks in her palms, waiting for the blow he's going to deliver.

Herb spits the fire from his lungs like a dragon. "None of this would have happened if . . ."

"If what Herb?" she says, her voice low and hard.

"Why did you give her away? She lived in poverty. And you've been waiting for our child, who has been dead for twenty years—"

"No, Herb. No, please don't say that." She blinks away tears. "I tried."

"She's dead." He clenches his jaw and turns away. "My child is dead. And I need to grieve for her now."

"Oh, Herb," she says, shaking her head. She crouches down and holds her face in her palms, pushing away her memories.

Myra doesn't know how not to love Herb.

"My intuition was wrong. Everyone else was right—I was in denial."

"Elizabeth lived in that trailer? Where Rosie lived?" His voice is harsh. "You gave her away to live in poverty."

"I did it for our marriage." She whispers, but her words are taken by the wind and tossed in the ocean. "I gave her money."

Herb clears his throat. "I would have forgiven you. I'm the one who left, Myra. To find myself in California." He laughs bitterly.

"Why can't you forgive me now?"

"You gave away a little girl and pretended she didn't exist. And that is a weak thing to do. At least I could respect you choosing her over me."

Her gaze trails away. Never in their marriage has he spoken to her like this. He's taking this so far they will never return from it.

"You should have told me and dealt with the consequences. How much planning did such a lie require? You gave birth to another man's child, gave this baby away. And managed to keep it a secret. For over thirty years?"

"Rosie loved her. I gave her to a loving mother."

He rubs his temples in circles. "Does Kenneth know? That he has a daughter?"

"Yes," she says, "but there was Adele to consider." She closes her eyes.

"Of course. Adele! Kenneth is such a stand-up guy. Is that why he's hanging around now?"

"Not exactly. I didn't know Elizabeth wasn't Charlotte. I haven't seen Elizabeth since she was four years old—I swear it."

"I suppose I shouldn't be surprised," he says, "with all of this." He waves his hand in the air.

Myra bites her lip, as if steeling for a blow to the chest. "And why do you feel that way, Herb?"

"You gave us all away to obsess over Charlotte. That's the truth of it. And I'm not sure I can forgive you for that." He turns his back to her, and before he goes, he says, "I'm sorry for all I've said. But you've gotta face this shit. Otherwise, there is absolutely nothing I can do for this marriage."

Her silver hair blows in her face like it always does on the pier. She grits her teeth. Drops of rain plop on the deck and hit her face. The cold still surprises her after all these years. The smell of fresh rain intermingles with the saltwater, and the air is thick with the marine layer.

"Get your kids. Put your living children first, for once in Elizabeth's life, for once in Jimi's life. And dammit, fix things with Gwen. That's my advice. As far as you and me—Myra, I can't speak to you another minute."

She hesitates. "Sarah thinks she's out for revenge. That we should find her, let the cops question her."

Herb looks at her squarely. "Someone has been spying on us for years. Someone nearly killed you. And it's a damn good thing this man is already dead . . . or I'd have killed him myself." He takes a breath. "But Elizabeth *is* your child." He leans closer, whispers, "Do not fail her now. Let her go."

"That was low, Herb."

He rolls his eyes. "Let's find out who's been stalking us. It sure as shit isn't Elizabeth. Maybe when she turned up, it instigated someone—I can't say."

"You're right," she says hoarsely. "I can't betray her. I need to let them go."

He turns his back to her and leans on the pier, staring out at the choppy sea. "Jimi needs you too."

A dull ache wedges itself in her head, the start of a migraine. "Do you have to pluck out all my failings in one day?"

Herb doesn't move, doesn't speak.

"I'll give you time." She walks away, watching the flickering lights from inside the house. And she wishes she could be young again, go back in time and sew her family whole.

CHAPTER THIRTY-THREE

GWEN

Gwen smooths her sweater. "I can't believe all of this. I just can't. It's been an insane few weeks." She shakes her head. "And this girl—my sister? Not Charlotte, but a sister my mother kept secret? I'm livid." She shivers.

"It is shocking," Kevin agrees, reaching for her hand.

She takes a deep breath. "Do you think she wants revenge, Kevin?"

He thinks a moment. "I actually don't think she did anything. You can tell she loves that little boy and that she's traumatized by what happened to them." He shrugs. "Anything is possible, I suppose. I just don't get that vibe."

"Don't you think it's a really fucking strange coincidence that my biological sister showed up in town right after killing that man?"

"Look, I'm not a cop. I think she decided it was her damn right to come home to family. And the abusive douchebag had friends."

"Maybe," she says, gulping her coffee, "maybe." She stands for a moment, watching the rain drip down the awning, and concentrates on the sound of water clanking against tin.

"Oh, come on, don't be mad. It's just a theory. I prefer to think there are a few decent people left on the planet."

"Why did she leave like that, then?"

"We would leave if our children were being chased by a lunatic," he says dryly. "At least I would."

"That's a shitty thing to say."

"I'm sorry all this is happening," says Kevin. He looks at her with placid blue eyes. "Really."

"That's why she consented to the DNA test." She nods to herself. "I bet she knew who she was."

He leans against the counter. "Well . . . if she hadn't gotten cornered at the hospital, she might not have consented regardless. And only stayed around 'cause Myra was so insistent we didn't need the test. You know?"

"I was so worried about my mother. And she's not innocent in this at all. I made Jimi apologize to her for his childishness, insisted he was wrong about her. And what happens? I have to explain that she's not actually Charlotte. But she *is* Mom's secret baby from an affair."

He shakes his head. "Let them work it out. We have our own children to parent. You aren't responsible for Jimi or your mom."

"You don't understand. Your parents spend most of their time golfing," she says bitterly.

"Stop. I keep my mouth shut around here—"

"Golfing and vacationing in the Bahamas."

"Ninety percent of the time," he continues. "I keep my thoughts to myself most of the time. Stop this battle with your mom. It doesn't matter if Myra still blames you. Or if she's just lost in her own world. This is our family, and it affects—"

"What? What does it affect? I do so much. So much to be a good mother, a good wife."

"It affects us all." He exhales.

"Whatever, Kevin." Her stomach twists. She loops her thumb around her jean pocket so she won't punch the man. "Kids and I are going sledding. The feng shui people are coming by your office at two." She stomps loudly up the stairs.

"Jesus," he mutters, "Have 'em feng-whatever this place too. You're stressing me out."

She swivels on her heel. "I heard that!"

*   *   *

Each time Gwen steps in the deep and crunchy snow, her foot sinks. It takes all of her strength to pull her boot out of the hole. Her fingers are like frozen sausages inside her gloves, and the vapor from her own breath is the only warmth. Rays of sunlight cut sharply through the trees, illuminating patches of snow where shimmering crystals of ice hide in the shadows. Gwen isn't a fan of coldness. It is so damned inconvenient, dressing children in fourteen layers of clothing, only to deal with half-frozen clothes melting all over her trunk.

It is time to go home. The girls will freeze in this.

The girls grumble and complain, but there are only a couple of hours of daylight remaining. They can't afford to stay outside as dusk sets and the temperature dips even lower. The sky fades to a powdery shade of blue, darkening with each passing moment. A hint of persimmon feathers the horizon, and swirls of wind smack her cheeks. The kids don't feel it yet. They've spent the past hour running like wild cheetahs with sleds.

The smell of pine and the richness of the earth wafts through the crisp air. But the thought of getting caught in the forest at night sends a chill through her. The fear is so intense that her hands shake and sweat runs down her neck. She tells herself not to be silly. It's only this stuff with Charlotte-Elizabeth that has her on edge.

They trudge for the SUV, which is less than a half mile from the deep woods. The girls drag their sleds, scraping them into tree branches, whining about the walk. Gwen ducks around low hanging pines. Occasionally she bumps into a branch, and it whips back. Crystals of ice smack at her cheeks. The inexplicable panic deepens with each flick of icy water. She should speak to Lisa, her therapist, about this. Her mother is driving her insane. She thinks of her girls, her sweet girls, and how she has worked so hard not to traumatize them. At least all their problems won't be her fault. They might develop bipolar disorder. But that's simple genetics. She sighs.

"You don't know how lucky you are," Gwen says, though she is annoyed at her frozen toes. "So many kids would kill to play in the snow like this."

Cora scoffs. She does this a lot lately.

Gwen ignores her. With night approaching, she focuses on returning to the car. They need to get back home. Kevin is waiting, probably roasting fresh salmon on his new George Foreman grill. He must be so excited about his new appliance. Gwen purchased it for him as a makeup gift and left it on the kitchen table with a bright red bow. Her love language is gifts.

It has gone quiet, except for the light scrape of boots and sleds against the slick ground. She clenches her fingers to help the blood circulate through her extremities.

"Gwen!" A voice echoes across the frosted landscape. She can't make out who it is, and she's not in the mood for socializing. Kevin probably sent one of the Girl Scout moms.

"Who is it?" she yells back.

The person darts toward her, dragging a child by the hand. Gwen's heartbeat speeds up. Why are they coming so fast?

"Savannah! Cora!" calls the child.

She squints, shading her eyes from the blood-red sun. The figures are shadowy against the backdrop of the setting sun, but she puts together the voices and the silhouettes.

Elizabeth and Theo. *Shit.*

Gwen waves as the distance closes between them. She pastes a smile on her face.

Elizabeth arrives at her side, out of breath, cheeks pink. Her face is dewy with sweat. She pats Theo's head. "We need to talk," she says, trying to catch her breath. "Kevin said you were up here."

"Right." She offers an apologetic shrug. "But we were just about to leave. Have you spoken with Myra?"

"No," she says warily. "Not since we left."

Ah. So she doesn't know that her lies have been exposed. Gwen decides not to get into it, not in front of the kids. "Anyway, we need to get going."

"That's fine," Elizabeth says in a low, cold voice Gwen hasn't heard from her before. "But first, we have something to discuss."

She shivers, rubs her hands together. "What do you want from my family—" Gwen notices Theo, standing right there. She bends down to his level. "Hey, buddy. Wanna play with the girls for a bit?" Gwen spies the girls, squealing just ahead. She waves them over. "Look, Theo is here," she says. "Why don't you go play?"

Savannah and Cora exchange a glance.

"I thought you left," Cora says to Elizabeth.

"Nope, we just had some errands to run." She narrows her eyes at Gwen. "We're back. Go on now, Theo. Stay where I can see you."

The three children dart off. With her gaze fixed on her son, Elizabeth says, "Tell me more about Jared Henderson."

"What are you talking about? I told you, he was my high school boyfriend." She's never heard Elizabeth speak so directly. Her tone is challenging, and Gwen doesn't like it. "You bailed town. Why don't you tell me about that?"

Elizabeth laughs. "Did you find your half of the necklace, Gwen? The piece engraved GB?"

"I . . . no, I haven't yet . . ." Her cheeks burn. Why is Elizabeth so obsessed with that necklace?

She reaches into her coat pocket and pulls something out of her pocket. She opens her palm, revealing a pile of coiled silver. Gwen recoils; she feels dizzy.

"What's that?" she says uneasily.

Elizabeth holds up one chain, lets it slide through her fingers. "This one I've been wearing all my life," she says softly. She holds up another chain. "And this one is yours."

"What the hell?" She snatches the necklace out of Elizabeth's hand and inspects it. GB is engraved on the heart. "Where did you find this?" she whispers.

"In Peter's things, at the cabin. Or, I should say, Patrick Jared Henderson."

"What? You could've gotten that necklace engraved anywhere. Maybe you got 'em both engraved to pull a scam on my mom," she hisses, anger flooding her veins. How dare this woman find her out here and spout accusations?

"Who the hell is this man?" Elizabeth screams. "You knew him. His rich parents uptown said you were his girlfriend."

Gwen freezes. She leans forward, palms on her jeans. "His parents?"

Elizabeth takes a newer photo out of her pocket, one where she and her husband are sitting together. He is clean-shaven and smiling, with his arm around her. It must have been taken shortly after they met. Elizabeth holds it inches from Gwen's face. "Is this Jared?"

She cannot take her eyes away from the photo, from Elizabeth sitting with him. "Yes, that's Jared. But I never gave him that necklace. I don't understand what you're talking about."

Elizabeth flinches, tears caught in her eyelashes.

"You have to believe me."

"I don't know if I can do that," Elizabeth says. "You were with him that night when he took her." She digs her heels into the snow. "And yes, I admit I'm not Charlotte. But you knew that, Gwen, didn't you? You knew that because the two of you did something to her. Why did he have that necklace?" She is shouting now, trembling.

Gwen takes a step back. "I swear . . . I don't know what you're talking about. Please, calm down!" She cups her hand around her ear, tuning out what Elizabeth is saying. "Wait . . ." She puts her finger to her lips.

Elizabeth goes silent, stares at her.

The landscape is darker, the smell of snow thicker. The children's laughter and bickering has stopped. She is no longer cold. Fear sends a shock of heat to the tips of her frozen fingers.

"Wait a minute," Gwen says. "Do you hear the kids?"

Elizabeth whispers, "No."

A bird creeps through the evergreen trees. Branches crack, breaking the silence.

"Savannah! Cora! Theo! It's cold. We're almost to the clearing," Gwen says.

"Careful not to slip on the ice," Elizabeth yells.

No one responds.

They pick up their pace. The thought of walking through the trees after dusk intensifies Gwen's fear, but she tries to act calm. The snow is less deep and crunchy, but the ice is slick and dangerous. She trudges cautiously, making sure each boot is firmly planted before moving the next. She wraps her arms around her chest, trying to warm herself.

"I'm sure they're just playing," she assures Elizabeth. Gwen calls again, annoyed.

No response.

Standing still as possible, she listens for the scrape of the sleds.

Nothing.

"Girls!" A wave of panic settles in her chest.

"Theo!" Elizabeth turns to her. "Why aren't they answering?"

Gwen's pulse accelerates. The eeriness is replaced by full-blown panic.

She watches, numbly, as Elizabeth takes off, running and slipping, falling and pulling herself up, into the woods. The photo of Jared slips from her hand, landing right in front of Gwen.

She picks it up and begins to move. "Elizabeth? Slow down."

The last thing she hears is one sharp sequence of noises: one piercing scream, scrambling bodies, a thud . . . it slips through her consciousness like a song playing too fast, with no pause, no mute, and certainly no way to rewind.

"What's happening?" she says, or maybe she just thinks this is what she's saying, because the next moment catapults her into action.

The red sled lies ahead, as if kicked off into the trees. Now she is running, running, the short distance to the heap of red. Shards of plastic from the broken sled scatter from the edge of trees onto the icy path. She yells the children's names and calls for Elizabeth. The words escape her lips without her permission. She operates on animal instinct.

Cora lies in a crumpled heap of pink—her snowsuit—with her blonde hair spread in waves around her.

"Cora!" she yells, stumbling over her boots to get to her child more quickly. Every move she makes is slow, numb. Cora seems to be miles from her. Gwen sinks to her knees. Her daughter is unconscious, a thin snake of blood running from her forehead and down her face. Her cheeks are flushed and sweaty. Gwen moves her head tenuously, not wanting to worsen Cora's injuries. The snow beneath her head is frosted crimson. The crystals shimmer with her daughter's blood. It is unreal. This cannot be real. She runs her fingers through Cora's hair and kisses her cheek, sobbing. "Cora, baby! Wake up. Wake up, please."

She is watching a movie of someone else's life. This must be someone else's life.

And when Cora begins to stir, she turns her head and scans the area. *Savannah,* she thinks. *Where is Savannah? Theo? Elizabeth?*

Cora's eyes flutter and she murmurs, "Mommy?" She groans, reaching for her head. "My head hurts."

"What happened? Where is everyone?"

Gwen fishes in her pocket for her phone. She dials 911. "My daughter is injured."

She remains calm, as instructed. She holds Cora's hand and reassures her that she will be okay, even as the sun fades into an inky night, and the deep forest shrouds the moon.

It is not until the ambulance sirens grow close and EMT's trample through the quiet woods with flashlights and flood-lights that she falls into despair: Savannah hasn't come back. She scans the area, but she can't see beyond the lights directed at Cora. The forest is cold and wet. Savannah is somewhere. Theo is somewhere. Elizabeth must have them. Gwen chokes on her tears. Elizabeth will bring the kids here soon. There was an accident. That's all.

"Where is Savannah? Cora, where is your sister?"

"I don't know," she says.

"Where is Savannah?"

This is unthinkable. This moment is absolutely unimaginable.

"I don't remember Mommy. I don't remember anything at all. I'm just so cold."

* * *

That's when Gwen hears tires shriek and crunch on the ice. She peers into the darkness, unable to make out anything. "Savannah!" She screams until her voice is raw. "Elizabeth," she screams, thinking how, this feels like déjà vu, like the moment on the beach is happening all over again.

"Mommy!"

Gwen is running again. She glances behind her at the EMTs caring for Cora. Gwen trips over her boots and falls, pulls herself up, falls again.

Cora is with the EMTs, but her mother has left her. Gwen is caught between her children. She cannot make it to either of them quickly enough. The push and pull—it is a band squeezing her heart.

The sequence repeats a million times.

Savannah meets her halfway. Fluorescent lights spread over the snow, casting an unnatural glow over her eldest daughter's face.

Savannah manages to climb through the thickening snow and into her mother's arms. "There was a man." She is out of breath, panting. "In a truck. He tried to grab Cora and she fell. He tried to drag her away from me, and I threw a big rock. The sled slammed into the tree."

"Savannah," Gwen says softly, "where are Elizabeth and Theo?"

"Mommy, that's the thing." Her voice trembles; she is so out of breath Gwen can hardly hear what she says. "They're gone. Elizabeth and Theo are gone."

Charlotte . . . Charlotte . . . Charlotte.

I've lost her again.

Gwen unclenches her palm to see Jared staring back at her with sea-green eyes.

The EMTs' words swirl outside Gwen's brain. She is watching. Their lips move in a jumbled cadence that resembles speech, but all Gwen hears is, "A man tried to grab Cora." Her daughters are with her, and it registers that their breath is hot. They are speaking.

They are alive.

"I threw a rock and chased him."

Savannah saved her sister's life.

"I threw a rock at him just like he threw one at Cora, Mommy. But then when Cora fell, he took Theo—he had a gun. And the next thing I knew, they were gone."

"Where was the truck?" says someone. It may be Gwen's own voice, but her brain is so muddled she cannot tell.

"Over where we parked," she says, breathlessly. "I know we were supposed to wait. I'm sorry."

That was why the sleds stopped scraping the packed ice. But he was here for her sister. He took her sister again.

Gwen folds Savannah in her arms. The EMTs lift the gurney up, with a click of metal, and slide it over the embankment to the ambulance. But the police move fast. It must be a good sign that the EMTs are moving slowly to avoid slipping on the ice. Someone tucks an aluminum blanket around Cora. She shivers, her lips milky-blue. Gwen runs her fingers gently over her cheek. "You're okay." They lift the gurney into the ambulance. Savannah and Gwen hop into the back, and her mind opens up, like it is defrosting. She comforts her children as she is supposed to. She transcends her fear and slips back into logic.

"Find my sister and her son." She kisses Savannah on the forehead. "Wait. Wait here. She's okay, right?"

"Yes, and the police are looking—"

Gwen backs out of the ambulance. Red and blue lights swirl through the parking lot, shining against the snowy embankment. The parking lot is filled with them. Sweat drips down her neck. She approaches the police, huddled around a small car. Hadn't Savannah said there was a truck? Maybe she'd heard wrong.

She approaches a cop who is speaking into a walkie-talkie. "Well, are they here? What about the truck my daughter mentioned?"

He shakes his head. "No ma'am. We're searching, I promise. But nothing yet. And this small car is the only vehicle in the area."

Gwen's stomach roils, her limbs go numb, and she feels herself losing her balance.

CHAPTER THIRTY-FOUR

MYRA

Myra watches quietly as her daughter paces back and forth in her dining room. She isn't about to question Gwen when she's in shock like this. Myra is trembling and confused, trying to piece together what the hell happened. The kitchen is a blur of blue uniforms. Fear oozes off Gwen and penetrates the pores of everyone buzzing around the granite island. Everyone fills up on coffee and attempts to keep up with each new issue Gwen finds to be angry about. Myra puts her hands over her eyes and tries to clear her mind. Even Kevin speaks softly and keeps his distance.

Myra realizes that Gwen is terrified. She's experienced it herself. She just doesn't understand why Gwen is so vicious when she's afraid. Why she seems to hate Myra for this.

"Explain what happened again, ma'am."

Gwen tells her story again. This picture of Jared Henderson, her high school boyfriend, lies on the table. With both necklaces.

The sight of him makes her cry. He took her child. She knows it now, must face it now. But at this moment, she takes a breath because it is Gwen who needs her, who has to get these cops to understand what happened, when she's damn near hysterical.

Elizabeth and Theo. Someone has them. Yet Myra is so numb, shocked. She can't quite wrap her brain around this. *Is this real?* The fresh grief and terror roll through her, because she's lost two children in one day. They have to find Elizabeth. They have to find Theo. This cannot be happening again. She'd thought somehow her family was inoculated against another loss. No. Lightning statistically rarely strikes twice. This cannot happen again.

The cop begins once more. "So let me get this straight. Your high school boyfriend kidnapped your sister. And then he came back and kidnapped another sister. Except he's dead. With all due respect—"

"Don't speak to my daughter that way," Myra interjects. "Find Elizabeth and Theo."

"We're on your side, here, I promise," he says. "We've put out an Amber alert. I need the details right. That's all."

Myra sighs. "I know it. This is all so stressful. All so devastating. And we have lived with it for decades." Maybe it is time to shut down the inn and move on. Maybe they should all change their names and move away. Where might they go? If Myra and Herb give up the inn, who will they be?

Savannah and Cora sit together, holding hands, on the sofa and answer the myriad of questions thrown at them. Little Cora's head is wrapped in white gauze, and her lip is swollen and red. The dog yips and scurries toward the couch. She hops on Savannah's lap and licks her face.

Herb focuses on the girls, stroking his neck.

Myra watches Gwen, dazed by it all herself, before she finally says, "What happened with Charlotte wasn't your fault at all. And what happened today is not your fault either. We will find them." She clears her throat. "We will."

"What the hell are you talking about, Mother?"

"Maybe you feel badly that Savannah found Cora—"

"And I just left Charlotte to die? Is that what you're saying? 'Cause even if that's how you feel, I hardly think this is the time to bring it up."

Myra sighs. "Why must you be so mean? I'm trying to help—"

"I lost Elizabeth. And Theo. He's a little boy. I am losing my shit, and you bring up Charlotte now?"

Myra bites her lip for a moment and finally whispers, "Let's just get through this moment. Okay?"

"Let's get through this *together*?" Gwen shakes her head. "Interesting. Because I don't remember there being a 'together' between you and me. Not ever."

"I admit, I was distracted. But right now, we are focused on solving this problem." An overwhelming sadness sinks and spreads within her like a disease, because this is true. It's all true. She gave all her love to a ghost.

She had thought Gwen was an independent child, one who didn't need as much nurturing as she'd expected. Other toddlers seemed glued to their mother's legs, craved attention, whereas Gwen would lean in for a hug only now and then. Otherwise, she was quite content to play alone or with her little friends. Myra remembers watching those cuddly babies—clingy! said the mommies, nodding at one another, commiserating—and she felt a bone-deep envy.

"*Oh, but you're so lucky,*" they said. "*To have a bit of time to yourself. My little one won't let me use the bathroom alone!*" Myra could tell this was only a half complaint. Beneath the neediness was a hard truth. "*My baby,*" they said without words, "*loves me. Maybe yours just doesn't love you all that much.*" Myra found herself jealous of the tantrums the babies threw when their mothers dropped them off with a sitter. "*Separation anxiety,*" the other mothers said. "*It's completely normal.*" Was it normal that Gwen simply hugged her goodbye and ran off to play?

That was what Myra took from it anyway. Gwen wanted Herb's attention aplenty. Her eyes glowed when he was present. She tugged at his finger to show him one painted glitter-glue project or another and insisted he build big towers of blocks for her to send crashing to the ground, giggling with delight.

The year Herb was gone, Gwen suddenly wanted her attention. The little girl would climb into the king-size bed, in Herb's spot, and cuddle up to her mother. Herb had not only left his wife but his daughter too, and Myra was furious about it. Gwen followed Myra around the inn, wanting her to play tea party and Candyland, and this sent an unexpected swell of joy through her. Gwen stroked her mother's cheek with her tiny fingers and said, "Don't worry, Mommy. It will be all right."

Myra decided she didn't care if Herb ever returned. She and Gwen had each other. Gwen was the little girl Myra had expected to have. Her cheeks burn with shame, thinking back on that time. Because if Herb never came back, Gwen would love her best. She would hate her father for leaving, take her mother's side. Myra would have a Velcro child, just like the other moms. And she could commiserate with them, all while an incomprehensible delight rose in her chest.

When Herb returned, Gwen reverted to her catlike independence, except now her coldness extended to her father. He felt so lost, so guilty. And Myra patted his back, assuring him that Gwen would be back, would love him with the same intensity as she had when she was three. Myra said tenderly that she was oh so sorry.

Secretly, she could hardly keep her lips from curling upward. Herb deserved this. It was his own doing.

* * *

Now, Gwen stares blankly, shoulders slumped. Her tears seem to catch and dry before they can slide down her cheeks. Myra braces herself for what Gwen will say next.

Herb gets up from the coach and pads toward Gwen. "Please don't speak to your mother like that." He puts his arm around her. "Don't say things you can't take back," he says, addressing both Myra and Gwen.

Myra steadies her posture. She tells the police, "He kidnapped my daughter and grandson. He nearly kidnapped my granddaughters. Whoever he is."

She can hear the policeman's radio crackle. His eyes are empathetic and soft. She squints to get a look at his name. "Officer Richardson. Can you imagine if this was your child?"

"No, ma'am. I can't. I'm just trying to get an accurate assessment of our perp so we can cover all our angles. The kids escaped. That helps." He sighs. "But the first day or two is vital in terms of catching him—"

Myra winces, a familiar pain radiating through her chest. "Or we won't find them alive."

"The chances are significantly lower," he says softly.

"All right. What now? What do we do now?" Gwen's voice rises.

Myra puts an arm around Gwen to steady her shaking body. "It's okay. You thought quick. It's all going to be okay."

"Savannah, what did you see again? Do you remember what this man looked like?"

"He threw the rock. And he took Theo. That's all I saw." Savannah's lower lip quivers. "I can't remember anymore, Mommy."

Officer Richardson says, "Right. Which means man is involved with Henderson, somehow. I've got someone headed to the parents' house, now that his body has been identified. We have to notify them, of course."

Myra stands up, paces to the kitchen. "Herb, what do we do?" she says, before realizing they aren't partners; there isn't a "we" anymore.

Herb shakes his head, and she can't tell if he's trying to dispel her fears about their marriage or if he's just in shock. "We wait," he says softly. "Like last time."

She puts her head in her hands and cries. This can't be like last time. It can't.

Gwen rakes her hands through her hair. "Where do we go? Nowhere is safe. This crackpot son of a bitch is stalking us. All of us."

Officer Richardson paces the length of the kitchen and finally continues, "I think we need to keep officers here on alert." He turns toward the other officers. "Keep that Amber alert. Question the parents. These things are usually very closely linked to the home."

Gwen meanders into the living room and settles between her girls. "Are you saying Jared's whole family is in on this? Maybe they wanted Theo back. He's technically their grand-kid." She stops for a moment and then holds her pointer finger in the air. "Maybe that's it. They wanted Theo and Elizabeth."

Myra's stomach swims. "What if they walked into the arms of a family of killers?"

"Let's not make that leap," Officer Richardson says.

"Okay," Gwen says. She puts her arm around Cora. "It's probably best not to talk anymore here. To let the girls rest."

"Agreed." Richardson takes his coffee cup into the kitchen. "I'll get the squad cars here to keep watch." He raises his voice. "We will find them, Mrs. Barkley. We have to."

CHAPTER THIRTY-FIVE

GWEN

A cop car waits in Gwen's driveway to protect her daughters from this hell she's caused. Her children are traumatized—Gwen has already called Lisa for a referral to a child psychologist—maybe she can fix her daughters. But she thinks Elizabeth and Theo may be dead by now, and she's not sure how she's going to live with herself. *Please, please let them be found.*

The neighbors are probably on the phone with real estate agents in case the Barkleys have spread their curse farther and wider than before. She can hear her mommy friends whispering about her. The news has gone viral, and the kidnapper is closing in on them.

Jared is Peter. He *was* Peter. Gwen understands, sees it now. She has always known he had the answers, somewhere in her consciousness. Why else would he disappear like that?

She remembers how he screamed at her. His jealous messages. But when Gwen complained about him, her friends had said how lucky she was to have a boy like Jared. They said she had unrealistic expectations.

Boys are just like that sometimes, they'd said knowingly. *You should be grateful. He's right, you are kinda demanding.*

Gwen hadn't felt respected, hadn't felt loved. After Charlotte disappeared, she questioned her intuition again and again. She remembers that spark of rage in Savannah's eyes when she announced she had thrown a rock at the man who stole her sister. Pride bubbles through every molecule of Gwen's body. Oh, how she wishes she were that strong. All the primal screaming in the world will not heal her soul, not this time.

She pads into the closet and rams her face into a soft stack of laundry and screams. Gwen needs to put all her coping strategies to use and stay strong. The cotton is streaked with her saliva. Her girls are home, but Elizabeth and Theo are gone. She shoves her face back into the pile of clothing.

Gwen's ears perk up at the sound of footsteps knocking up the stairs. She holds herself straight and peeks through the sliver of light that illuminates the bedroom.

"God, are you okay?" He scans the bed, where the girls sleep, cuddled up against one another. Cora sucks her thumb, a habit she'd stopped two years before.

She lays her head on her husband's shoulder. He runs his fingers through her hair. "I thought I heard screaming," he whispers. His neck is moist with sweat. "Can we go downstairs and talk? I don't want to wake them."

She bites her lip, thinking. "The cops are still outside?"

"Yes. Come down and have a glass of wine with me, babe."

They step around the one creaky floorboard in the house, right beside their bed. This always annoyed her, but tonight she simply steps past it. She turns to take one last look at her children before they sneak down the stairs. Gwen squeezes her eyes like the shutter of a camera, trying to superimpose the image in her brain so she will never forget. Someday they will be teenagers; they might not be best friends, but she will have the memory of the time they loved each other more than anything. That time has passed for Gwen and her sisters.

She takes a bottle of white wine out of the fridge and plunks it between her and Kevin. He uncorks it and flashes her a tired smile. She inhales the crisp scent of rose. Sinking into the barstool beside him, she stares at the counter. The wine glugs as he pours them each a generous amount. He clinks his glass to hers. "Here's to my wife's smart thinking."

Gwen offers a weak smile. "What if they can't find them?"

"They will."

"I have something to tell you," she says, raising her chin. "This is my fault."

A series of images flickers through Gwen's mind. She remembers playing at the inn with her friends. Her mother insisted that she play with the maid's daughter. Gwen didn't want to. She was just one of those children. Her mother had tried—in Gwen's mind—to force her to play with this girl, who was far too little to be any fun. Gwen hadn't understood it. Gwen called her names. Made fun of her. Really, she said anything she could think of to make the small toddler go away.

She had been a *bully*.

"How can this possibly be your fault?"

"Kevin, I was terrible to her as a child. I bet she remembers. And I might never have a chance to apologize."

He holds her shoulders firmly. "You were just a little girl. A mean thing to do? Yes. But that isn't why Elizabeth is here now."

"I'm one of the evil bullies I give talks about. I didn't even feel guilty at the time, Kevin. It wasn't till many years later." She grips the glass tightly. "I was not a good person." The glass slips from her hand and smashes onto the ceramic tile. She paces across the kitchen, ignoring the shards of glass scattered in all directions. Blood drips from the soles of her feet, smearing on the white flooring and then the carpet as she moves.

"Gwen, you're bleeding." The edge in his voice ripples through her mind.

"Charlotte will never be found," she whispers. "Not ever. I can never go back and change that night."

"This is not then," Kevin says. "Hope is not lost."

Kevin guides her into the bathroom. She crouches on the floor beside the toilet, watching droplets of blood trickle into puddles. "Where could they be? Something has happened to them. This won't end well."

"You might need stitches," says Kevin, focusing on her foot.

"Ouch! Dammit it. I do not need stitches." Numbly, she moves her ankle into her lap and digs slivers of glass from her foot, tossing them methodically in the garbage.

"Your left foot is bleeding a lot."

She catches his despairing eyes. His parents are so incredibly normal. His mother plays fucking bingo at the community center, and his father is a lawyer. Kevin must have felt so damned secure as a child. He's in over his head. She is out of his scope. Gwen tried to be a normal mother. She runs a Girl Scout troop and teaches those kids their value; they read intersectional literature. They march together and learn important lessons such as how to change their own flat tire. She has analyzed every angle about how to survive life as a woman in this world, and the other moms respect her for it.

But now? Well, who wants to send their kid sledding with an unfit parent who attracts kidnappers? This does not instill confidence in her ability to organize a playdate. Raising strong girls is all good until real danger puts little children in harm's way. Not only will Cora and Savannah have PTSD, they'll also be friendless.

Like Elizabeth.

She is so very dizzy.

"Hon, can you do me a favor?" she says, hanging her head between her knees. "Check on the girls. And bring me my phone."

Kevin finishes inspecting her foot. She hadn't noticed him working out the rest of the slivers with tweezers or wrapping the left foot in gauze. She smiles. "Thank you for being you."

"I'll be back with the phone. I'm sure the kids are fine. Asleep in our bed. That's what the cops are here for." He kisses the top of her head, and she wonders why he loves her. She has spent so much time rebuilding herself that she's not sure which Gwen she is anymore. Is she the jealous bully who snuck her kid sister out at night over a boy? Or is she the Instagram brand she has curated? Her head pounds.

Oh, the roles we play, Gwen thinks. We act so many parts. Elizabeth is a human on a stage, just like the rest of us. She has manipulated no more strings than Gwen or her mother or even her father. Gwen molds herself to meet the expectations of others. And she has also expected too much. From herself. From her mother. And now, from Elizabeth Lark. Both of them have been forced to contort and twirl like marionettes on a stage.

"Here's your phone." Kevin interrupts her racing thoughts. "Maybe we can move to the couch. You don't need to sit here on the bathroom floor all night."

"I'm fine," she says, glowering.

"What?" He throws his hands up.

She clenches her jaw. "I just want to sit here with my phone. Maybe you should go lie down with our daughters. I'm not a very good mother, it seems."

"Come on."

"Seriously, just go. I want to be alone."

"All right," he says, and heads toward the stairs. "Have it your way."

Gwen limps into the kitchen and pours herself another glass of wine. Something isn't sitting right with her. Elizabeth mentioned Jared's parents. Is it possible they'd know a little more than they told the police? Maybe if she went to the doorbell and begged, feigned some sort of grief over Jared's death? She has to do *something*. She can't just sit around and wait for the cops to find Elizabeth and Theo's bodies. Because if they aren't found alive now, they never will be. Maybe his parents will give her information about that night. Or where he went twenty years ago. Gwen could tell them that she was his old girlfriend. The word sends a chill down her spine.

Girlfriend. Goosebumps prickle her flesh.

A short drive up the hill—that's all it is. She wraps her foot in another bandage and leaves.

*   *   *

The clouds smother the moon tonight; not a speckle of light punctuates the darkness. Her headlights are insufficient to illuminate the road ahead. She travels through a deep wooded area, up the hill toward the parents' house. It's just beyond this stretch of wilderness. Gwen tightens her grip on the steering wheel and switches the radio off. She can hardly see. This road wouldn't be easy under any circumstances, as she can't remember the last time she drove alone at night. She and Kevin hardly leave the girls after dark, and when they do, he is behind the wheel. This thought, in itself, fuels her desire to do something, to fix this on her own.

The wind buffets the car, and it takes all of her concentration to keep her car aligned with the curves of the road. Her tires hum over the wet asphalt. It smells like rain, thick and heavy in the air. She wants to get through this patch of darkness before the storm catches up to her. A splinter of lightning whips across the sky, but it is far off. Gwen isn't afraid of storms—of course she isn't, growing up in Oregon. It's just so very dark.

As the car winds up the hill, she tries so hard to put the pieces of that evening together. The bits are scattered; from the instant she realized Charlotte was gone, the urgency intensified and so did her panic. The same feeling had pulled at her in the snow when everyone went missing, leaving her alone, trying to find them before sunset. She rolls down the window a couple of inches, lets the air cool her face. The houses get larger, the lawns more expansive as she drives. She had no idea her boyfriend's family was so wealthy. Staring ahead, she pushes away the inadequacy she feels around one percenters and tries to form a plan. Elizabeth had said the Hendersons remembered she had dated Jared. She can use this.

Gwen pulls up beside the Hendersons, grateful that the cops have left. She will offer them condolences, really use this ploy to get information. They must know who he was friends with more recently, right? Maybe, as his first love, she can dig more out of them. Yes, this is what she'll do.

She sits in front of the house, car idling, hands sweaty and gripping the steering wheel. It takes her a moment to gather her courage. Her sister is the missing one, she reminds herself. The Hendersons *have* to talk to her.

She climbs out of the car and moves confidently down the long path to the front door. The neighbor's light flickers on. Probably nervous from all the police activity today. Someone steps outside, craning their neck her way. Gwen squints, tries to get a look at the neighbor who had no clue who she was living next door to. Shit, if they've lived here long enough, they've probably heard of Charlotte's case.

The woman continues to walk swiftly down her driveway, as if she's coming over to speak with her, and Gwen is not in the mood to gossip with the neighbor. She feels the expletives working their way up her throat, but she pushes them down. No need to be rude because of her own fucked-up life. It's not the neighbor's fault she lives in a mansion. She's also wearing a dress and heels at this hour. Gwen focuses on the Henderson's door. This is where she's going; she can't get distracted now.

And then the woman is waving at her. As the distance between them closes, she looks very familiar. Gwen steps closer. The woman is calling her over. Her auburn hair glints under the porchlight. God who *is* that?

"Gwen?"

She freezes, locks eyes with the woman. "Adele?"

"Why, yes," the woman says, "come over, dear. I can't believe all that's happened today."

She sighs. Not now. "Why don't you drop by the inn? It's been an awful day, and I need to get home soon."

Adele's face falls. "Ken is staying there. I can't possibly come by. But if you have to go . . ."

That's right, Gwen thinks. *Ken's at the inn.* She hadn't known precisely where he lived, but she's not exactly surprised either. Rocky Shores is a very small town. And this is the only multimillion-dollar neighborhood, unless you count the three or four houses directly on the beach with lots of property. Everyone knows the families that live there too.

He's at the inn *often.* And he's about to be permanently in the doghouse. She wonders if Adele knows yet. Gwen groans. She hopes this won't be a discussion about Ken and her mother.

"Okay," she says, "but just for a moment." She'll drop back by the Hendersons in fifteen minutes, max.

Gwen follows Adele into the house. It's even more impressive inside. The house extends backward; she couldn't make out how huge it is from the driveway. Oak floors gleam, polished to a shine. Buttery leather couches surround a roaring fire. A circular staircase leads to the second level. She peers into the kitchen. It's the size of her entire first floor. Mom said Kenneth was wealthy, but she hadn't said he was *this* rich.

"How are you, dear?" Adele says. "I heard about Charlotte. And that she is missing again. I am so sorry." She shakes her head. "Why are you up this way?"

"I have an appointment with your neighbors," she says, unsure what Adele knows about her neighbors, about how much to reveal.

"I saw the cops there earlier." Adele smooths her dress. "I wondered what might be going on."

Gwen relaxes. So that's what this is about. The woman is curious. Still, she's not supposed to say anything about the investigation. "Right," she says. "Not sure about that." Her voice is thick. She blinks away tears. "I'm not at liberty to say anything."

"I'm so sorry. This must be hell. Here I've been, all worried about Kenneth, about my marriage. And you have real problems." She shakes her head. "What do they say? Count your blessings? Check your privilege?"

"Something like that. I need to do it too." She is distracted, not in the mood for this. "I should go. It's been a very bad day, looking for Elizabeth and her son."

"I understand," Adele says. "Tell Kenneth I miss him, if you see him."

"Sure." She turns on her heel, about to leave, when she stops herself. "Have you noticed anything about your neighbors? About their son maybe?"

"Not much." She shrugs. "Years ago, I guess there was some trouble with him. Ken tried to help, to mentor the boy. I thought it was because we never had kids. He hadn't wanted them, but maybe he regretted our decision? Can't say, really. Too late to speculate. Why?"

"Ken mentored him?" Gwen's brain starts moving. "Like they worked together?"

"I guess. Kenneth has a garage. He has a classic car collection. I guess he was just showing it to Jared. Boys like that kind of thing." Something in her face clouds, something very subtle, but Gwen catches it.

"Cool," she says, beginning to shake. "Could I see? I love classic cars too."

"Oh no. I'm afraid Ken keeps that all locked up. I don't even have a key." She points to the wall. "See, the wall there rolls open. So does the one on the other side of the room, in case he ever takes one of those vehicles out. He says it's his man cave." She laughs. "We have bigger problems than his car collection, I'm afraid."

"So he never lets you in, but he let the neighbors' kid in?" Gwen cocks an eyebrow, scans the living room for anything out of place.

She's paranoid again. *Stop it,* she tells herself.

"I suppose so," Adele says. "Men are weird. I have my craft room, though. My walk-in closet. He doesn't go in there."

"Makes sense." Gwen smiles. "I'd better get going."

She waves goodbye and takes a few steps down the path. Again she stops. "Adele?"

"Yes, did you forget something?" Adele stands in the doorway, rubbing her shoulders because of the cold.

"I was just wondering. For all this time, all I've been told is that Ken works for your father. What exactly do they do?"

"Oh, that's all very complex. Computer systems for large companies, security. They have contracts with Boeing and Amazon."

She perks up. "Security? You mean like security cameras and computers?"

"I think so. I don't really keep up with it all—"

"Thanks, Adele. I'm sorry, I was just curious. I really ought to get going. Need to visit your neighbors really quickly." She waves again, moves swiftly down the long driveway. Except she doesn't go to the Hendersons'. Instead, she leans against her car and pretends to scroll through her phone. She wishes there was a way to get into that garage. But there have to be cameras everywhere, alarms. There isn't a way to go skulking around Ken's property without getting caught.

But Ken is Elizabeth's father. Ken is always at that inn. He lives next door to Jared.

Pretty much anyone who has a connection to Jared is suspect. It's just a feeling. Feelings are not facts, her therapist says. But she's ignored her gut before, and that didn't end well.

Gwen doesn't need to talk to the Hendersons. She needs to find Ken.

She gets in the car and squeals down the road. To the inn. She's got to get to her mother. The mantra repeats, over and over. *Get to that inn. Get to Mom.*

Jared had liked Charlotte, she remembers. He had commented on her cuteness and said things like, "Oh come on Gwennie, let her go with us." Probably he liked her because Gwen didn't. This is what she understands now. It was more manipulation, designed to create a deeper chasm between her and Charlotte. Charlotte was so little, so sweet, but her charms didn't work on Gwen. But that only made Charlotte try harder. All the pictures she painted for Gwen—tossed in the trash. The engraved necklace—lost.

Wait.

Gwen had worn the necklace that evening. She did! Yes, it was how she got Charlotte to come with her.

She applied her makeup while Charlotte complained.

"We'll wear our new necklaces," Gwen said. "We'll be like twins. I'll put lip gloss on you too."

Charlotte reluctantly agreed.

Where did the necklace go? Jared slapped her. She swung back. It must have come loose during their scuffle. Gwen is not one to endure such bullshit at the hands of a man, yet she didn't think to mention that he'd hit her when she spoke to the police.

But he'd helped with the search. He seemed heavy with remorse.

Then he disappeared.

"This isn't a kidnapping," Sarah Marlow had said. "There's no evidence of that, and abductions are incredibly rare. We are looking at a little girl who disappeared within yards of rough water."

Kidnappings may be rare, but rare things have to happen to someone. Where did he take her sister when she was commiserating with her friends? Could Gwen have saved her if she'd told the police these brutal, buried truths?

It's important to break the pattern, Lisa says. Or did Lisa say that? Maybe this has been Gwen's mantra all along. Is it true that Myra loved too little?

No, Gwen realizes. Her mother loved her plenty. She gave all she could. And that was enough.

Kenneth could be inside her mother's house right now. She can't bear to think like this. Her head aches. She arrives at the inn, releases a breath. Rushing for the door, she hopes with all her heart that her instinct is wrong. That she's overreacting, taking things to the nth degree again.

The door is locked, enveloped in blackness. Probably no guests. Her parents must be at the house. There is a key under the flowerpot—or there was, when she was a kid. She lifts the heavy ceramic and reaches into muddy water until she hears the plunk of a small piece of metal on cement. *Aha!* It's a little rusty, and she fiddles with the door for a moment before it flies open. A weird, almost electric instinct rushes to the tips of her fingers, and Gwen can't ignore this feeling. Not this time. She flips on the light switch and steps into her father's office. The key to his safe hangs on the hook beside the cards to the guest rooms. Inside is a gun. Gwen opens the safe, loads the gun, and shoves it in her coat pocket.

Gwen uses her father's landline to call Kevin. It's late. She considers what to say, but mostly she wants to make sure he's okay before she calls the cops.

Christ, her hands tremble.

One ring, two, three . . .

"Hello?" His voice is thick with sleep.

"I'm at my mom's."

"Did something happen?" he asks, a bit more alert.

"I was just upset. I don't feel like driving home. Okay, sweetie?"

"If you're sure."

"I hear Mom. Gotta go."

She hangs up and calls 911.

CHAPTER THIRTY-SIX

ELIZABETH

She wakes beneath a crisp white duvet, swallowed by a bed as large as any she's ever seen. Her fingers instinctively reach for her cheek, which is hot, tender, and scraped. Everything spins; translucent colors dance in her vision. Pieces of things, a sliver of a moment, a microcosmic bit of a conversation—they are torn, almost unintelligible now. A mosaic she can't put together.

Where are they?

Theo is holding her hand. She senses the worry in his downcast eyes, so she squeezes it, tries to reassure him. His eye is black, but he is wearing a fluffy white robe, and they're in a giant room that smells clean and new. She sees a beveled end table and a crystal-clear glass of water sitting on it. Using every muscle in her body—oh god, her muscles, flesh, bones throb with pain—she pulls herself to a seated position. She turns her neck a millimeter at a time and says to Theo, "Are you okay? Did they catch him?" This must be the hospital. Elizabeth reaches for the water.

"No!"

She turns around too quickly, wincing in agony. "What?" Her vision sharpens. Alice's voice echoes through the mostly bare room. Two giant beds. Two glass tables. White walls. She runs her fingers down her soft, terry-cloth robe. It's thicker and more luscious than any piece of clothing she's ever owned. *What the hell?*

Alice's dark-brown skin looks pinched. Her lip is bleeding. "Don't drink the water," she says hoarsely.

Elizabeth stares at Alice. Her stomach lurches. A memory comes to her. The snow, yes, they were in the snow, trudging after Gwen. The children, missing. How she'd run and run, only to be dragged to that truck. She takes a painful breath; her bones must be bruised. Theo is with them. He is alive, doesn't appear injured except for his eye.

"Who hit you?" she asks, checking him over.

"The guy who wanted me to shut up."

Savannah. Cora. Gwen. Her heart pounds, breath catches. "What about—"

"The girls escaped. He didn't want them anyway. He wanted you and Theo." Alice coughs violently into her elbow. "And I wasn't letting you go, so here we are." She waves her arm. The stark white paint is suddenly macabre. "And whatever that shit was, some drug . . . my head is pounding like I've been on a weeklong bender."

"Who is *he*?"

"Beats the shit out of me. What the hell are we dressed for? Indoctrination into a religious cult, maybe. This is so creepy." There is one square window in the middle of the room. She climbs out of bed, stomps toward it, and bangs on the glass. "Hey! I know you can see us. Come out and tell us who you are."

The cameras in Myra's shed. This person put the cameras there. Hacked the system. And he's watching them right now.

Theo grabs Elizabeth's sore arm. "We're at some rich person's house, and I'm not staying here." His eyes are fiery. He follows Alice to the window, pounds on it. The sound reverberates through the room. "I want *out*."

It occurs to Elizabeth that he's on the verge of a tantrum. She shrugs. He's not going to behave anymore, and she's *proud* of this.

They're being held hostage, just like before. "Alice," she says, racking her brain, trying to remember. "Who took us? I remember running for the kids. I remember being jabbed with the needle. The rest is blank as these walls."

"I was at the car, waiting for you," Alice says. "And I heard screaming. I don't think he expected me to whip out my gun. But he was fast . . . it was all so fast. He knocked the gun from my hand, shoved the needle in my arm." She addresses Theo. "What do you remember?"

"He just talked. On and on. I kinda blanked out what he was saying because Mommy looked so sick."

"Well, did you recognize his voice?" Alice presses.

"I don't know." He stomps his foot. "I don't know."

"Shh, it's okay," Elizabeth says. She pulls herself up. Every muscle in her body feels tenuously attached. "Look at that." She shivers uncontrollably.

In the center of the wall is a single painting. Charlotte Barkley's infant face, cut out from Myra's canvas, with frayed edges, is pasted crudely on a blank canvas. It is so white it would blend in with the wall if not for its thickness. Only a light shadow spills off the edges.

"Oh Elizabeth. What the fuck are we into?"

"Doesn't matter. All that matters is getting out." Her throat is constricting, the walls restricting, consuming the air.

Theo looks faint.

"Sit down," Elizabeth says. "Please."

He ignores her, looks through the window and bangs again, over and over, screaming, "Who are you?"

No answer.

The first thing they need to figure out is where they are. Clearly not a cabin in the woods. But something about this place feels colder than a frozen winter. She senses finality.

She can't panic—*won't* panic—not now. There has to be a way to escape. But she can't know how till she finds out the location. Theo and Alice are asking the wrong question.

"Where are we?" she says, addressing the window. Her voice is steady.

A speaker crackles. She jumps. "Where are we?" she repeats.

"Don't you want to know who I am? How this all happened?" A voice bellows through speakers in each corner of the empty room.

"Not really," she says honestly. "Maintain your anonymity, asshole. You think it's safer. I relish in the fact you have no identity. Not to me."

He laughs, not a deep and threatening laugh, but as if this amuses him. It sends a flicker of anger through her, a spark that could burn this whole place down.

Alice is wide-eyed, speechless. Theo kicks the wall. Elizabeth stares straight ahead, right through the window. She focuses; she can't let her focus waver.

"You sure about that?" he says.

None of them speak. It's what he wants: to be begged, to be important. Elizabeth isn't giving him what he wants. Alice and Theo are not giving him a damn thing.

"I gave you so many chances, darling."

An image is projected on the wall. She gasps, looks at Alice. It's a house, a huge house with sculptured rose bushes in the front.

Peter's parents' house.

"Holy shit," says Alice. "Are you—"

"John Henderson?" After a long pause, he says, "No. They don't know a damn thing about where their son disappeared to, and if you'd told them he was dead, they would've probably paid you for killing him," he says. "They're scared of him. You're currently next door. I'm a concerned neighbor is all. That disturbed boy's been in some trouble, hasn't he?"

She grits her teeth. "What chances have you given me?"

The projector cuts out. The crackling speaker goes silent.

The wall slides open, slowly, revealing a sprawling living space. A double fireplace is the centerpiece, surrounded by leather couches. The contrast between the home and this room is sharp.

Kenneth stands between the two rooms.

"Adele must have decorated the house," Elizabeth says plainly. "Your side is stark white."

Theo grasps her arm, digging his nails into her flesh. He recognizes Kenneth from the inn.

"Since you're neighbors, you must've known Jared. And Gwen, obviously. Tell me the rest."

"Don't speak to me like that," he says.

"What happened to Charlotte, Ken?" she says. "You must know."

"What did you know about the Barkleys before you left Washington?" he says.

"Rocky Shores is my hometown. I used to live up the road." She takes a breath. "I had just left the cabin. And I stopped at the inn because it was so familiar."

"Wait a minute." He furrows his eyebrows. "This is your hometown? That's interesting."

"I remember when Charlotte was kidnapped. I found her necklace in the sand when I was twelve."

"In the sand?" He raises his eyebrows. "Come on. That makes no sense. It's creepy."

"That's creepy?" He is turning this on her, just like Peter—Jared—always did. She glances around the white prison. "You're insane. We grew up in this tiny town together. But her piece of the necklace was in Jared's safe. How would he have gotten it? I think you know, don't you?"

He shakes his head. "How can you not remember coming to the inn with your mama?"

Her throat constricts. Her blood slows, creeping through her veins. "I figured someone would remember. But it's not what it seems." Her voice is hollow; it rings ominously in her ears.

"Let's be honest, here. Please. We all just have to tell the truth. You came with her to work. Played with Gwen while she cleaned. Remember the Cabbage Patch dolls?"

"How would you know any of that?" Elizabeth's cheeks burn. Little beads of sweat crawl down her neck, but she doesn't wipe them away.

A wry smile forms on Kenneth's lips.

"Who are you?" she whispers.

"I've been around a lot more than you know." He smiles, white teeth gleaming. "Your husband did something to Charlotte, didn't he, Elizabeth? How long have you known him? And you must know who you are." His light smile sends a chill through her teeth. "DNA tests and all."

"What do you mean by that?" Elizabeth's body trembles. Her feet wobble from side to side.

"You murdered him. I think that trumps anything he ever did to you, right?"

"What the hell is going on here? I didn't murder anyone. And why are you after Myra?" She shudders from the inside out.

"That's on you, darling. Why did you come here? Think about it. If you were actually Charlotte, you'd have a life free from Jared Henderson. And since the whole charade started before you knew you'd killed the man, I understand your motive. Really." He lets out a laugh.

"How do you know anything about me?" Anger rises from the pit of her stomach.

"You're completely in the dark about the whole thing?" he says, staring at her with a frightening intensity.

She doesn't respond.

"Wow." He sighs. "I did the best I could for you. But you had to come back and make things rough."

She steps backward, holds Theo behind her. Alice seems frozen.

"I suppose I should tell you who I am. I owe you that. Thirty-two years ago, Myra and I had a brief affair. Herb was away, doing his existential crisis thing in Los Angeles." He rolls his eyes. "It's a man thing."

"What does this have to do—"

"With you? Well, I'll tell you. And you wouldn't be in this position if you'd left things alone." He clears his throat. His charismatic brown eyes have turned to steel. "I never wanted a kid. But we had a baby."

"I don't know what you mean," she says, though somehow she does.

"That baby was you."

Elizabeth stares at him, unable to fathom this. And yet, this crazy revelation makes sense of the discord in her life. It lines up zigzagging bits of information she'd tried to ignore—the lack of other family besides her parents, why they were so close with the Barkley family, and her mother's curt response to Elizabeth's question: *Why do I have to come with you? I don't go to your other jobs. And Gwen is mean to me.*

"*They're our friends.*"

They weren't Elizabeth's friends. But her mother's nonsensical relationship with Myra Barkley created intrigue in her mind.

"I was adopted," she says, locking eyes with him. "And Gwen had no idea we were sisters." She inches toward Kenneth. "But Jared did."

"Right," he says. "And Jared and the Barkleys shared a maid." He smiles wide. "Your mama."

"You're a bastard. A cold son of a bitch," she hisses.

"Oh, come on. Adele would have killed me if Myra found you and wanted to . . . reconnect. Plus, Adele's family owns my businesses, at least while they're alive. That's a lot of money. Hard work. I couldn't give that up. You are a married woman. You understand." He pauses. "Well, you were."

"You don't give a shit about Adele," she says. "All you care about is money."

He looks genuinely confused at this. Theo puffs up his chest in anger.

"What is wrong with you? Jared Henderson kept us locked away for years." Her gaze shifts to Theo, standing beside her with angry tears in his eyes. She changes tack; she needs to get her son out of here alive. *Focus,* she tells herself. She won't be distracted by the audacity that drips from his mouth.

"I promise, I won't tell anyone. Let us go."

"Exactly. We won't say a word." Alice presses her fingers to her lips. "Promise."

Kenneth laughs. "I don't believe in taking people's word for things. I'm a businessman, remember?"

Focus. Don't react.

"Jared was not a bad man," he says. "His main problem, and his downfall, really, is he lacked self-control. As you've experienced."

"And he was just . . . your neighbor?"

Kenneth chortles. "And Gwen's boyfriend. Charlotte's killer. I helped him understand that you were a Barkley girl too. He was quite interested in that. That we could help each other."

Her insides quake; she peers into the house, trying to find an escape.

"The point is," he continues, "I had to keep watch on you for your entire childhood. Mostly, it was fine. Rosie loved you. I doubted she wanted you to know about Myra or me. I kept watch, but I grew complacent."

Elizabeth exchanges a look with Alice. What the hell is he talking about?

"I'm sorry. Is this confusing you? Let me get to the point." He steps toward her. She flinches. "Poor Rosie died. This threw me. I knew about the house Myra left you, wondered if Rosie would tell you. Maybe to reconnect, or for legal matters regarding that dump."

"The trailer," she says dumbly. "That was Myra."

He waves his hand, dismissing the comment. "Right, right. But this isn't my point." He smiles. His gleaming teeth are suddenly menacing; he's had too many facelifts.

"Go on," Alice says.

"I needed to ensure that didn't happen. And Jared was happy to take you up there where no one would find you. To get rid of my problem without a body to deal with," he says, pointing his finger. "Especially for a little money and the promise I wouldn't tell anyone about what he did to Charlotte. You were safer then. A hell of a lot safer than you are now."

"You hired him? To hold me hostage?" She can hardly breathe.

He shrugs. "More or less."

"Look at this child." She points to Theo. "You can't do this. Not to a little boy. He's your grandson." She wants to throw up. Between that drug and this realization, her stomach is swimming.

"You shoulda left Jared alone," he says. "Really, that would have been better for us all. 'Cause now, you're risking everyone's life. This is on you."

"No. Leave Theo and Alice alone. Let them go." She is pleading now, and she hates it. Elizabeth will beg for her son's life—she's done it before.

She will kill this man. If she gets the opportunity, she will make him suffer.

Kenneth crosses his arms against his chest. His jacket shifts, revealing the gun in its holster. "Myra's probably home. Now that she's got that DNA test. And I can't let her and her wimp of a husband spread that around town."

"You don't need to hurt Myra," Elizabeth hisses.

"Catch up with me. I had higher hopes for my own genetic material. You must take after your mother." He shakes his head.

"Come on." Alice trembles beside her. "You said yourself, you've got self-control. It's Peter . . . Jared . . . whatever his name is, who had the problem. You aren't a killer. You're a businessman. Respected, attractive." She shakes her head. "You don't want blood on your hands."

He tosses his hands up. "You're right. You are. I mean, you see this beautiful room? The lovely clothing I bought you?" He gestures toward the robes they're wearing. "This would've been a nicer place for you than that cabin, by far. But you went and talked to the neighbors. Soon enough they'll go nosing around to see why their kid is wanted by the cops. And that will cause a shitstorm for me."

"We're so fucked," Alice says under her breath.

"I've grown weary of this too, Alice. Trust me, I have. But I promise, if you do what I say, I will not hurt you."

"You're worse than him!" Theo shouts.

"Watch your mouth there, kid." He steps toward her son. "Didn't your mother teach you to respect adults?"

"Don't speak to my child," she says, seething. "Ever."

He scoffs, smug as hell. "Now, why don't we invite Alice to join us on our trip to the Barkley house? It's only polite."

"Please leave Alice out of this." Elizabeth's lip quivers. "She has nothing to do with any of it."

"I didn't bring her," he says, with a laugh. "But since you've brought her along, it would be rude not to take her with us." He shoves the gun into her back. "Let's go."

He pushes the three of them through the house and into the rain, which is streaming now, hitting brick-colored puddles so hard they bubble like a witch's cauldron. The barrel of a gun is shoved in her back and it's dark. But the Hendersons are next door. Other neighbors surround them. Yes, these lots are large, but if she screams loud enough, someone could hear. Kenneth is wrong. He's either not that smart or he's underestimated her. Otherwise, he'd have taken them out through the garage.

If they don't escape now, right now, he'll kill them all. She screams, sharp and loud. He puts his hand over her mouth; her screams are muffled, but he's not going to shoot them here. Theo kicks him hard in the groin, and he starts falling, falling. The wind is knocked out of him. He coughs, trying to catch his breath, and though he can't speak, his free hand grips the gun even tighter.

This time, he aims it at Theo's neck. He has an SUV sitting in the driveway, idling. She exchanges a look with Alice. The glance is quick, but the question is deep. He shoves the gun harder into her son's flesh; Theo begins to cry.

"Okay," she whispers. "Don't hurt him, and we'll go wherever you want." They slide into the backseat.

"I'm going to get rid of Myra and Herb. That's all. And you, Theo, and Alice can take my car anywhere in the world," he says, putting the car in drive.

"You're going to frame us," she whispers.

"Your choice, darling. Your son or your mother. I think it's pretty damn simple." He hits the gas. The SUV doesn't barrel down the highway; the tires don't hug the road so tightly they have to grip their seats to avoid being tossed to one side of the vehicle with each curve in the road. Kenneth rolls slowly over back paths to avoid getting pulled over by the cops. And because he's concerned, Elizabeth surmises, that the gravel might scratch his paint or nick a window. He is ever calm, humming along to an Elton John song playing on the radio. Kenneth is in control of his car, in control of his captives. And this time, Kenneth is driving a practical car for a storm.

Theo leans against her, trembling. She whispers, "I will get us free."

He looks at her intently, fiery eyes strong and sure. He believes her. This time he believes her. Hope swells inside her. They've done this together before. But she can't do anything yet. The car doors are locked on the inside, same with the windows.

Soon she can smell the water. They are close.

"I'm going to let you out," he says, pulling into Myra's drive-way, hidden back from the road, from directly in front of the inn. For privacy, of course. Both of their cars are parked out front. "But if you move a muscle, I'll put a bullet in Theo's head."

Her son whimpers. Rage flashes through her. She says, through gritted teeth, "I understand." She surveys the parking lot, searching for guests, for anyone that can help them.

"Sorry. Maybe there's an undercover at the inn. But the guests have been evacuated. Myra and Herb are home alone." He opens his door and steps out into the rain.

"How do you know that?" she says.

He chortles. "How do I know most of what I know?"

"Cameras," Alice mutters.

He smiles. "Come on. Let's go say hello to your mother."

CHAPTER THIRTY-SEVEN

MYRA

The house is hollow, so quiet it has lost its soul. The flesh torn from her home leaves but a skeleton and it kills her. Myra organizes her collection of teabags as if she's throwing a party. She vainly tries to forget about the psychopath, her daughters, her dying marriage. She peeks over the barstools at Herb. His skin is chalky. He cracks his knuckles, taps his left foot. Myra looks away. He purposely does the little things that irritate her. Why should he care? They are finished. Even if he were to forgive her, this marriage has gone through more than what is fair to ask of a relationship. It is a loved dog in pain. Sometimes it's better to let it all go, to scatter the last ashes in the wind.

Myra bites the inside of her cheek. "God," she murmurs. The room is so thick and viscous with blame and regret. She pushes this feeling deep down and puffs her chest out like a mama bird. This home was once her nest.

Wind flurries against the house. The distant sound of thunder vibrates through her. She tells herself this is any winter night in Oregon.

She watches Herb. Myra can hardly imagine breathing without him. We can't always have what we want. And there's no room for regret because she doesn't regret having her daughter, and she cannot imagine Elizabeth not having Rosie. And yet, perhaps she should have told Herb—but who can know? He might have left her then. One mistake collided with another, and some of them led to outcomes she wouldn't erase even if she could.

But Myra understands, as tears and snot run down her face, that life is messy. Decisions are complicated. And dammit, you can't change the past. Something sharp rises in her chest. She and Herb lost their eight-year-old daughter. There was no instruction manual on how to handle that correctly.

So, all she says is, "I'm sorry."

Rain taps against the metal awning, and the full storm gutter spills onto the patch of ivy in the front yard. Mesmerized by the sound, she leans her cheek against the kitchen table.

There is a shift in the wind. She holds her breath. "Herb, do you hear that?"

He doesn't look up from his book. "It's just a storm."

The rain intensifies, but she hears something else—like a stiff broom sweeping cement. Or footsteps smashing wet gravel. The sound moves toward the house, picking up in tempo.

"You don't hear that?" She tilts her ear toward the door.

Herb finally sets the book down.

Shadowy figures displace the porchlight. Voices penetrate the staticky sounds of the storm. "Who is that?" she whispers.

"Maybe it's Sarah." He meets her eyes.

"I didn't hear a car pull up," she says.

He steps toward the door and looks through the peephole. "It's just your boyfriend," he says with a sigh.

Kenneth stands in the door. Elizabeth and another woman are crouched behind him, drenched and shivering. Theo hangs onto his mother's leg. "Can we come in?" Kenneth says.

"Herb, she's here! They're okay. What happened? Who kidnapped you? Call 911." Relief courses through her. She almost laughs, filled with joy. "We are so lucky, so lucky you're back."

Herb holds his chest. "We were so scared. I'll call the police." He envelops Theo in his arms. "Buddy, you're trembling. Come inside."

Myra closes her eyes tightly, wanting to jump up and down with excitement. "Oh, Elizabeth." Tears roll down her face. "I was terrified I'd lost you. What happened?"

"This is Alice. Remember the woman who has been helping us?" She sounds so distant. Probably still in shock.

Myra blinks. "Kenneth told you the truth?"

"Yes," she says hoarsely. "I had no idea. You have to believe me." She covers her face with her hands. "I'm so tired."

"Herb, get the phone. Call Gwen. Poor Gwen, she's been incredibly upset. Blaming this on herself."

The four of them are silent, serious.

"Wait a minute." She furrows her brow. "Who took you? Herb? Get the phone." She is certain she must be missing a crucial detail. Theo's lips are blue. He's quivering. They are wearing identical white pants and button-down shirts, with initials sewn onto the front pockets. She steps into the kitchen for a couple of dishtowels.

"The cops are on the way." Kenneth smiles and squeezes Elizabeth's arm. He plops down like he owns the place, which is not atypical for Kenneth. "Sit, ladies. Theo, have a seat with your mother."

"Who took you? From the mountain with Gwen. Kenneth? Where did you find them?" she says.

Elizabeth's teeth chatter; her face is as pale as the day she arrived.

"I don't understand . . ."

"Hello," Alice says, voice shaking. "It's good to meet you."

"What's going on?" An ominous feeling spreads through Myra's body, from her chest through the tips of her fingers.

Theo widens his eyes like he's trying to tell her something. He is gripping his mother's hand more tightly than she's ever seen.

"You all must be in shock," Herb says.

Alice visibly stiffens. "That's right."

Herb picks up his cell phone. "Here, I'll make the calls. To Gwen, the cops. We need help here."

"Exactly," Myra says.

Kenneth bursts into laughter. "No one is going anywhere. No cops will be called."

She leans on the couch. "Kenneth, what are you talking about?"

"I didn't want Adele to get caught up in this mess. It's very simple."

She takes a sharp breath. "But you told her. That's what you said."

Kenneth shakes his head. "I did not tell her. Adele would have found out years ago, when Rosie died. Because of that damn trailer. Elizabeth could've found out and wanted to reconnect."

Herb rubs his forehead. "We need the police—"

"What the hell, Kenneth? That was a long time ago. She'd gotten married." She stares into his eyes, which are suddenly vacant and hard. "Wait. You're behind this whole thing—"

He smiles. "I wonder why Elizabeth would leave so very quickly. Why is that?"

"You tell me why Peter showed up at that bar." Elizabeth stands up.

He pulls a gun from his jacket. "Let's all sit tight, and I'll tell you what we're going to do here. Put the phone down."

"Kenneth!" Myra's stomach roils. "What is wrong with you?"

He clenches his jaw. His soft face dissolves into anger. "No one is leaving this room."

Tears run down Elizabeth's face.

"This won't work," Alice says calmly. "You won't get away with this. Now, why don't you pack up your things and get going? I'm sure no one here wishes to ruin your marriage."

He nudges Elizabeth with the gun. "You caused this."

Myra thinks fast. The pieces are jumbled before her. How does Kenneth know Jared Henderson? Her mind races. He showed up at the inn right after Elizabeth came. He knew. How? She can hardly see straight.

Herb clutches Myra's hand; he meets her eyes.

Kenneth turns the gun on Herb. "Don't move."

He was the one who locked her in her shed that night. The one who's been watching them. Myra looks to her tea kettle. Steam shoots from the spout. She wants to smash that kettle into him, to burn his wicked face.

She focuses on his wool coat, his leather shoes. A narcissist, a liar. He is more menacing than Jared Henderson. "How did you know he killed Charlotte?" she says numbly.

"He helped with the search." Kenneth laughs. "A stupid attempt at a cover. He's my neighbor. Was blubbering about this terrible mistake he'd made. Killing his girlfriend's sister."

"I cannot believe you. Why?" Tears drip down Myra's face. "Why?"

"Because as panicked as he was, I told him who Elizabeth was. A Barkley girl. He'd always wanted Gwen, you see. Elizabeth was the next best thing."

Myra cannot speak. The betrayal is too hard to fathom.

Herb places his hand on hers. His watery blue eyes are warm, familiar, forgiving. So much you can tell about a man, by his eyes. After all these years of marriage they can communicate in the deep quiet. He will always be her Herb.

Elizabeth whispers, "Let him take me. Alice—"

Myra won't let this happen. Can't do it. Not this time. "Who are you?" She steels her voice. "Tell me where Charlotte is. Tell me everything."

"Don't look at me like that." His Adam's apple bulges. "Gwen's a tough one to crack. As you can appreciate. She broke up with him that night and went blabbing to her little friends, trying to embarrass him. This is what he told me. But the thing about Jared—well, he became Peter Briggs the day he met Elizabeth. The man can't control his temper. I apologize for that." He shakes his head. "He took off for his truck. Planned to go home and punch a wall, baby that he was. But there was little Charlotte. And he was holding that necklace of Gwen's, I guess. Too damn sentimental. He should've gone home."

Myra can hardly stand this. Her legs wobble, vision swims. "What happened next?"

"Now, Myra, Jared's not here to defend himself, so this isn't fair. But according to him, he took her for a little ride. To scare Gwen. Except she went crazy. Biting and kicking. He supposedly snapped her neck. By accident." He pauses. "Well, as accidentally as one can do such a thing. Really, he's the one who caused this for you."

"You monster." She wants to gouge his eyes out.

Kenneth laughs. "When Rosie died, Elizabeth needed to leave town. I couldn't have Adele finding out about this. Her father owns my business."

"This isn't even about Adele. It's all about money," Herb says.

"Shut up," Kenneth yells. "Just shut the fuck up, Herb, or I'll shoot you."

Herb tightens his grip on Myra's hand. "In the end, *everything* comes down to money with you."

"Shut. Up." Ken waves the gun at Herb.

Myra curls her hands into fists. She focuses on the spit dribbling from his lower lip.

Myra's heart drums so quickly she feels she might faint, have a heart attack. The sound of police cars, lights whirling and sirens whining, grows closer. Trees swish in the ocean squall; the scent of pine and salt rush in the door. Ambient rain patters in the distance.

Police rush to the door. This is her home. He killed her daughter.

She lunges at Kenneth. Her skin blisters with rage. Myra once heard that when you have a baby, you carry bits of their DNA inside your blood for the rest of your life. Her daughters live in her flesh. Three daughters.

She catapults into his muscled body.

The sequence of events is blurry. It is like a car crash you see coming, and yet you can never prepare for its velocity. People scatter. Kenneth fires a round. She puts her hand to her side. Droplets of hot blood slide through her fingers.

Herb is beside her. He drops to the ground next to her, tears landing on her cheek. He holds her hand gently, like they did during their first dance. They speak in the deep, dark silence.

I forgive you. I love you . . .

Her flesh burns; it feels as if her body has been set ablaze. She slips in and out of consciousness, from total darkness to colors merging together and spinning, then back again. Vomit spills from the corner of her mouth. Blood drenches the carpet.

She is going to die; she accepts this ending.

A body lurches inside, slow, so slow. In one of the swirls of light, so surreal, she sees that it is Gwen. She points a gun, yelling, "Kenneth, you did this. You and Jared, together."

She opens her mouth to speak. The question lingers in the air: "Why not me?" Gwen is about to ask, when everything spins again. Myra feels herself on top of the ceiling, yet the carpet is underneath her.

Gwen pulls the trigger. The bullet tears through the house, and the motherfucker collapses to the ground. Half of his head flops beside her.

Elizabeth, Gwen, and Alice crouch beside her, arm in arm. Their faces slide together, joining and separating. One collective identity. The sequence repeats itself.

Women. We save ourselves and we save one another. Women.

This is enough. It is all she needs. She drifts out of consciousness. A little opalescent wisp of Charlotte passes through her mind. Then she is gone.

SIX MONTHS LATER

The cherry blossom trees are in full bloom, and their tender buds flutter in the breeze. The sky is a wild blue, only a shade lighter than the water. Elizabeth wipes the dewy sweat from her brow and scrapes at the layers of paint on the walls of the inn— from the dreary shade of green to buttercup-yellow. The outside will be sapphire-blue with white trim.

"That was her color," says Herb. "We had it painted when she disappeared. Your mother couldn't handle the memory."

Elizabeth is startled when Herb refers to Myra as her mother; it is still so hard to fathom. "When are the people coming to install the floors?"

"Next week."

During the dark and lonely nights. Herb went through Myra's magazines and listed every circled item, recreated every dog-eared page. The thick curtains have been removed, and lacy ones to match the walls will be put up once the paint dries and the dust from the wood clears. "This is good flooring," he says, "the kind with no squeaky boards."

"Herb, she knows how much you love her," she says, and scrapes at the paint again.

"I do." He thinks a moment, and adds, "I'm so glad I got to say so. I once told my wife, if we can get through this, we can survive anything."

Charlotte finally had a memorial service. The cops excavated the cabin, and her bones were found under layers of earth. The family scattered her ashes in the ocean, to fly wild and free. A sort of peace fell over them all. They will never fully heal, but this small bit of closure helps. Myra does not have to wait. Her child is swimming in the ocean she loved.

New mahogany, just like Myra planned. She was hospitalized for three months, with a bullet to her kidney. After four surgeries, she is finally home. She does physical therapy daily and walks with a cane. Herb and Elizabeth sat with her, comatose. A tube breathed for her. Five pints of blood were drained from her abdomen. She wasn't expected to live, but as usual, Myra defied expectations. Jimi and Gwen came to say their goodbyes, and she blinked that very day.

Elizabeth's phone pings. Myra.

"Can someone help me?"

Herb lifts his eyes up, hands covered in dust.

"I'll go," says Elizabeth.

She steps through the gravel, toward the house. The sun is high in the cloudless sky, though that ever-present ocean breeze sends a chill through the air. Elizabeth zips up her hoodie. Cherry blossoms and freshly unfurled blue cornflowers grow wild by the evergreens.

Myra is in the kitchen, sitting at the table and slightly breathless. The tea kettle wheezes. "I'm making Earl Grey," she says. "Got a little tired."

Elizabeth pours Myra a cup and dunks the teabag in the steaming water.

"Want a cup? I feel bad for dragging you over here."

Elizabeth feels her face flush. "I'm actually a coffee drinker."

"How come you never said so? There's a Keurig right beside it."

"Okay," says Elizabeth, and places a pod in the machine. "How are you, Myra?"

"Some days are better than others." She smiles. "I flash on that night a lot. Wake up in cold sweats." She looks distant. "I'm glad you stayed."

So much is different. Gwen, especially.

But Elizabeth saw something inside her change that night when she shot that gun and collapsed on the floor. "You are a strong woman," Elizabeth said. "And it isn't about how many followers you have on Instagram." Besides. Elizabeth has never used Instagram or Twitter or Facebook. It didn't exist while she lived in that cabin. Often, she ponders, who would she be, if not for Peter? What type of person would she be if she'd known she owned that house?

A tenderness developed between them, and it isn't because Gwen saved her life, or maybe it is, in a strange way. It's like Gwen has held her breath from the moment she lost Charlotte, and she's finally let out her guilt in a primal scream. Theo likes her girls. "Cousins," he says, "I have cousins, which are kinda like best friends except better."

And Jimi. He spends so much time with his mama, helping her pick out patterns for Herb to work on and showing her that he needs her. Jimi was the outsider of the family, born after Charlotte's disappearance. Now, he's brave enough to crawl over the edge sometimes, be a part of their lives. Go fishing with Herb. Barbecue with the family before rushing off to a concert with a new girlfriend.

Elizabeth had planned to move up to Washington with Alice, but in the end she couldn't bring herself to move Theo again. Elizabeth and Theo rebuilt the trailer she grew up in. And sometimes, in the dark of night, she opens the window in her old bedroom and leans her cheek against the sill, letting the scent of the ocean waft inside and linger in an opaque fog. Like she did that summer evening before she trudged down to the beach and plucked her sister's necklace out of the sand. It's coiled in her bedside table, and it will stay with her for the rest of her life.

ACKNOWLEDGMENTS

Though a writer may seem to draft a story alone, producing a novel that readers will enjoy takes a collective effort. There are so many readers and writers in the community whom I'm indebted to, who've helped bring my kernel of a story to life. Jenny Chen, my editor, first fell in love with my little cast of characters and pushed me to layer their family mystery in ways I never thought possible. I thank her immensely for all the work she put into this book. Her guidance has made me a better author. The entire Crooked Lane team has been a dream to work with, especially Madeline Rathle and Melissa Rechter. My agent, Lauren Spieller, has been the best champion for me and my work, and continues to help build my career and my confidence. She's the best agent an author could ask for: passionate, enthusiastic, and knowledgeable. I am incredibly grateful to have her as well as the rest of the team at Triada US Literary Agency.

There are so many other authors who've read, critiqued, and offered moral support during the long hours I spent drafting and revising Elizabeth, Myra, and Gwen's story. Thanks to my critique partners, early readers, and author friends who encourage me to keep writing: Swati Hegde, Sara Kapadia, Megan Collins, Vanessa Lillie, Wendy Heard, Daniela Petrova, Eliza Nellums, Ed Aymar, Tara Laskowski, Maureen Connolly,

Noelle Salazar, Suanne Schafer, Eva Seyler, Preslaysa Williams, Olivia Arnold, Jamie Beth Cohen, Nicole Mabry, Nicole Bross, Jerri Schlenker, Samantha Kassé, and many more. I also thank the students and faculty in the creative writing department at Boise State University, where I've not only honed my craft, but made wonderful friendships in the writer's community.

I have the greatest family ever, and I'm especially grateful for my husband, Anthony Woods, for how hard he's worked, caring for our six children so I could write. I love you so much. My children inspire me on a daily basis. I am so incredibly fortunate to be mom to Hunter, Julianna, Harley, Dylan, Piper, and Emmett. This book is also in memory of my father as well as my aunt Linda, both of whom passed away while I was revising this book. Also, it is in memory of my first husband and father to my oldest two children, Brad Rosen. I thank you for loving me, for helping me through the darkest times of my life, and for showing me that I could handle anything—even losing you far before I should have. And a deep, heartfelt thanks to my mother and sister: you are the strongest women I've ever known, and all that I do is because I saw you work hard and achieve your dreams, how you've struggled through hard times and managed to continue on.